W0019444

What They Are Saying About
The Door in the Fog

The Door in the Fog

Just in time for Christmas, Dorothy Bodoin's new Foxglove Corner mystery, entitled *The Door in the Fog*, will be published on the first of November. I have already marked this date on my calendar, for any day that begins with a Bodoin book is a special day. It is not only the perfect gift to give yourself but to others, as well, and remember, you are not only giving a book but hours of pleasurable reading – the best gift ever.

The Door in the Fog marks the sixteenth book in Bodoin's series and once again, readers will be thrust into the life of Jennet Ferguson, her husband Crane and their many friends and neighbors, not to mention their precious collies. After sixteen books, they will have established themselves as friends and the reader will wait from book to book to see how they're doing and what complications they have in their lives. No doubt about it – Jennet always manages to find herself in the midst of murder, theft, curses and problems, with a touch of the supernatural woven throughout the stories.

Suzanne Hurley

The Door in the Fog

A cornflower blue door appears and promptly disappears on an old, abandoned barn. A wounded collie stumbles into the fog and vanishes. Another dog, fashioned of lightning, flashes in and out of existence. A cursed painting of a girl with collies wreaks havoc in the lives of anyone who owns it. The history of a ghost who haunts the new Inn.

There are enough spooky and irrational happenings in the town of Foxglove Corners to set Jennet Ferguson adrift in a sea of mysteries. And seeing things that weren't there was getting to be a habit with her. When Terra, the leader of the Lakeville Collie Rescue League, disappears along with her collie and all the League's money, Jennet and her friend Annica start sleuthing once again, this time undaunted by a psychic's warning to be careful.

The Door in the Fog is another *delightful* novel in the Foxglove Corners mystery series with all the familiar characters and places, and a few new ones thrown in to make things interesting. The twists and turns keep the reader in suspense until all the mysteries are solved and everything that can be explained is, in a satisfying, albeit somewhat mystifying, ending. I really enjoyed reading this novel and I highly recommend it to all cozy mystery lovers.

Evelyn Cullet

Other Works From The Pen Of

Dorothy Bodoin

Where Have All the Dogs Gone?—July, 2011

A young activist who calls herself Rima frees shelter dogs to save them from being destroyed, thereby setting the stage for a deadly encounter.

The Secret Room of Eidt House—March, 2012

A rabid dog that should have died months ago from the dread disease runs free in the woods of Foxglove Corners, and the library's long-kept secret unleashes a series of other strange events.

Follow a Shadow—September, 2012

A shadowy intruder haunts Jennet's woods by night, and a woman who can't accept the death of her collie asks Jennet to help her find Rainbow Bridge where she believes her dog waits for her.

The Snow Queen's Collie—March, 2013

During a Christmas Eve snowstorm, a white collie appears on the porch of the Ferguson farmhouse, and the painting Jennet's sister gives her for Christmas begins to exhibit strange qualities.

Wings

THE DOOR IN THE FOG

Dorothy Bodoin

A Wings ePress, Inc.

Cozy Mystery Novel

Wings ePress, Inc.

Edited by: Jeanne Smith
Copy Edited by: Leslie Hodges
Senior Editor: Jeanne Smith
Executive Editor: Marilyn Kapp
Cover Artist: Pat Evans

All rights reserved

Names, characters and incidents depicted in this book are products of the author's imagination or are used fictitiously. Any resemblance to actual events, locales, organizations, or persons, living or dead, is entirely coincidental and beyond the intent of the author or the publisher.

No part of this book may be reproduced or transmitted in any form or by any means, electronic or mechanical, including photocopying, recording, or by any information storage and retrieval system, without permission in writing from the publisher.

Wings ePress Books
http://www.books-by-wings-epress.com/

Copyright © 2013 by Eileen Harris
ISBN 978-1-61309-840-0

Published In the United States Of America

Wings ePress Inc.
3000 N. Rock Road
Newton, KS 67114

Dedication

For H. Susan Shaw and Marja McGraw, my friends and critique partners

One

The shot fractured the morning silence, a single firecracker pop followed by an anguished yelp.

Someone was shooting in the woods. The gunshot had come out of the fog, which was madness on a day with visibility reduced to a few yards. My black Taurus had been inching down the lonely country road, navigating a series of curves afloat in thick white condensation.

How could the shooter see his target? What creature had uttered that cry?

In the back seat, Misty, my white collie puppy, scratched at the window. She wasn't afraid; Misty was never afraid. But I was.

A stray shot could well find me inside my car, supposedly safe, traveling an unfamiliar woodland route because my usual road had been inexplicably closed.

I didn't even know the name of the road, couldn't see a sign even if it existed, but I was aware of woods to my left, farmland on the right, and another curve ahead. With every turn the fog had seemed to thicken. It was as if I were doomed to travel this road forever while the fog enveloped me and every mile took me farther from home.

I didn't like driving in fog, didn't like curves. Curves in the fog were a dangerous combination. One never knew what lay ahead.

Keep moving, I told myself. *You should come to a crossroad before long.*

I heard another shot, then another.

Tuned in to my apprehension, Misty began to whine.

I followed the present curve and, when the road straightened, spied an animal body lying at the roadside, wreathed in mist and motionless. It looked like a deer. A doe slain out of season, or a fawn? No, that wasn't right. It looked like a dog.

I pulled off the road behind the body. Leaving the Taurus idling and Misty fussing to accompany me, I made my way through high wet grasses to the still form.

It *was* a dog, an adult collie with a mahogany sable coat and no collar around its neck. Now the shots made sense. A careless shooter, a stray dog. Death. This kind of tragedy happened all too often in the country where many dogs ran free.

I should move it farther from the roadside, lest it be run over. But as I neared the fallen collie, it lifted its head.

The dog had been wounded or stunned. Which changed my approach. As an experienced member of the Lakeville Collie Rescue League, I knew that a frightened, possibly wounded, dog was unpredictable. While I had no desire to be bitten, leaving the collie to die alone at the roadside was unthinkable.

I believed in being prepared for all eventualities. Knowing I might find a collie in distress at any time, I had the tools of my trade in the car's trunk: a muzzle, a long leather leash, blankets, and a canine first aid kit, together with a small box of dog biscuits.

"Hold on baby," I said. "Just a minute."

Before I could turn to go back to the car, the dog scrambled to its feet, stood unsteadily for a moment, and limped into the fog. Blood smeared the grass where it had lain. Not an overwhelming amount, but blood nonetheless.

The dog was wounded; it couldn't go far. A few more yards, perhaps, before weakness overcame it. Then I'd seize my chance.

With luck, the rest of the story would unfold quickly and neatly. I'd coax or carry the collie to the car, move Misty to the front seat, drive back to Doctor Alice Foster at the Foxglove Corners Animal Hospital, and hope for a happy outcome.

I hurried to the car and grabbed the muzzle and leash. Misty set up a feverish yipping, demanding to be taken along on this new adventure. Telling her to hush and stay, I headed past the pooling blood into the fog.

Undulating wisps of cottony condensation whirled around me. They clamped moist tentacles on my arms and legs. What I could see of the terrain appeared to slope gently uphill. This was a farmer's meadow, I imagined. There was no fence, no sign banning trespassers, and, in any event, no one to challenge me. At least none I could see.

In spite of the warm April morning, I felt a chill. If only I could see through the fog, my search would be easier. I plodded on, calling softly, "Lassie? Where are you?"

Lassie? All of my dogs were females. For some reason, I'd never owned a male.

"It's going to be all right," I said.

Misty's howl followed me, adding to my unease.

I stood still for a second and listened. There was no sound, not so much as a rustle in the grass or a faint whimper. Only damp white fog, thick and secretive, swirling over the ground and spreading to the sky. It rolled back in waves as I advanced through clumps of blowsy white flowers, Queen Anne's Lace or a white weed resembling it.

I held on to the muzzle and leash, ever hopeful but expecting at any moment to stumble over a dead collie.

The uphill grade grew steeper. Minutes passed, and reason struggled to assert itself. This foray into the fog-shrouded countryside was well-intended but futile. I'd left my car on a lonely country road with the engine idling and my puppy in the back seat.

My husband, Crane, would be angry—if he ever found out. A deputy sheriff who was well acquainted with danger on the roadway, he'd be incredulous at my recklessness.

I could hear him then as I always did when doing something ill-advised. "Never stop your car on one of these country roads, Jennet." I knew that lecture by heart, as well as its companion piece. "If you're ever in trouble, stay in the car, lock it, and call me on your cell phone."

It was too late, alas, to heed his words. He knew about my work with the Rescue League, had often said he was proud of me. I couldn't rescue collies without leaving my car.

A thorny plant slashed at my leg, making me wish I'd worn blue jeans to the animal hospital. I almost tripped on a rock.

Only then did I remember the shooter. He might still be in the area, hidden from my view by the all-encompassing fog. Who knew what his intentions were? I'd better go back to the car and call Crane or Terra Roman who had organized the Rescue League and kept it running smoothly. Still, I hated to abandon my search.

One more time, I thought. "Lassie, where are you? Speak."

My labored breathing was the only sound in the mysterious white world. I couldn't help thinking that the dog had already died.

Should I go on? Just a few more steps?

I scanned the wall of fog, willing it to part, letting me see what lay ahead.

I took those few more steps and saw a splash of blue perhaps three yards in front of me. If I continued in this direction, I would run into it.

When I was close enough, I saw that it was a door painted cornflower blue with brass hardware. Could this be somebody's house without a walkway leading up to it? How odd.

It seemed as if the door were slightly ajar, offering a silent invitation. The dog would have crept inside, having found a quiet place to heal in private or to die. But no sound indicated the presence of an animal.

I reached for the doorknob and touched a smooth surface. It wasn't a knob, and this wasn't a door but a realistic image of one painted on a wall, complete with specks of mud at the base. As for the door being ajar, that was an illusion.

I'd come to a weathered structure whose brown wood exterior contrasted with the clear color of the painted-on door. I stepped back in the moving fog and saw the simple lines of an old barn. Tramping through encroaching weeds and grasses, I found the real door, secured with a rust-encrusted lock and chain.

Whatever was inside, it couldn't be the wounded collie. Probably nothing was inside, nothing alive at any rate.

Why would anyone paint a door on the side of an old barn? Certainly not to deceive a trespasser on foggy days.

It didn't matter. The dog did, but finding it in the fog was going to be impossible. I could still hear Misty, although her voice was muffled. She was howling, certain I'd abandoned her. The eerie wolf wail added to my unease.

This was no place to linger. There was something strange about the barn with the false blue door. Something that verged on the unearthly. The entire morning had been strange, beginning with the sudden formation of the fog and the closure of my familiar road home. I felt the chill again, more intense this time, and remembered the shooter in the woods.

Had Fate conspired to bring me to this place at this time?

I retraced my steps and found the Taurus still idling, where I'd left it.

Of course. Where else would it be?

Misty ran from one side of the back seat to the other, ears flattened, tail wagging. The blanket I kept for the dogs to snuggle on had ended up on the floor with her favorite toy, a little stuffed goat, once as white as Misty herself. Her joy at my return shone in her eyes and her joyous yips.

Misty had been a rescue. I had a house full of rescued collies, together with one dog I'd purchased from a breeder. I'd been in the League long enough to know how our organization worked. We saved one dog and lost the next one, but I wasn't ready to give up on the collie who had run away from me to be swallowed by the fog.

Two

After a mile of traveling through dense fog, I saw a road sign. It appeared to waver beyond drifting strands of fog, but I could make out the words: Deer Leap Trail. I'd never heard of it and only hoped the name wouldn't prove to be prophetic.

Another mile brought me to a crossroad. Pulling over, I consulted my map of Foxglove Corners and pinpointed my location. If I made a left turn there, I should be heading in the general direction of home.

Misty had fallen asleep in the back seat, and the silence in the car was deep and deadly. I didn't turn on the radio, knowing I needed every shred of concentration to navigate the road. Fortunately there were no other cars on the trail which was dangerously narrow, and the dead animals along the way were small wild ones.

How strange that woodland creatures would get run over on this little-traveled by-road.

Seeing the road kill, I couldn't help thinking of the dog I'd left behind. The mission of the Rescue League was to save every collie who needed our help. We'd sworn to leave no collie unaided unless offering that aid was impossible, as in the instance of the rabid dog who had once attacked me.

With that single exception, I had never encountered a true impossibility. Had I been too quick to abandon my search for the wounded collie?

I toyed briefly with the idea of turning around and making my way back to Deer Leap Trail. But the fog showed no sign of dissipating anytime soon. It would be difficult to find the exact location again. Then, once I reached home, my usual Saturday chores and my own dogs would claim my attention. As they should.

The next day was Sunday. I could return to the area then and hope the collie had survived its wound and remained in the area.

I had no cause to feel guilty. But I did.

~ * ~

At last I reached Jonquil Lane and my green Victorian farmhouse with its stained glass windows and graceful twin turrets all veiled in wisps of fog that floated high above the earth. The daffodils and jonquils on both sides of the lane were in full bloom, in shades ranging from bright yellow to palest ivory.

My section of Foxglove Corners was a magical place, never more so than in the spring with fresh greens everywhere and fragile new blossoms on the fruit trees.

Sensing or scenting home, Misty woke and nudged the window with her nose. I parked the Taurus, took her leash, and led her down to the ground.

The barking of the dogs in the house quickly dispelled the illusion of fog magic.

I had a rainbow collection of collies: Halley and Candy with their showy tricolor coats; Raven, a rare bi-black; Sky, a blue merle; and Gemmy whose fur was often described by those unfamiliar with the standard as "Lassie colored."

They converged on us with wagging tails, prancing paws, and raucous barking. I should teach them to sit and stay and offer paws, one dog at a time, to say hello. This loving onslaught, however, was more fun for them.

Misty, still tired from her ordeal at the animal hospital, still a puppy, made a beeline for her crate, carrying the toy goat in her mouth.

The kitchen looked the way I'd left it with no tell-tale food wrappings littering the floor and every item within view in its proper place. My brood deserved treats from the Lassie jar. Well aware of rewards for good behavior, they sat in a semi-circle and waited.

I passed out dog biscuits, poured fresh water, then sought the nearest comfortable chair where I could plan the rest of my day. First I had to call Terra to make my dog-in-distress report. She might send another rescuer to the Deer Leap Trail area later today, perhaps Sue Appleton who lived near Jonquil Lane on a horse farm.

But Terra wasn't home. I left a message on her answering machine and set the problem aside for the moment. I had to make a beef stew, write the week's lesson plans for my English classes at Marston High School, and mark off another day on the calendar in my countdown to Easter vacation.

As I contemplated a whole week of wondrous free time, I glanced out the bay window. Fog still filled the air, obscuring the yellow Victorian house across the lane where Camille Ferguson, my neighbor and aunt by marriage, lived with her husband, Crane's uncle.

Secret, silent fog veiling roads and walkways, hiding objects and landmarks, distorting reality.

How could I have thought for even a second that the painted-on blue door in the fog was ajar?

~ * ~

I always knew when Crane was near before I saw his Jeep on Jonquil Lane because the dogs did. Especially Candy. She regarded Crane as her special person, long having forgotten that I was the one who had brought her into our circle.

A dog's superior sense of hearing never failed. Crane must be rounding the last curve on the lane, turning into the driveway, parking. Candy stationed herself at the side door, yelping and generally going berserk.

Through the kitchen window I watched Crane cover the distance to the house in long sure strides. The morning fog had cleared hours ago, but it was re-forming, draping the landscape in a mist as fine as gauze. The woods across the lane were already retreating behind a white wall.

I always said a silent prayer when Crane arrived home safely after long hours patrolling the roads and by-roads of Foxglove Corners. Once he had been shot. While we lived in a comparatively peaceful section of Michigan, one never knew when a routine traffic stop would lead to tragedy.

Apparently nothing untoward had happened today.

He opened the door and waded through exuberant collies to give me my greeting. With his blond hair and frosty gray eyes, he brought his own energy wherever he went, together with a breath of the wood-scented outdoors. Instantly the house burst into electric life.

I made our welcome home kiss last a little longer than usual.

"It's like pea soup out there," he said as he locked his gun in its cabinet. "It's shaping up to be a dangerous night on the freeway."

"It was touch-and-go this morning on the way home from the vet's."

Because we avoided shop talk and serious discussions during dinnertime, I waited until afterward when we were in the living room relaxing over coffee before telling him about the collie and my thwarted rescue.

"Are you familiar with Deer Lake Trail?" I asked.

"Sure. Not much goes on there."

"Did you ever see an old barn with a blue door…fairly close to the road? The door looks real but it's just painted on."

He took a sip of his coffee. "I've seen plenty of old barns, but no blue doors."

"At first I thought the dog had gone through the door because it looked like it was open. Then I saw it up close. Who paints a fake door on a ramshackle barn?"

"An artist?"

"Or an artistic farmer. I could hardly see through the fog. There could be other barns nearby and a house. The collie may be dead by now," I added.

"Maybe not if he had the strength to run away from you."

She, I thought. *Lassie*. But I hadn't seen her clearly. Only the pain and terror in her eyes.

"It's so frustrating," I said. "Terra hasn't returned my call. That's not like her."

I thought Crane had overlooked the shooting; I should have known better.

"The land on either side of Deer Lake Trail is private property," he said in his strict deputy sheriff's voice. "It's a 'No trespassing/No hunting zone.' You said somebody shot the dog?"

"I heard gunshots. One, then two more."

"Then you got out of the car and walked over to the dog—and this barn?"

"Guilty," I said. Then, "I couldn't just drive on, Crane, even if I wasn't a rescuer. I thought the dog was dead. There was blood on the ground. Why would anyone shoot a collie?"

"Maybe it was preying on livestock. There are still some feral dogs in the neighborhood."

I nodded. What had been a major problem, thanks to a delusional animal activist, had dwindled down to isolated incidents. "But firing a gun in the fog is idiotic," I said.

"That's why you should never have gotten out of your car in the first place."

"But the dog might have been dying."

"Okay. Once you saw that it wasn't, wandering away from the road was taking a chance."

"I know."

Crane was right. I was inclined to act first and think later, a habit that could have proved lethal this morning. On Sunday, after tonight's fog had burned off, I'd be able to see the barn and, I hoped, the dog.

Lying in the meadow, miraculously healed, wagging its tail at my approach?

Not likely, but I could dream. Certainly the man with the gun would be gone.

I drank my coffee slowly, thinking of the Queen Anne's Lace that grew in the meadow. The blowsy white flowers were the only landmark I remembered. The door with its bright blue color should be visible from the road even if it was farther than I'd estimated.

I realized that the dog might be long gone by tomorrow, that the time to act had passed, and I felt anxious and conscious of failure.

Why wasn't Terra Roman returning my call? Unless Sue Appleton or another rescuer had found the collie, but then Terra would have let me know.

At this point, all I could do was wait.

Three

Sunday morning dawned clear and warm with a sky of pure cerulean, drifting white clouds, and vibrant spring color in the fields. It was a perfect April day without a hint of fog to hinder my search for the wounded collie.

As soon as Crane left for his patrol and I brought the dogs back from their first walk of the day, I set out with Candy for Deer Leap Trail with extra biscuits in my jacket pocket. I had debated the wisdom of taking her. Usually I could accomplish more without one of the collies in the car, but Candy had a gift for ferreting out the world's secrets. Perhaps she could lead me to Lassie.

The road was even narrower than I remembered, but chances were I wouldn't encounter another vehicle coming toward me. I drove slowly enough to watch for leaping deer and still observe the countryside. This, too, was as I remembered. Farmland on one side and woods on the other with a glimpse of silvery blue water beyond close-growing trees. Yesterday the pond or lake had been hidden by the fog.

Today I was able to see signs posted at intervals. 'No trespassing' and 'No hunting.' Unless the shooter owned the property, he had no right to tramp through it with or without a weapon. Neither did I, for that matter.

At last I came to an old barn. Not the right one because it didn't have a blue door, or any door, on the side. Still, I pulled off the road and studied it. It was the approximate size of the barn I'd seen yesterday, and it was old although sturdy.

A profusion of white Queen Anne's Lace grew near the road's edge up to the barn as if to border an unseen walkway. It seemed to beckon to me. Although this couldn't be the right barn—for where was the blue door?—I left the car with Candy in tow and walked toward it, keeping her a safe distance from the white flowers.

Not far from the barn, I spied a white farmhouse equally old with simple classic lines and no ornamentation. It stood in a surround of riotous floral color: yellows, blues, reds with white for contrast. The owner had allowed wildflowers to grow close to the very foundations of the house, and a tangle of vines climbed up the side visible from the road. The place had a secretive fairy tale ambience.

Then I saw the dried blood on the grass. Candy sniffed at it and whined, trying to tell me a wounded creature had passed this way, which, of course, I knew.

The collie had lain here eyeing me warily, then stumbled to her feet and disappeared into the fog. This had to be the right place because here was the blood. Except…

There was no dog, living or dead, in sight and no blue door.

I couldn't possibly have imagined the door. Could I?

No. Although I had thought for a moment that it was ajar… But I couldn't have conjured that bright, cornflower blue shade. It had been real. I wasn't going to second guess myself. I had seen stranger things in Foxglove Corners than a vanishing door.

Chalk it up to the aura of strangeness and mystery that hung over Foxglove Corners like an alien cloud. If it hadn't been for the blood on the grass, an undeniable sign, I'd have driven on in search of another patch of Queen Anne's Lace and another barn.

I remembered the real door, then, the one secured with a rusty lock, and led Candy around the structure to its front.

The lock wasn't there. Curious. With a cautious glance toward the house, I opened the door and peered into a dark, empty space, not unlike my idea of a mausoleum. The interior was swept clean of everything except cobwebs, and the air was chilly and damp. It didn't look as if any living creature had ever made its home inside or any farm implement had been stored here.

You're supposed to be looking for the collie, I reminded myself. *Or a collie's body.*

Somewhere in the flower-filled meadow that stretched as far as I could see, meeting that cerulean sky miles away? In the house perhaps?

I set out to walk to a stand of blue spruces where the meadow began its uphill slope. Ahead was dark evergreen forest, a place of refuge for a suffering dog. For me, it was impenetrable.

Instead of continuing on this course, I turned toward the house, marveling at the vigor of the multi-colored wildflowers, and climbed the eight steps to the wide, empty porch. I knocked on the door, an alarmingly loud sound in the quiet countryside. No one was home, and indeed, it looked as if this farmhouse might be one of the many abandoned residences in Foxglove Corners.

Candy lay down, seemingly oblivious of the mystical ambience I'd sensed. Certainly there could be no canine in the vicinity or she wouldn't be so calm.

"Candy, up," I said. "We're going home," and we walked back to the car, Candy tugging eagerly on her leash.

Once again I had to admit defeat, and my thoughts turned to Terra Roman. I expected to find a message from her on my answering machine when I returned home. It wasn't like her to ignore a message about a collie in distress.

~ * ~

There was no blinking light on the answering machine. Thoroughly frustrated, I left another message for Terra, this one laced with impatience, and consulted the clock. A long walk with the dogs, Sunday dinner, and the weekend was over with a collie who might still be in need and all of my attempts to help her thwarted.

Crane's report, delivered later as he hung his uniform jacket in the closet, only added to the puzzle.

"I checked out Deer Lake Trail for you, honey," he said. "The only barn didn't have a blue door. Could you have been on another road?"

In my mind I saw the sign again, white letters wavering through fog. Deer Leap Trail.

"No," I said. "I think we have another Brandymere Road in Foxglove Corners."

He smiled. "That's one explanation. Did you see anything that looked like world's end?"

"No, and no ghostly wayfarer who disappeared while traveling on it. I can't explain the blue door, Crane. And it wasn't aqua or teal but cornflower blue, a fresh, bright shade."

"I don't know what to say, except I didn't see any stray collies either."

"Well, then…" I let the sentence trail away. There was no point in dwelling on the mystery until I heard from Terra.

In the meantime, I would deal with reality. The chickens I was roasting for Sunday dinner, the ever-present question of which vegetable to cook, the apple pies cooling on the counter well away from Candy, Raven, and Misty, my trio of food bandits.

As I was setting the table, the dogs flew into their 'Company's here!' frenzy and somebody knocked on the front door. It was an imperious sound, and there in the driveway a gleaming blue convertible caught the last rays of the sun. Brent Fowler's car.

He always knew when dinner was about to be served at the Ferguson table, even when I varied the hour. I reached for another plate and opened the door. Candy rushed out to the porch and danced joyfully around his feet.

Brent was one of Foxglove Corners' beloved icons, a wealthy fox hunting bachelor with hair the color of an autumn maple leaf. He held many a female heart in his hand but appeared to be unattainable. At present, his fist was clutched around a bouquet of spring flowers, all of my favorites, tied with a trailing yellow ribbon.

"For you, Jennet. Happy spring!" He thrust the flowers at me. "And for you, too, Sheriff," he added for the benefit of Crane who had come up behind me. "A little decoration for your dinner table."

I accepted the bouquet and buried my nose in a cluster of pink lilies. How I'd missed the fragrance of fresh flowers during the long winter. "We haven't seen you in ages, Brent," I said. "Come in. Sit down. Where have you been?"

He flopped into a chair and divided his attention between Sky, his old favorite, and Misty, who had been a small puppy when he'd last seen her. "Out of town. Along about mid-February I grew mighty tired of snow every day, so I threw the dogs in the car and headed south. I came home for the Michigan spring. Michigan is the only place to be in April."

"Early spring is my favorite time of year," I said. "You'll stay for dinner, won't you?"

"Thanks. Wouldn't miss it."

While Brent and Crane caught up on each other's news, I finished setting the table, thankful that I'd roasted two chickens—one for leftovers—and baked two apple pies. With fresh asparagus, a salad, and biscuits, we would have a veritable feast.

I was glad Brent had made one of his unannounced appearances tonight, was happy to see him looking so well. We hadn't seen him in weeks and from time to time, I was plagued by a fear that something had happened to him, that I'd passed on my own bad luck to him, although he'd taken it willingly. Insisted on having it, and in fact, looked to the ownership of it as a challenge.

I was thinking about the haunted painting known as *Ada's Litter*. The mere thought of Julia's Christmas present to me created a coil of chill in my cozy kitchen.

The painting, a charming depiction of a golden-haired girl, a collie, and her litter on a blue Victorian porch, appeared to be the essence of charm. It was so lifelike you could imagine yourself stepping into the scene, feel the summer sun on your arms and smell the flowers that grew amid the grasses. At least that had been my reaction to it.

But strange stories swirled around the painting, tales of disaster and deadly fires ruining the lives of whoever owned the painting.

Did I believe this?

Not at first. But the day came when I had to accept the truth. '*Ada's Litter*,' that re-creation in oils of a girl and her dogs on a sweet summer day, was evil.

Its creator, artist Aura Lee Larkin, had advised me to burn it. I was ready to do that, but Brent had rescued it.

That had been a few months ago, time enough for *Ada's Litter* to work its evil spell.

But Brent seemed the same as ever. Blustery, blundering, brimming with enthusiasm for his new hot air balloon, the *Sky Dancer*.

"Do you still have *Ada's Litter*?" I asked him.

"Well, sure. It's hanging next to my other Larkin, the fox painting."

"And has everything been all right?"

"Never better," he said.

"It hasn't brought you bad luck then?"

"Not yet."

Well, he'd been away for the second half of the winter. Presumably the curse or whatever it was didn't pursue the painting's owner from state to state.

"Annica persuaded me to take her for a balloon ride one day," he said. "I think she has designs on me."

"You do?"

I knew she did. Annica, the pretty red-haired college student who worked as a waitress at the restaurant, Clovers, to pay her tuition, made no secret of her crush on Brent. He was several years her senior, though, and a man of the world, not the best match for a young girl like Annica.

"I thought you'd like to come along," he added. "Seeing Foxglove Corners from the air gives you a whole new perspective."

"That would be nice," I said. "One day."

At one time I'd wanted to go for a ride in one of Brent's hot air balloons. Now I wasn't so sure. Annoyingly, I couldn't explain why I had changed my mind. It wasn't that I was afraid. Not exactly. 'One day' was nice and vague. In the meantime, I had plenty to occupy myself on *terra firma*.

"Dinner is served," I said and lit the tapers in the heirloom candlesticks that had belonged to Crane's Civil War ancestress, confident that they would cast their protective glow over our meal.

Four

Monday found me behind my desk at Marston High School wondering where the rest of my fourth period class was. Denver Armstrong, by far the most difficult of my students—and to describe him as 'difficult' was a kindness—hadn't appeared yet.

He might also be called a catalyst. When he was absent, the class was calmer. Usually. Well, change that to less turbulent. I wrote his name on the attendance slip and scanned the rows to make sure I hadn't missed anyone.

Denver had made my days miserable last semester. My heart had all but fallen in January when I saw his name on my new class list. Mine wasn't the only section of American Literature, but it was the only one that meshed with his schedule.

This time the stakes for Denver were higher. He was repeating the class which was required for graduation. So far he was failing it again and didn't seem to care. In truth, the class, composed mostly of juniors, cared for little aside from spring break and their planned jaunts to Florida.

Ah, spring! The sweet-scented breezes of April wafted through the open windows, drawing everyone's attention to the outside world of blue skies, green grass, and frozen treats. Even mine.

This class and three more, I thought. Then freedom to escape to that beckoning other world, my Victorian farmhouse where my husband and collies lived.

I picked up the literature text which grew heavier every day. At long last we'd reached the twentieth century and were reading Thornton Wilder's play, *Our Town,* with parts assigned to volunteer readers. Three cast members were among the absent.

"Hey, Teach."

That voice… I recognized it.

Denver sauntered in, carrying a sandwich wrapped in greasy orange paper and a can of pop, two forbidden items. No notebook, no textbook. He wore a sleeveless black tank top, also forbidden, and a smirk on his mildly attractive face.

"You can't bring those in here." I drew a heavy line through his name on the attendance slip and added 'T' for tardy.

He sneered. "Why not? It's my lunch."

Here we go again.

"I don't doubt that, but lunch is over," I said. "It's time for class, and you know the rule. No food or drink allowed in the classroom."

"'Kay."

He strolled in front of me, and, perching on the windowsill, started to unwrap the sandwich. A gob of Ketchup dropped down to the floor. He smeared it with his foot. Someone laughed. Someone else, said, 'Go, Denver!' in a loud voice.

Denver Armstrong and the teacher. We gave our audience a better show than Thornton Wilder.

"Leave the room, Mr. Armstrong," I said. "You can eat your lunch in the office."

I opened the top desk drawer and pulled out a discipline referral, which was something I hated to do.

At the last faculty meeting, our not-so-beloved Principal Grimsley had complained bitterly about the number of referrals that landed on the assistant principal's desk. Often he had to take time out of his hectic schedule to handle them personally. Maintaining discipline was part of our job. One referral a month was acceptable. A dozen a day indicated that we weren't efficient educators. Hundreds of hopeful young teachers were waiting for a chance to prove their worth. His implication? We were dispensable.

Let's see how those untried hundreds would handle the Denver Armstrongs of the school.

I scribbled: 'Arrived late to class; brought sandwich and pop; refused to part with them; attire unsuitable for school.' Denver was still sitting on the windowsill, bare arms soaking up the sunshine. More gobs of ketchup had dripped down to the floor.

"Go," I said, and handed him the referral. "Now."

He took an enormous bite of his sandwich and dropped the rest of it in the wastebasket as he stamped past me. The pink referral, which he had crumpled, lay atop the half-eaten bun.

I'd have to write another referral and send it to the office with one of my trustworthy students. But it could wait until the end of class. I knew there was no chance Denver would report to the office. He'd sail out of the building and most likely buy another burger.

I picked up the anthology again and turned to the class with what I hoped was a calm demeanor. No need to let them know I was seething.

"Please turn to page two hundred," I said.

Today's reading included the heart-wrenching scene in which Emily revisits a day in her past after her death. At least I considered it heart-wrenching. Unfortunately Cheryl McCormick, who had been reading Emily's lines, was one of the day's absentees.

"We're going to need a new Emily," I said. "Would anyone care for an extra credit reading grade?"

The class fell silent. Not a hand went up.

"Okay," I said. "Becky Lane, will you be our Emily today?"

"I guess." With a dramatic sigh, Becky opened her book.

Fifteen minutes into class, we started reading.

~ * ~

My friend, Leonora, was a fellow English teacher at Marston. We taught in adjoining rooms, and ever since Leonora's move to a pink Victorian house in Foxglove Corners, we had shared the hour-long commute to Oakpoint, half of it on the freeway, half on country roads.

This week it was Leonora's turn to drive. I sat back and watched scattered suburban houses give way to rolling hills topped with evergreens. The day had lost none of its allure.

"I can't wait for Easter vacation," Leonora said. "The kids are wearing me down."

That surprised me. Leonora, a pretty, vivacious blonde, enjoyed enviable control in her classes, even her large section of rowdy freshmen. She hardly ever sent disciplinary referrals to the office.

"Everyone has spring fever," I said and told her about the latest episode with Denver Armstrong.

"What nerve! Maybe they'll suspend him again."

If only they would. He shouldn't be allowed to continue his disrespectful, disruptive behavior. For a moment I contemplated the wondrous peace that would descend on my fourth period class with Denver gone. Then I felt guilty for he was, after all, my student.

Leonora slowed to exit the freeway. Before long, we were traveling on a quiet road lined with woods and lakes and frequent 'Deer X-ing' signs. The road to home.

"Tell me more about the mysterious blue door you saw," Leonora said.

"There's no more to tell. I saw a blue door. It was definitely there, painted on the side of the old barn, but when I went back yesterday I didn't see it."

"Do you think the fog created the illusion of a door?" she asked. "It was pretty dense."

That was true. Fog could be deceptive, but mainly it concealed structures and landmarks and caused accidents on the freeway.

"Fog is white," I said. "This door was bright blue. Cornflower blue. I couldn't possibly be mistaken. I know what I saw."

"Why don't we swing by Deer Leap Trail now?" she asked. "Maybe, as a bonus, we'll see the collie."

The collie, I feared, was long gone, perhaps dead.

"Not today," I said. "That's out of our way, and I have so much to do tonight. Cook dinner, walk the dogs, and I have to call Terra again. I can't understand why she isn't returning my calls."

"She might have gone away for the weekend," Leonora said.

"I hope it's as simple as that."

"You may find a message from her on your machine."

I was beginning to have a bad feeling about the entire sequence of events. The unseen shooter, the wounded dog, the vanishing door, and, most of all, Terra's puzzling unavailability.

"It's like I'm tumbling into a mystery again," I said. "A many-faceted mystery."

I had no hope of identifying the shooter and little hope of finding the dog and the blue door. But I was determined to make contact with Terra. As the Rescue League's founder, she had always responded immediately to a collie-in-distress report, often investigating the case personally. Why was this one different?

"If you're free on Saturday morning, we'll drive out to Deer Lake Trail," I said. "Maybe by then I'll have some answers."

~ * ~

There were no messages on the machine. All I could do was call Terra again. This time I added that I was worried about her and hoped everything was all right. Then, on an impulse, I dialed Sue Appleton's number. Wonder of wonders, I found her home. I told her about the collie who had run away into the fog, bleeding from a gunshot wound, and my unanswered calls from Terra.

"That's odd," Sue said. "We have a meeting on Wednesday."

"We do? I didn't know about it."

"Terra sent out a postcard last week. Didn't you get it?"

I glanced at the basket where I tossed mail that I didn't want to deal with until a future date. The postcard must be in there.

"I can talk to her then," I said. "Of course it'll be too late for the dog."

"This is no way to run an organization," Sue said. "If I'd known, I could have driven out to Deer Leap Trail when the fog cleared."

"I should have called you," I said, feeling pangs of guilt again.

"I'm not blaming you, Jennet. It's Terra. She's not as thorough as she used to be. It's like she's lost interest in rescue."

I was loath to criticize Terra with another member of the Rescue League. So far, we had all worked together in harmony to achieve our common goal. While I was annoyed with Terra's apparent indifference, it was only fair to give her the benefit of a doubt.

"I'll see you on Wednesday then," I said.

When I hung up the receiver, I rifled through the basket and found the postcard from Terra. If I hadn't talked to Sue, I wouldn't have come across it until after the event. Now that I thought of it, this, too, was strange. Terra hosted an annual Christmas party in her home and a picnic in the summer, but she rarely called meetings.

What was going on here?

Five

The mystery deepened on Wednesday when Leonora and I arrived at Terra Roman's house to find members of the Collie Rescue League milling around in the front yard and on the porch. The house was dark and silent. No one had set out a welcome doormat for a gathering or prepared a pitcher of lemonade to counteract the discomfort of the warm, muggy afternoon.

I recognized Emma Brock and Liz Melbourne. An unfamiliar woman with red hair sat in one of Terra's wicker chairs. She must be a new member. Sue Appleton stood beside her car, drinking a milkshake. We walked over to join her.

"Is this the right night for the meeting?" I asked.

"It's the date and time Terra wrote on the postcard," Sue said. "This infuriates me. I cancelled a dinner engagement tonight. Here's my dinner." She drained the shake and reached into the car to set the empty container in the cup holder.

"What do you suppose happened?" Leonora asked. "Did Terra have some emergency?"

"With her dog, maybe?" I added.

Terra had adopted one of her own rescues, a tricolor collie named Shadow. If Shadow was inside, she was quieter than any collie I'd ever known, especially with people so close to the house. And would Terra leave Shadow in the dark? I didn't think so.

"No one knows," Sue said, not bothering to hide her annoyance. "If something came up, she could have let us know. She never used to be so inconsiderate."

Terra's puzzling absence explained the unanswered phone calls. But not to be home for her own meeting was strange.

I glanced at the porch. "Her mailbox is full. She must have gone away."

There were other signs of neglect. The forsythia bushes needed pruning, and the grass was too high. Wild blue and white violets bloomed amidst the blades. The recent warm weather and rain had encouraged growth. Next to the Rescue League, Terra loved to work in her yard.

"What do you want to do?" Leonora asked.

"We can wait awhile. About fifteen minutes."

"I hope she shows up. I've been looking forward to this meeting."

Leonora had only recently expressed a desire to join the League, had yet to save her first collie. I was afraid she had a romanticized idea of the work the members did and would shy away from the unpleasantness and heartache that often accompanied rescue. I'd hoped she would hear some stories from the other, darker side this evening.

"Darn it all." Emma Brock strolled over to a silver Honda with collie-themed decals. "I wanted to ask Terra's advice about my Lacy. I'm afraid I bought a vicious puppy. I heard her mother was a fighter."

Leonora looked at her in alarm. "A collie?"

She nodded. "My new puppy. She looks as sweet as pie, but she keeps showing her teeth and growling at me. She's only a baby, just three months old."

"She'll need training and a strong hand," I said. "Let her know you're the boss."

"Yes, but what if she's still aggressive after that? I don't want to have to give her up."

"Good heavens, no!" Now I was alarmed. "You can't do that, Emma. You're in rescue."

"Does Lacy bite?" Leonora asked.

"A little. They're puppy bites, but she breaks the skin." Emma extended her arm with a bandage circling her wrist.

"She'll outgrow that," I said, remembering Halley as a puppy.

"I hope so," Emma said. "I was counting on Terra to give me some advice. No offense, Jennet."

Emma was a small woman with a soft voice who appeared fragile and wore prints with soft floral patterns. I imagined that sweet little Lacy already saw herself in the role of alpha dog.

"Well, it doesn't look like Terra is going to show up," Emma said. "We must have gotten our signals crossed. I'm going to take off. Lacy has a temper tantrum if I leave her in her crate too long." She said goodnight and opened her car door.

"Emma sounds like she's afraid of Lacy," Leonora said. "We might as well go home, too, Jennet."

I shrugged. Crane was bringing a take-out dinner from Clovers and the dogs' needs had been met. I had no reason to hurry home, but there was no point in standing in front of an empty house.

Others were drifting toward their cars, mumbling their discontent, and Sue was getting in her car.

"Has anyone stopped to wonder whether something happened to Terra?" I asked.

Sue turned her key in the ignition. "Like what?"

"Maybe she went away for the weekend and had an accident, or she might be lying in the house, unconscious."

"You've been reading too many Gothic novels," Leonora said.

"And listening to Annica."

The young waitress-college student had a penchant for telling gruesome tales and giving the most mundane of facts a nightmare twist. She would have had a field day with this aborted meeting.

"We could ask one of the neighbors," Leonora said.

The nearest houses were as dark and silent as Terra's. It was seven-thirty, an hour when many families would be in their yards enjoying the lingering daylight or an early barbecue, but I didn't see a soul.

"I don't know if that's a good idea," I said. "Terra might not like our raising the alarm, and there's a chance that she doesn't even know her neighbors. When I lived in Oakpoint, I only had a few friends on my street. It's only marginally different in Foxglove Corners."

"I'm sure there's a simple answer." Sue seemed to have gotten over her annoyance with Terra. "One that doesn't involve blood and mayhem."

I recalled that Terra was a teacher. It was the middle of the week. If she had arranged for a substitute, surely somebody at her school would know where she was. But where did she teach? I couldn't remember. And why call a meeting when she planned to be away?

I took one last look at her house. "I wish I knew what she did with Shadow," I said.

~ * ~

After the meeting that hadn't happened, I didn't expect a message from Terra on my answering machine when I got home. I felt certain she would explain her absence in her own time. Meanwhile, the wounded collie was a lost cause, although I still planned to watch for her. Well, I was always on the lookout for collies running free on the roads and in the wooded areas of Foxglove Corners. It had become second nature.

Without Terra at the helm, we'd have to work alone. It wouldn't be easy. Any organization needs a leader. Terra was the one who kept a list of foster homes. She knew how many collies were ready for adoption and who would be available to investigate prospective buyers. Fortunately Liz served as the league's treasurer.

But I was getting ahead of myself. How much could happen in a couple of days? Terra would turn up with apologies and an explanation. She'd reschedule the meeting, and all would be well again.

~ * ~

That night I dreamed of the blue door. I was wandering through a dense white fog, stumbling over prickly low-growing bushes, when I saw a cornflower blue door in the distance. It appeared to be half open, and light poured from the interior, creating a path.

I gravitated toward that path and walked more easily over the terrain, but it seemed that cold, clammy hands reached out to grab me. I couldn't let myself be captured by these loathsome appendages or I'd be lost forever in the fog. Lost and doomed.

As I moved closer to the door, it retreated farther back in a field of fog until it was no longer a door but a sapphire winking in a damp, mist-begotten world.

When I woke, abruptly, I felt as if those ghastly hands had touched my skin. I imagined I saw a distant glimmer of deep blue and rubbed my bare arms, expecting them to be wet with unholy condensation.

It was morning, still dark, and the alarm clock was blaring. Crane was downstairs starting breakfast. An enticing smell of pancakes wafted up the stairway. I should get up, but I lay in bed trying to figure out what the dream meant before it faded.

I could think of only one interpretation. The blue door was an illusion, born of the fog and vanished in the fog. It wasn't something I was destined to find, no matter how many times I drove past Deer Leap Trail; and, strangely, that knowledge filled me with sadness.

Six

The headline in the evening's *Banner* fairly screamed at me. 'Search on for Foxglove Corners Woman.' Above the article was a photograph of Terra Roman. It was a mediocre likeness. She looked solemn, not like herself.

Quickly I scanned the article, then reread it. Terra's sister, Tina, had reported her missing when she didn't show up for a movie date. Terra had been in her classroom on Friday, but no one saw her after she walked out to the school parking lot at the end of the day with a friend. That friend had provided lesson plans for Terra's classes.

The school's policy required a teacher to inform the office what day she expected to return to her classes. That call hadn't come from Terra, so the administration had no reason to suspect foul play. Marston had a similar policy which had never made sense to me. How could I tell on one day how I would feel the next? At any rate, the office assumed she had a two or three day illness.

"She must have gone home that Friday," Tina said. "Her collie is missing, too."

None of the neighbors on White Pine Street had seen Terra; no one admitted to having more than a passing acquaintance with her. They remembered occasional collies running and barking in the backyard, though.

Today was Thursday. Terra had been missing for six days.

I was right. Something had happened to her, but she wasn't lying dead in her house. Tina, who had a key, could attest to that. It appeared that Terra had come home, made a cup of tea, and gone out again, leaving the cup to drip dry in the sink. She hadn't slept in her bed, and the dog's dish was on the counter filled with kibble. The leash was gone.

Another mysterious disappearance in Foxglove Corners.

According to Terra's principal, she had been wearing a pink dress with long sleeves and a white collar and a pearl choker on Friday. Which, I imagined, she would have changed for a casual at-home outfit. Unless she'd had to go out again immediately. In other words, the pink dress wasn't a very good clue.

You're forgiven for the meeting fiasco, Terra.

I remembered the mutterings of the inconvenienced League members. We should have had more faith in Terra, should have known she'd never summon us to a meeting and absent herself from it without a serious reason.

Along with concern for Terra, I couldn't help speculating about the future of the Collie Rescue League. What did Terra's disappearance mean for us? What if someone came across a collie in need of emergency medical care? Or a foster home? Or what if one of us encountered a rescue problem she couldn't solve?

With six collies, one of them still a puppy, and a full-time teaching job, I couldn't possibly foster a canine foundling. I could pay for veterinary care, though, knowing Liz Melbourne would reimburse me. But in order to survive, the League needed someone knowledgeable and diplomatic in charge.

The women, while caring and dedicated, were inclined to gossip and criticize one another. I could see them floundering and arguing among themselves without Terra to smooth over bruised feelings.

The situation could well spiral out of control, and the collies we should be helping would suffer.

There was, however, one tiny bit of encouraging news. Wherever Terra was, I assumed that Shadow was with her.

~ * ~

On Saturday morning, Leonora and I set out on our jaunt to Deer Leap Trail. We planned to search for the elusive blue door and the collie. To be accurate, Leonora hoped to find the dog. I was more realistic. Too much time had passed since the day she'd been shot. As for the door, I was still convinced that I'd seen it and still mystified.

"It's exciting to go someplace new on a glorious spring weekend," Leonora said. "Even though we're not that far from home."

Leonora liked to travel. So far she hadn't announced any plans for Easter week. I wondered why. I knew she was seeing Deputy Sheriff Jake Brown again. He'd courted both Leonora and my sister, Julia. Jake favored beautiful blondes and apparently couldn't decide which one he liked the best.

If Leonora had Easter plans with Jake, she had been uncharacteristically secretive about them.

She was right, though. In spite of Terra's disappearance, in spite of the gravity and probable hopelessness of today's mission, an air of excitement blew in through the open windows with the April breezes. Something was going to happen today. Something good, I hoped.

The morning was warm and sunny with only a light haze to distort our vision. Vibrant wildflowers bordered the road. If only I could transplant those tall purple flowers to my garden or stop and gather a bouquet. But this could be privately-owned property.

The detour signs were still in place, so we followed a winding by-road that was little more than a path cut through woods and ultimately came to Deer Leap Trail.

Leonora squinted into the sunlight. "Is that the barn?"

The structure she pointed to was relative new and sported a coat of red paint that gleamed in the sunlight. Nearby three horses grazed behind a white plank fence. The scene was tranquil and typically country.

"No," I said. "I don't remember seeing a red barn."

Not on the morning of the fog, which was understandable, nor on my second trip, which was not. If I hoped to solve the mystery of the blue door, I had to be more observant.

I recalled the woods and the lakes, though, and the 'No Hunting' and 'No Trespassing' signs. When we came to the patch of white Queen Anne's Lace, I slowed down. Although wild—considered lowly weeds by some—they grew as if planted up to the side of the old barn. *The* barn.

"That's it," I said. "I'm ninety-nine percent sure."

"But it doesn't have a blue door."

"No. Not today."

"The barn must belong to that white house," she said. "Did you check with the people who live there?"

"No one was home. I think the house is vacant."

I was certain of it. There were no vehicles in the gravel drive, and the barn, I recalled, had been swept clean. Also, on the day of the fog, the door had been secured with a rusty lock. On my second visit, the door was unlocked. Somebody must have at least visited the property. But why leave the barn unlocked?

The house had a desolate, forsaken look, and the wildflowers and untamed vegetation seemed to be growing even closer to the foundation. I had been here only a week ago, hardly long enough for such an invasion.

"Let's drive on and see if we can find another barn," Leonora said.

"We won't," I said, but I steered back to the trail, and we reached the crossroads without seeing one.

"This is where I turned," I said.

"If it's still Deer Leap Trail on the other side, let's keep going."

I humored her, even though I knew I hadn't ventured in this direction. The trail beyond the crossroad wound through a quiet stretch of woods and water, of darkness and green. Then the scenery changed. We passed a palatial white mansion built far from the road, then another. Eventually we came to an elaborate sign: Sapphire Lake Farms, an obviously pricey development of custom-built houses. The foremost of them sat on a velvety expanse of lawn with a pond at its center. After we passed it, we were back in deep country.

"There's nothing mysterious here," Leonora said. "Should we keep going?"

"Why not?"

"If we see a restaurant, we can stop for lunch."

"Out here in the wilderness?" I asked. "I don't think that's likely."

"You never know. If we don't find one, we can always go to Clovers."

And regale Annica with tales of the vanishing blue door. I smiled at the thought of her eagerness to help solve the new mystery.

Leonora said, "Do you know what I think? The barn with the blue door wasn't on this road after all. You got turned around in the fog and ended up on a different road entirely. Maybe it runs parallel to Deer Leap Trail. So there's no real mystery. We're just in the wrong place."

"That makes sense," I said. "But it didn't happen."

Still, Leonora's idea of parallel roads made me think of a parallel universe. On Deer Lake Trail in the alternate universe there was an old barn with a cornflower blue door painted on its side and a collie whimpered as she waited for somebody to find her. This was, after all, Foxglove Corners, a place of strange and mysterious happenings.

"I saw the road sign clearly," I said. "Even through the fog."

We had come to one of those wooded stretches where the leaves of the trees on either side grew into one another, forming a canopy plunging the road into a curious dimness. It seemed that we were in an endless green tunnel. When the road curved a few miles later, a distant rumble of thunder mixed with a new darkening of the sky.

"What happened to our bright day?" Leonora demanded.

"It's going to storm," I said. "We'd better turn around and go home."

Seven

I had never known a storm to develop so suddenly. It was as if a giant hand had abruptly extinguished the world's lamps. Even as I looked for a place to turn around, the thunder crashed overhead. A lightning bolt electrified the sky, illuminating the thorny roadside vegetation just waiting to scratch my car's finish.

"This wasn't in the forecast," Leonora said.

"No matter. It's here."

The road was too narrow to make a complete U-turn safely. With no other option presenting itself, I drove on, hoping to come to another crossroad. The next instant, sheets of rain poured down from the clouds, stealing my visibility. The windshield wipers swished back and forth, all but useless in the deluge.

There was something unnatural about the way the storm had sprung to life so suddenly when a short time ago, the day had been clear and bright.

This is Foxglove Corners weather, I thought. *Strange and menacing.*

"I can't see where I'm going," I said. "If a deer leaps out in front of the car, I'll never be able to stop in time." Instinctively I slowed to twenty-five. To twenty. It felt as if I were speeding.

Leonora said, "What deer in its right mind would dash across the road in this rain?" Then in an excited tone, she added, "I see a light up ahead. A tiny one."

I saw it too. A lone, brave beam shining through a wall of rain. "If there's a house, it'll have a driveway," I said. "We can park and wait out the storm in comfort."

The light originated in a lamppost placed close to the road. A wide drive curved to the right. Thankful for any respite, I turned in, drove a few yards, and brought the Taurus to a stop in front of a tall, trellised arbor.

In a flash of lightning, I could see a house. Large, brown with towering gables, built close to the road. A sign swung madly in the wind, but I only made out one word: 'Inn.' The first floor windows were brightly lit as if to scare off the storm.

We'd found our refuge. Maybe.

"It looks awfully spooky," Leonora said. "Like the kind of house you see in a horror movie."

"Any port in a storm," I said. "If they're open, we can have lunch. By the time we're finished eating, the storm should be over."

"I don't like the looks of the place. It's supposed to be an inn. Where are all the other cars?"

"It's still early. Anyway, you can't see properly in all the rain. We can stay in the car," I said. "There's a chocolate bar in the glove compartment. We can split it."

"I *am* hungry but for something substantial," she said. "Do you have an umbrella?"

"It's in the trunk."

"Then let's make a dash for it."

It was impossible to race around to the trunk, open the umbrella, and run up to the brown house without getting drenched. At last, we stood in the vestibule, staring at an untenanted reception desk and an empty dining room.

"There's nobody here," Leonora said, trying to pat the water from her long blonde hair. "What kind of place is this?"

A chalkboard announced the day's luncheon specials in colored chalk:

Chicken Pot Pie
Chicken salad sandwich
Beef barley soup

Beneath these offerings a pink cartoon bunny pleaded: *Please join us for Easter brunch and Easter Egg Hunt! Prizes and surprises and fun for all ages!*

"Comfort food," I murmured. "Exactly what we need."

I peered into the dining room. The tables were set with white linens and china. Spring bouquets in canning jar vases served as centerpieces and lamps in sconces threw fantastic shadows on paintings, mostly country landscapes. Lakes and forests and waterfalls. All this splendor and not a soul in sight, not even a hostess.

"This," Leonora said, "is creepy. Maybe we'd better go back to the car."

As she spoke, a young girl came through an archway. She had a cap of tousled blonde curls, and her earrings were lacy white disks that resembled crocheted doilies.

"Welcome to the Spirit Lamp Inn," she said with a shy smile. "I'm Diana. Two for lunch?"

Now this was more like what I'd expected. The unusual had just become mundane. We might have been at Clovers except for the absence of a dessert carousel and the bubbly red-haired Annica filling it with pies and cakes.

"We'd like lunch, yes," I said, and she led us to a table in front of a window. Not that we could see the view.

The girl rattled off the day's specials.

"This is a soup and sandwich day, if ever there was one," Leonora said. "That's what I'll have with coffee."

"The same for me."

When she had left us alone in the cavernous dining room, Leonora said, "The Spirit Lamp Inn. What kind of name is that?"

"A shivery name," I said with a smile, remembering all the Gothic novels I'd read that began with the heroine seeking shelter from a storm in a sinister house. Nothing could be stranger than the Spirit Lamp Inn's dining room, prepared to host a crowd, about to serve two women.

"Something's odd," Leonora said. "It's too quiet. It's like there's only us and Diana in the whole inn."

I'd felt the strangeness too. It practically washed over me in waves, but I determined to stay in the real world for once. "That can't be. There must at least be a cook. As soon as the rain stops, a few customers will drift in. Otherwise, how could a restaurant stay in business?"

"Even so." Leonora continued to fuss with her hair; it was already beginning to dry on top. "I'll be glad to get out of here. Let's eat and run."

"Before we leave, I'd like to ask Diana a few questions. She's the first person we've seen since we left home."

Leonora and I had the dining room to ourselves. We ate without further conversation and listened to the rain beating on the window. It sounded more like hail. When Diana came back to recite the dessert menu, we ordered blueberry pie, and I seized my opportunity to engage her in conversation.

After complimenting her on her earrings and discovering that she'd crocheted them herself, I said, "There's an old white farmhouse on Deer Leap Trail, south of the crossroads. It looks empty. I wondered if it's for sale."

She stared at me, fidgeting with one doily earring.

"Do you know who lives there?" I asked.

"I'm not sure I know the house you mean," she said.

"I only saw one house. There's an old barn on the property."

She continued to look blank.

"Fields of flowers grow wild right up to the house," I added. "They're pretty, but it looks like there's no one to cultivate a garden."

"I wouldn't know," Diana said. "I'm not from around here."

She made her escape but came back to serve the pie and refill our coffee cups without an extraneous word. When she was out of earshot, I said, "I find it hard to believe she doesn't know what house I mean."

"She *did* seem evasive."

"There's something mysterious about that place," I said. "I'm going to ask her about the blue door. I don't have anything to lose."

It was still raining by the time we finished our pie, but the thunder and lightning had moved on to threaten another town. We could drive safely home. Having accomplished nothing? I saw one last chance to add to my information.

When Diana brought our check, I said, "Have you ever seen a barn with a blue door in the vicinity?"

"No, but there's a little blue house a few miles down the road," she said. "It might have a matching door." She paused. "Why do you want to know?"

"No particular reason. I thought I saw one the other day." Quickly I changed the subject. "I imagine you see a lot of stray dogs out here in the country. We're looking for a lost collie that might have been hurt. It's a sable."

She looked puzzled. "A sable?"

"That's a color. Brown and white."

I might have anticipated her answer.

"We're a restaurant. We don't encourage strays of any kind."

I wasn't going to let her get away with that half answer. "So, did you see a collie?"

"Only on television," she said. "My grandma has all the Lassie DVDs."

With a smile, she set our bill down on the table. "Whenever you're ready," she said.

~ * ~

It was still drizzling as we drove home on Deer Leap Trail, past the white house and the barn and the Queen Anne's lace, all of them fresh washed and sparkling after the hard rain. A rainbow arced across the sky. The bands of fragile color made everything seem brighter, almost magical. But something of the dark mystery that permeated the Spirit Lamp Inn seemed to travel with us. Something was wrong there. I couldn't figure out what it was.

"Diana knows more than she's saying," I said. "I wonder why all the secrecy?"

"Maybe her boss doesn't approve of gossiping."

"There was no one around to hear us talking. I still think that's strange."

"It is, a little," Leonora admitted.

"I don't think Diana made the sandwiches and the pie herself. I'm going back to the Spirit Lamp Inn someday soon. In the evening maybe."

Diana had skipped merrily around my question about the collie. Of course they didn't encourage strays. Of course they were a restaurant. But had she seen this particular collie? I wished I knew. DVDs indeed. It seemed as if Deer Lake Trail were steeped in mystery.

"I'd like to see the spirit lamp," Leonora said. "Does it have anything to do with ghosts, I wonder?"

"I doubt it."

I wasn't sure exactly what kind of lamp had given the inn its name. A few minutes on the Internet could clear up that mystery.

But what of the blue door I'd seen? And the farmhouse? What was its story? And the collie? Could she still be alive?

"Let's go back for their Easter brunch, and see what their idea of fun is," Leonora said.

"Or before that."

Mysteries were falling like the storm's last raindrops around me. I had to start taking action.

Eight

One click at the computer keyboard took me to a definition of spirit lamp: *a lamp that burns alcohol or other liquid fuel.*

It had nothing to do with ghosts. I should have known that. *Beer, Wine, and Spirits.*

In fact, I owned a spirit lamp, a pretty glass luminary that resembled an overgrown perfume bottle. I couldn't remember where I'd bought it and had only used it as a decoration.

Would that all of the day's mysteries could be so easily solved.

For a moment, I slipped into the role of Devil's Advocate. Suppose the young waitress, Diana, was not evasive but merely shy, a new employee eager to please her customers and earn a nice tip. She really didn't know anything about the white farmhouse on Deer Leap Trail, had never even noticed it, and the only collie she had ever seen lived on a television screen. It was possible.

As for the Spirit Lamp Inn, the place was probably crowded today with Sunday afternoon diners. An electrical storm would naturally keep customers away.

But the door in the fog continued to puzzle me. Then there was Terra. The Sunday *Banner* carried a brief update of her disappearance with two sightings, both of which had proved to be false.

Feeling that Leonora and I had been sidelined by the thunderstorm, I began to plan my next visit to the area. It wouldn't be today, though, as my Sunday was already crammed with chores and activities which included a long walk with the dogs. Then tomorrow was Monday, bound to be a difficult day with Denver Armstrong and company.

Don't think about anything unpleasant now, I told myself. *Go out with the dogs and enjoy the fresh spring air.*

~ * ~

After yesterday's stormy weather, Sunday was sunny and warm with a robust wind that whipped my hair in my face and set the dogs' fur blowing. It blew through the wildflowers that grew along the lane, creating ripples of glorious color, and sent whatever wasn't anchored to the earth sailing through the air.

Who doesn't love a warm spring wind?

With Candy, Raven, and Gemmy leashed and the other collies trotting sedately in our wake, we walked all the way down to the horse farm on Squill Lane where Sue Appleton lived. She was outside, dressed in jeans and a bright red sweater, taking pictures of a colt, while three horses grazed happily on new grass.

"Come see our new addition," she called. "This is his first time outside."

I led the dogs to the fence, and Sue walked over to greet them "What gorgeous collies!" she said as Candy yelped her displeasure at being restrained. Sue aimed her camera at Halley, Sky, and Misty who gathered at the fence reveling in the admiration of a friendly human.

"That's a good one for my album," she said. "I guess you heard about Terra."

"Is she still missing?"

"So far as I know. What do you think happened to her?"

"I can't imagine."

Neither of us raised the possibility that Terra and her dog might have met with foul play, even though that was the most obvious explanation.

"The League is going to fall apart without her," Sue said.

Which was exactly what I'd been thinking. But I said, "It doesn't have to."

"Liz picked up a surrendered tri male in Maple Creek yesterday. She's keeping him for a few days but doesn't have room for another long-term rescue. Terra would have found a foster home for him. She has the A and the B list."

"There's a B list?" I asked.

"The last resort people. They only want the best dogs. The clean, handsome ones who don't need vet care."

"We should appoint a temporary leader then," I said.

Sue backtracked. "I agree, but let's wait a while. I'm hoping this is all a terrible mistake. We don't want Terra to come home and find she's been replaced."

"She would want us to carry on."

What if she never came back? It was well enough to hope for Terra's safe return, but I couldn't think of a legitimate reason for her absence. In the interests of the imperiled collies who depended on us, we'd have to put emergency measures into place soon.

"As the League treasurer, Liz keeps track of the funds," Sue said. "We're in fair shape financially, but we planned to sell collie memorabilia at a yard sale next week. Terra has been collecting all sorts of figurines and art. They're locked in her house."

"Maybe her sister will let us take them. She has a key."

"That's a thought."

The wind was picking up. It tossed a handful of dust and grit in my face. Candy began scratching at the ground, and Raven and

Misty were barking at the horses. I didn't know much about the equine race, but the noise and perceived aggression of the dogs couldn't be good for their nerves.

"We'd better move on," I said.

"Before you go, Jennet, I think we should call everybody together and have a meeting. We can brainstorm and maybe come up with solutions to some of our problems."

"Just let me know when and where," I said and called my brood to heel, hoping it wouldn't be necessary.

~ * ~

I was never surprised to see Brent Fowler on my doorstep near the dinner hour. The red-haired fox hunter appeared later that day, for once without wine or flowers or candy. That was so unlike him that I suspected something was wrong.

But he seemed to be the same Brent, jostling with Sky who forgot to be timid in his presence and roughhousing with Misty. He addressed Crane as 'Sheriff' and announced his latest endeavor: a children's book about two boys who had an adventure while flying over the woods in a hot air balloon.

It seemed an unlikely endeavor for Brent, who was always in motion. Writing required long, quiet hours at a desk. I'd started a book on supernatural experiences in Foxglove Corners, but it remained unfinished because, I told myself, I'd run out of ghost stories.

"We set May first for our hot air trip," he said as he grabbed a cracker from a hastily-assembled appetizer tray.

I'd forgotten about it. Rather, I'd shelved it in a back corner of my mind.

Now as Brent described the ultimate thrill of cruising in the sky in a hot air balloon, I decided I had to make my feelings known to him. Some powerful inner voice was issuing an unmistakable warning. What would be a thrill for Brent and Annica would be wrong for me.

It wasn't that I was afraid. I'd faced danger before. But that voice was persistent, and foreboding was thick in the living room tonight. It felt like a rapidly rising mist, and I knew well that disaster could creep about unnoticed in the mist.

Instead of floating high above Foxglove Corners in a colorful balloon, I could see myself falling through the air, out of control. Out of time. To be sure, my imagination was in overdrive. Still…

"I'm not sure I want to go," I said.

"I did, Jennet," Crane reminded me. "You'd be safe with Fowler or I'd never allow you to go."

Not even that dictatorial sentiment swayed me.

"I don't even like flying in an airplane," I said. "If anything goes wrong, it's a long way to the ground."

"The *Sky Dancer* will be safer than any plane. I'm the skipper. And this will be better. We can fly low. You can touch the treetops if you want to."

That mental picture amused me. My hands trailing through rustling leaves that ordinarily would be beyond my reach. But was that an experience I needed for a full and satisfying life? I didn't think so.

"I just feel I can live happily enough on land," I said.

"If you bail on us, Annica will be disappointed."

I doubted that. With me out of the picture, Annica would have Brent all to herself, which was a cherished dream she'd never realized.

"She'll get over it," I said.

Brent knew when to capitulate. Or to appear to do so. "It's still April. You'll have plenty of time to change your mind."

"I think the ham is ready," I said. "Who's hungry?"

Candy woofed her answer and dashed to the kitchen. Brent got up and stretched, and I resolved not to let the subject come up again.

However, with talk of the planned hot air balloon jaunt finished, my earlier impression that all was not well with Brent returned. Brent was a man whose zest for life reached out to encompass anyone who crossed his path. He was a little less jovial tonight, a little quieter and serious. If I didn't know him better, I'd describe his face as haunted.

Nine

After dinner, as we relaxed in the living room over coffee and lemon meringue pie, I said, "Is anything wrong, Brent? You seem subdued tonight."

He let his fork linger over the last piece of pie on his plate. Candy sat at his feet waiting to see if he was going to leave it for her.

"Me? Subdued?" He was incredulous. "Never."

"You seem unlike yourself. Not quite so hearty."

"What could be wrong?" Brent asked. "The horses and dogs are in tip-top shape, the hunting is good, and Skyway Tours is making me rich."

Brent, of course, had been wealthy before he started his hot air balloon business. What did they say? *The rich get rich and the poor get poorer…?*

Making money wasn't my primary concern in life. I smiled at Crane. He winked at me. Brent missed our exchange, and Candy whimpered, her eyes riveted on Brent's dessert plate.

"Have you found the vanishing blue door yet?" Brent asked.

"That remains a mystery," I said. "But Leonora and I discovered a strange inn. The Spirit Lamp Inn. Have you ever heard of it?"

"Can't say that I have. Is it in Foxglove Corners?"

"Yes, on Deer Leap Trail."

"It must be new," he said.

I thought of the old brown gables, the spooky façade, the dark atmosphere, and the empty dining room intended to serve at least two dozen. The Inn looked as if it had been there for decades, hovering over the road, casting its spell.

"It may be a new business, but the house is old. The food is good, though," I added. "Leonora and I are going back for their Easter Sunday brunch."

"Maybe I'll join you," Brent said. To Candy's chagrin, he finished his pie and scraped the plate clean with his fork. "Did you ever come across that wounded collie?" he asked.

"Not yet."

"It was a sable, right?"

I nodded.

"I saw a bunch of lost dog flyers for a sable and white female collie in Lakeville the other day," he said.

"Do you remember any details?"

"A few. The dog's name is Breezy. She's two years old, and there's a hundred dollar reward being offered. You might want to tell your rescue pals to keep their eyes open."

"That could be the dog I saw, but I'm not even sure she's still alive. Do you have a phone number?"

"I left the flyer at home. Sorry, Jennet. I'll drop it off tomorrow. But what are you going to do? Call up these people and tell them their dog was shot and maybe died?"

"I'm not sure."

Would I welcome news like that? No, but on the other hand, I'd want to know what happened to my dog. Still, I didn't have any proof that Breezy was the collie who had disappeared in the fog. There must be at least a dozen sable and white collies in the area. Maybe more. I had one myself.

Well, I didn't have the owners' phone number, which meant I didn't have to decide tonight.

As for Brent, he'd successfully turned the focus of the conversation away from himself. I still felt that something was troubling him, but if he wouldn't tell me about it, what could I do?

Just wait for further developments, and in the meantime offer him another piece of pie.

~ * ~

The next time I found myself with an hour to spare, I drove out to Deer Leap Trail. It wasn't the most propitious day for an exploration. The sky had been overcast all day with evening storms predicted. I thought of the deluge that had overtaken Leonora and me on our previous visit and didn't relish the prospect of a repeat performance.

Well, I'd be there and home long before evening. My plan was to drive by the white farmhouse and the barn. Then I'd stop at the Spirit Lamp Inn. I wasn't sure what I hoped to accomplish. See if there was any sign of life at the house, perhaps, and whether anyone else at the Inn would be willing to talk to me.

As I turned onto the trail, I watched for leaping deer and a wandering collie—sable and white female—but all I saw was a wild rabbit hopping through the vegetation that grew at the edge of the woods. Everything was quiet and peaceful, exactly the way a country road should be.

When I came to the old barn, I pulled off the trail and let the car idle while I surveyed the scene. The borders of Queen Anne's Lace had widened, and the wildflowers seemed to have tripled since my last visit. Waves of vibrant color spread over the meadow and flowed up to the very foundation of the house. Like enchanted waves intent on invading the structure. It was a chilling comparison, a fleeting impression, and I let it slide out of my mind.

How could anyone drive past the farmhouse and not notice this wild floral display? The waitress Diana was either lying or she always approached the Inn from a different direction.

A plaintive cry yanked me out of my introspection.

Then came the echo. Then silence. From inside my car, I scanned the acreage, trying to determine its point of origin. I couldn't. Nothing in my sight stirred. There wasn't even a breath of wind to set the wildflowers in motion.

All right. What creature had made the cry? A bird as it flew by and lost itself in the treetops? A small animal grabbed by a predator? A dog in peril?

Misty had uttered a similar cry the day she'd pulled a tablecloth and a vase of flowers down on herself.

Could it possibly have been the wounded collie? And could the wounded collie be the lost dog, Breezy?

I couldn't stay in the Taurus once these thoughts occurred to me. Heedless of my safety and Crane's warnings, I left the car and tramped through high grasses to the barn, taking care not to trample on the Queen Anne's Lace.

For a fraction of moment, I thought I saw the impression of a blue door on the side of the barn. The operative words were 'thought' and 'impression.' It would take the merest alteration in the air like drifting folds of fog or a haze to create such an impression. That and a lively imagination with which I was blessed—or cursed.

Still, when I reached the barn, I ran my hand along the section of the outer wall where the blue door would have been. Where I'd once seen it.

There was no anomaly there, no difference in the weathered surface, no raised area to indicate a door frame.

Back to practical matters then. Was the door to the barn still unlocked?

I went around to the front and spied the lock and rusty chain in place. Someone must visit the barn frequently. To unlock it and lock it again? If so, this couldn't be simply an unused out-building.

There must be something valuable inside. Something capable of making a sound.

I rapped on the door, hoping to hear another cry or a frantic scratching of an animal paw. Or—here was a new thought—a child.

"Is anyone in there?" I called and knocked again.

Nothing. I didn't hear a sound. This was the oddest place, but since I was here, why not see if anybody was inside the farmhouse, even though it looked as deserted today as it had both times I'd been here.

I stood on the porch, knocked loudly on the door twice, and waited. Finally realizing that I was wasting precious time, I turned to go back to the car and...

What was that?

In my peripheral vision, I saw a flash of light in the shape of an animal at the west side of the barn.

Rather, I thought I had.

As I stared at the barn, my heart pounding, I couldn't be sure. It had happened too quickly, appearing as a flash of lightning and gone in the same heartbeat. The silence was so thick I could practically feel it, and I sensed that I was alone in a wildflower-dotted landscape.

Still I cried, "Wait! Come back!" and stared at an empty space.

Was it that imagination of mine working overtime again?

That apparition, or whatever it was I had seen, had the shape and color of a sable collie.

I ran through the grasses and wildflowers back to the barn, stood still, and let my eyes sweep the road and the woods and the meadow. I didn't see another living thing.

Who is foolish enough to try and catch the lightning?

The same person who tries to find a mythical door she once saw in the fog.

Ten

On to the Spirit Lamp Inn. If I continued to sit in my car reliving the moment I'd seen the lightning flash collie, my heart would never stop pounding.

As I steered back onto Deer Leap Trail, I told myself that this was the second time I'd seen something that wasn't there. The second time this spring, that is. Maybe it wasn't my imagination but the place.

Strange things happened on this rolling expanse of land with its overabundance of wildflowers and empty structures. A blue door appeared and promptly disappeared. A collie stumbled into the fog and vanished. Another dog fashioned of lightning flashed in and out of existence.

Perhaps strangeness was the reason the house and acreage had been abandoned. Everything about the place conspired to warn outsiders away. I had ignored the warning and was left adrift in a sea of mysterious happenings.

At the crossroad, I checked both directions for oncoming traffic and drove across, noting landmarks recalled from our last visit. I saw the light first, the lamppost shining in the late afternoon sun, then the Inn with its sign, every word visible.

The Inn looked as old and spooky as I remembered, with brown gables outlined against a deep blue sky and small secretive windows. This afternoon there was an important difference. Perhaps a dozen cars were parked in the lot.

Inside a hostess clad in a black skirt and white blouse stood at the reception desk, pen in hand. She had the most luminous complexion I'd ever seen and brown hair that glistened in the dim overhead light. To her right, a tall clear vase of pussy willow branches provided seasonal décor but no real color.

I glanced in the dining room. Five of the tables were filled with people eating their meals quietly. The diners included three young children dressed in what looked like their Sunday best. All at the moment appeared to be well-behaved.

The hostess smiled. "Do you have a reservation, miss?"

"Well, no." Seeing the chalkboard menu with its invitation to Easter brunch, I had an inspiration. "I didn't come for dinner. Do you have to have tickets to attend the Easter brunch?"

"We advise it," she said. "The brunch is our most popular activity. Everyone wants to bring their kids to the Egg Hunt. The Easter Bunny is going to make a special appearance," she added.

"I'll take…" I broke off, considering. Would Brent really join us? I knew Crane wouldn't be able to, but Brent would be intrigued by the Easter bunny. Next year, he'd probably want to dress up in a rabbit costume and host an egg hunt at his mansion.

"Three tickets," I said, handing her a twenty dollar bill.

While she tore the tickets from a green roll, I said, "I've been looking at houses for sale in the neighborhood. Do you know that white farmhouse on the other side of the crossroad? The one with all the flowers in the yard?"

"The haunted house?"

"Haunted?" I echoed.

Her cheeks flushed with pink color. "I meant the old Haver house."

"Why did you call it haunted?" I asked.

"That's just an affectionate nickname. It isn't really haunted. It's been vacant for a long time and the location is so isolated... Well, people talk."

"Is it for sale then?"

She nodded. "Together with twenty-five acres. You must have seen the barn. Most of the land is woods."

"I didn't see a 'For Sale' sign," I said.

"I guess they've given up then."

Or changed realtors or were marketing the property on the Internet.

"I'd like to know more about it," I said. "For example, what condition it's in inside."

"From what I heard, all recently renovated."

"Good. I have six collies and need more room."

"Oh, my. Do you have a kennel?"

"No. I just accumulated them along the way. All but one is a rescue."

With that, I remembered to ask about the dog who might be Breezy. "Incidentally, I'm looking for another collie who's lost and may be wounded. She was last seen in this area."

"I can't help you with that, but if you're really interested in the house, you might try Victory-Royal Realtors in Maple Creek. They had their sign in the yard the last time I looked."

"I'll do that," I said. "Thanks."

Slipping the brunch tickets into my purse, I took a last look at the cartoon bunny on the chalkboard and thanked her. At last I was on the right track. I didn't believe a house acquired a reputation for being haunted lightly. Perhaps the mysterious blue door was part of a supernatural manifestation.

~ * ~

On the way home, I stopped at Clovers, planning to take home dinner and tell Annica about the new mystery. She would want to help me solve it. In the past, Annica's insights had been valuable. I'd come to regard her as my partner-in-detection.

I was in luck. Annica was waiting on customers, and the restaurant was steeped in the pleasant lull that occurs before the dinner rush hour.

A tall cardboard bunny directed me to seat myself. I found a quiet booth away from the dozen or more diners and studied the décor. It changed with the seasons. The shamrocks were gone, replaced by white rabbits, interspersed with yellow and pink tulip plants and baskets of decorated *faux* eggs.

Clovers would be closed for the holiday weekend, but the owner, Mary Jeanne, spread Easter cheer during the preceding days with a liberal hand. She would leave the tulip plants out until they fell forward on their long stems, after which she'd switch to red, white, and blue streamers for Memorial Day.

In the spirit of Easter, Annica wore a pale lavender dress protected by a novelty apron—more bunnies and baskets. When she moved her head, dangly Easter egg earrings jingled as if they had tiny bells inside. She strolled over to my booth, the bells making their faint music.

"Hey, Jennet. I haven't seen you in a dog's age."

I smiled. "A dog's age? What's that and where did you learn that phrase?"

"You know. A long time. Weeks. My grandma says it." She brought her pad out of her pocket. "What can I get you?"

"Dinner."

"The day's special is roast beef with potatoes and carrots."

Crane would like that, and I had half a pie at home. "I'll have coffee for here and two dinners to take out. Do you have a minute to talk?"

"I can take a break. Hey, Marcy."

Annica's fellow waitress emerged from the kitchen. She wore a duplicate of Annica's Easter apron.

"Can you hold down the fort while I visit with Jennet?" she asked.

"Sure thing."

Moments later, over coffee and mini muffins, I told Annica about the door, the lightning flash collie, and the house rumored to be haunted. "What do you think?" I asked.

"About the dog? That's easy. This collie died of her injuries. What you saw was her spirit. If she haunts this place, maybe you'll see her again. Maybe *I'll* see her."

That made sense. Still I liked to think of the collie alive and running through the wildflowers. She was Breezy, and I could return her to her owners who loved her.

"What about the door?"

"You said it's an ordinary old barn with nothing in it?"

I nodded.

"That's easy too. You imagined the door. Since it's imaginary, you made it one of your favorite colors."

"I don't think that's the answer," I said.

"Think about the function of a door. A door to what? Obviously not just an empty barn. How about this? A door to another world?"

"Mmm. Like Alice down the rabbit hole."

"Kind of. We'll look for the blue door then." Annica handed me a bowl filled with muffins the size of a thimble. I could eat six at once but only took one. "Are you getting excited about our hot air balloon trip?"

"Not particularly. I'm thinking of backing out."

Her eyes widened in alarm. "You can't do that. It's going to be a major spring event. I'm going to take pictures and make a video album."

"You and Brent can have your own party," I said. "Tell the truth. Wouldn't you prefer that?"

She sidestepped my question. "Brent will be disappointed."

"Not if you go."

She drained her coffee cup. "I don't understand, Jennet. This is something special that most people never get a chance to do. Why don't you want to go?"

That I couldn't explain, not in a way Annica would understand. A feeling of disaster was vague. I had premonitions all the time and lived with them, and once I had really wanted to fly over Foxglove Corners in Brent's hot air balloon. To know the heady freedom of flight, to look down and see my familiar world miniaturized. All right, to touch the treetops as we glided past.

"It'll be like a beautiful, glorious dream," she added.

Some of Annica's enthusiasm wafted across the table and infected me. Or maybe it was the fragrance of the lilies in the centerpiece.

"Okay," I found myself saying. "I'll go."

Eleven

Now why did I do that?

I didn't used to be so easily swayed. How could I possibly change my mind again? In spite of premonitions, I'd soon be flying over Foxglove Corners in the *Sky Dancer* with Annica and Brent. The first of May would be here before I knew it, soon after Easter.

The sky trip had been on my mind all day, even with the multitude of distractions in the classroom where the older students were mentally flying off to their spring break destinations and the younger ones were simply flying.

I glanced at my lesson plan book. In American Literature, Denver Armstrong's class, we were finishing the semester with a survey of the American short story. Ironically, today's selection was Ray Bradbury's chilling little tale of an emperor in ancient China who orders an early flying machine destroyed and its inventor executed in order to protect the kingdom from possible aggression.

I didn't need any reminders of danger and destruction. Thirty-three juniors still in back-from-lunch mode could provide their own version of that very well.

Except there were only half that many in class today. Attendance had been falling off steadily for the last few weeks. Understandably, the change coincided with the arrival of spring weather. After the long, snowy winter, the lure of sunny skies and blessed warmth was irresistible. I'd succumbed to that lure myself. Only not during school hours.

Today with sixteen students absent, I had to continue the list of names on the other side of the slip. One of the missing was my arch-nemesis, Denver Armstrong

Poor attendance reflected on me, and I suspected that Principal Grimsley had already taken note of it. I expected to find a summons to a conference hour meeting with him in my mail box any day. One more hurdle to confront.

On the other hand, a smaller class size was more manageable, better for my nerves, and better for learning. Once again I consulted my plan. Discuss the downside of modern inventions. Read story. Write composition. That should be enough work for the hour, and the assignment would be easy for the absentees to make up.

Seven minutes had gone by. It was past time to start the class. Alas, the talkers gave no indication of coming to order. The noise was deafening. If Grimsley were walking by my room now, he'd be sure to glance in. They'd fall silent as they became aware of his presence. He'd freeze me with one of his poison-laced looks.

Danger! Disaster!

Wouldn't it be a joy to fly away from Marston High School in Brent's hot air balloon, to soar high above the land, up, up, and away from the never-ending clamor that was fourth period American Literature?

Start the class!

"Everybody," I said. "Please quiet down. Open your books to page two hundred and thirty. *The Flying Machine.*

Another minute went by. The noise subsided slightly. If I couldn't hold them in thrall with my charms, surely Bradbury could with his magic. Of course I had to hook them first.

63

Picking up a piece of chalk, I said, "Let's make a list of all the inventions that enrich our lives today. Who wants to start?"

Answers flew through the air like missiles. Microwaves. Computers. Smartphones. GPS systems. Everybody wanted to speak at once, which resulted in a different kind of clamor.

"One at a time," I said. "Raise your hands. Debra?"

The wave of enthusiasm broke apart as Denver Armstrong entered with his signature smirk intact. It lay just beneath the surface of his mildly attractive face. He'd brought his textbook, but, fortunately, not a burger from a fast food establishment to eat in class today.

Back in school after his most recent suspension, Denver appeared energized and ready to make his requisite trouble. But he dropped into his seat with a minimum of disturbance. So far, so good.

I would amend the absence list later. If I stopped to do it now, I'd lose the precarious hold I had on my audience.

Quickly I listed an even dozen modern inventions on the board, including one I'd never heard of.

"Now," I said, "who can give me an example of how a wonderful machine can bring about disaster?"

Disaster was an appealing topic for my group. Cindy Granville raised her hand. "Texting is good, but if you text while driving, it can kill you."

I wrote 'texting' on the board. "Someone else?"

Denver raised his hand.

"Denver?" I said.

"Can I get a drink of water?"

Across the hall from my classroom was a water fountain, a favorite congregating place for students between classes, especially when the temperature began to climb. He'd just walked past it.

"Not now," I said. "After class."

"But I had pizza for lunch."

"That's irrelevant. Do you have a contribution to make to our discussion?"

"Oh, is that what this is? A discussion?"

His sarcasm netted him a few appreciative laughs from his female admirers.

I grabbed my temper with both hands and squeezed it until, had it been an orange, the juice would have drained out on the floor. Temporarily restored to calm, I said, "Anyone else?"

"Okay, be like that," he grumbled. "Wait till I tell the principal."

Somehow, some time later, I ended the discussion and started the reading with a simple description of a lush and peaceful land faraway and long ago. Ray Bradbury's exquisite prose could always soothe me. It seemed to have a similar effect on Denver. When I looked up to ask for a volunteer reader, I saw that he was asleep.

~ * ~

I loved to walk with my collies up and down Jonquil Lane when the sun was warm and the wind blew everything in its path—my hair, the dog's fur, and the flowers that grew along the lane. Near my house and the yellow Victorian where Camille lived with her husband, Gilbert, the flowers were jonquils and daffodils and yellow tulips, creating our own living yellow brick road.

Once past the abandoned development, still called the new construction even though the builder had gone bankrupt and left the state, the foliage consisted of wildflowers, lacy giant ferns and tall grasses spilling out of the woods.

Halley, Sky and Raven were allowed to walk free. Candy, my wild child collie, and Gemmy needed to be leashed. So did Misty, who had two role models, Sky and Candy, but had lately been acting more like Candy. Which meant I couldn't trust her not to run away into the woods. Misty was too young to hold her own against the wildlife she might encounter.

We rarely met anyone else on our walks, neither on foot nor behind the wheel, but in the sky… That was another matter.

When the dogs began barking, when Candy scanned the low-lying clouds and started to pull frantically on her leash, I suspected the approach of an intruder from above. Not a plane because I couldn't hear an engine, but a hawk or a balloon.

Moments later a magnificent yellow and red hot air balloon glided over the trees and into view. It was one of Brent's prized fleet. I recognized the *Sky Dancer*. He had taken us to see it when he'd acquired it.

So this was the balloon he planned to use when he took Annica and me for our May first sky ride.

It was truly beautiful, and it flew so low there couldn't possibly be any danger to the riders. If a malfunction occurred, one could simply bail out and grab a handy branch. But the hot air balloons were perfectly safe. Brent often said so.

The two young men in the balloon waved to us. Although I didn't recognize either one, I waved back. I knew Brent had hired a new assistant.

By now all the dogs were barking, the leashed ones leaping and twirling around, mesmerized by the sight. I could hardly keep them from pulling me off my feet.

Even when the balloon floated out of sight, the dogs' excitement continued. A quiet, civilized walk was out of the question then. We might as well head home.

As I turned my brood around, for some reason I recalled Ray Bradbury's doomed flyer, so proud of the flying machine he'd invented, so eager to share the wonder of flying with the Emperor. So soon to be dead.

Quickly I banished the thought. Death was incompatible with a golden spring day. Dying was for another season.

Twelve

Whenever I had a chance to read the *Banner* at home or the *Free Press* at school, I searched for updated news about Terra Roman. She had been missing for several days, and with each day the likelihood of a happy ending to her story diminished. When weeks passed without a mention of her disappearance, I was afraid the fickle public was losing interest in her case.

I also feared they would find her body in the woods one day, perhaps submerged in a pond far from a road. Chances are we would never know what had happened on the day of her disappearance.

This depressing thought always inspired another one. Would Shadow's body be found lying beside her? Or, would there be a happier outcome with both collie and owner biding their time in some secret location until they could return to the life left behind?

I couldn't imagine why Terra would vanish voluntarily, though.

It was discouraging not to know one way or the other. In the meantime, dogs still needed to be rescued. Since Terra had disappeared, five collies had found their way to the care of League members. At present, there was no room for more. The foster homes on Terra's A and B lists had dwindled, along with the funds which Sue had recently described as being in good shape. Food and vet bills for multiple dogs and an occasional treat or toy could quickly drain an organization's resources.

There was further trouble. Three long-time members had left the League citing family responsibilities, and an adoption had fallen through with no reason given, not even an obviously false one. I'd suspected this would happen if Terra didn't or couldn't return home. Without her, we were simply a band of women working as individuals to save our beloved collies from pain and loss. Frequent disagreements cropped up in the ranks. As a rescue league, we were foundering.

The only good news was the spring yard sale. With the help of Terra's sister, Liz had liberated Terra's collected figurines and art work from her locked house, and Sue Appleton had been busy advertising the event. Perhaps hoping to rekindle a spirit of camaraderie, Sue called an emergency meeting at her horse farm on Squill Lane for the following Friday.

Unfortunately Sue fell ill with a virus and phoned me in a desperate attempt to change the location of the meeting. To my house.

"I'm not sure that'll work," I said.

I wasn't fond of entertaining and did so only when I had ample time to clean house and cook. The rest of the week was crammed with tests to write, papers to grade, lessons to prepare, and two appointments at the animal hospital. The very thought of adding another item to my crowded schedule overwhelmed me.

My conscience whispered, *Can't you spare an evening for the welfare of the breed you profess to love?*

"Shouldn't we postpone the meeting until you're well?" I asked.

"I think we need to get re-organized as soon as possible," Sue said. "We already lost three people, and no one knows who to contact when they find an abandoned collie. They've been calling me. I have four dogs here at the barn."

"But who's going to lead the meeting?" I asked. "Not me. I haven't been a member that long."

"You'll do fine, Jennet," Sue said. "Just pick up some cookies at the bakery and serve coffee and iced tea. Nothing fancy. I'll have my assistant bring over my notes."

I sighed. The dogs would probably run wild with so much company. I could ask Leonora to help me, even though she wasn't an official member of the League yet. Did I have enough coffee mugs and chairs? I was sure I could manage seating.

"How many people should I expect?" I asked.

"About a dozen. Mostly you'll have to do some planning for the spring yard sale. Form a few committees."

"Where will that take place?"

"Liz volunteered her yard. I'll be better by then. I hope."

And what if she wasn't?

"If we want to last as a viable organization, we can't fall apart," Sue said. "Terra's been gone so long. We'll have to hold another election soon."

"Who could replace Terra?" I asked.

"I'm thinking you could."

"Oh, no," I said quickly. I could only be swayed to a certain point. "You're a much better candidate for president. You have more experience."

Besides, Sue didn't have a demanding job. She worked with her horses and student riders who certainly didn't defy her authority in a hundred little ways.

Sue had an excellent memory. "You once told me you thought about starting your own rescue group. Then you learned about us."

That was true; I couldn't deny it.

"Just pretend this is the group you founded," she said.

"I can do that. About the elections, though, let's wait a little longer to replace Terra and hope she comes home," I said. "And hope the parade of needy collies trickles down to a few."

~ * ~

Anyone would think I had enough to do without adding a visit to the Spirit Lamp Inn to my agenda, but the next day found me on Deer Leap Trail again.

It was going to be a quick visit, and it had a purpose. Our Easter brunch was turning into a party, and I needed two more tickets, for Annica and Lucy Hazen, Foxglove Corners' famed horror story writer.

Leonora had promised to help me with the Rescue League meeting, and I'd already bought cookies and quick breads at the Hometown Bakery. Everything was as ready as it could be. To be sure, I had an important mission today, but the prospect of ghost hunting added an element of fun to it. For of course I planned to stop at the Haver acreage.

In the late afternoon light, the haunted farmhouse and the barn glowed in their surround of riotous wild color. I pulled off the road hoping the blue door would materialize. It didn't happen. Perhaps it needed fog.

The entire area—house and barn and land—was steeped in a quiet so thick you'd have difficulty carving through it with a knife.

But something was amiss, a wrongness that hid in the play of light and shadow, perceptible only by a sixth sense. I felt the wrongness in the speeding up of my heart rate and the chill that spread over my body, turning my hands to ice.

Something wicked this way comes?

A favorite line dropped into my mind, one that seemed to fit the phenomenon. But why should I assume wickedness was abroad?

I slipped my keys into my jacket pocket, and headed toward the barn.

As I walked alongside the white Queen Anne's lace, I became aware of a faint sound floating across the wildflower fields. It sounded like someone weeping.

Where? I couldn't tell. More importantly, was the sound real?

I thought it must be. There was no wind to sigh through the grasses and wildflowers. To my knowledge, no bird's call sounded like weeping. What animal's voice could possibly be mistaken for that of a human?

Wind. Wildlife. What was left? I couldn't think of anything. But no one was there, unless the weeper lay on the ground hidden from view by high growing vegetation. That was a possibility.

"Is anything the matter?" I called. "Can I help?"

The wheels of my imagination spinning, I waited for someone or something to acknowledge my presence and my offer, waited for a figure to rise out of the high grasses and glide toward me.

Nothing happened.

You, Jennet, are going bananas, I told myself.

When I reached the barn, I went around to the front. The lock was in place, attached to its rusty chain. Not a sound escaped from the aging structure, and the weeping was weaker now, farther away. Could it originate in the woods? No, although faint, it was closer than that. Still, I couldn't pin its location down.

Then the weeping ended abruptly as if somebody had turned off a radio, plunging the area back into dense, eerie silence.

I turned my attention back to the barn, something concrete, something that was there. Why would anyone periodically lock and unlock an empty barn?

The answer was simple. The barn couldn't be empty, not all the time.

Belatedly I glanced at the house, half fearing someone was spying on me, peering through a window, outraged that I'd dare to trespass on private property.

That was unlikely. There was no car in front of or alongside the house. No sign that anyone had visited the place in months. Nothing but bands of multi-colored wildflowers that warred with one another for space and sun.

The haunted Haver House. Who would visit it except Jennet? Or a crying ghost?

Still, as I'd felt the wrongness, I was certain someone was inside the house, watching me. Someone I wouldn't want to meet.

You'd better get out of here.

Pulling the keys out of my pocket so they'd be ready when I reached the car, I hurried back to the road.

This was a haunted place indeed, and its attraction for me was strong. Even as I drove on, I knew I'd be back.

Thirteen

After dinner, Crane and I sat in the living room, he reading the *Banner* and I scribbling in a notebook. I was trying to decide what I could move to make room for the eight extra chairs I'd have to set out for the Rescue League meeting. Not the side tables. I'd need them for refreshments. And what on earth was I going to do with my collies?

Visions of pandemonium danced in my head, alongside bakery cookies and thin slices of nut bread. The living room looked nice, though, reasonably clean with all extraneous items stashed away and a vase of red tulips on the coffee table.

"I checked out your new haunted place this morning," Crane said, folding the paper. He paused to take a sip of coffee while I waited for his report.

"And what did you think?"

"It's a beautiful piece of property, but I didn't see anything haunted about it."

"I was there, too, a couple of hours ago," I said, "and I heard somebody crying. It sounded like a lost soul."

"Was it a child? Or a woman?"

"I don't know and couldn't tell where it was coming from. I guess the inexplicable only happens to people like me and Lucy Hazen."

I'd have to ask Lucy to go to the Haver property with me one day. I felt suddenly lonely in my ability to glimpse into the other world or, in this case, to hear an otherworldly sound. Loneliness, like misery, loves company. Lucy had the same talent, but hers was more diversified and fine-tuned.

Why not descend on the place with our entire Easter brunch party?

"I searched the meadow up to the woods," Crane said. "If the collie was there, it's long gone."

"I'm sure she is. Look how many days have passed." I frowned, realizing that Crane hadn't searched the woods, where scavengers roamed. But how could he? At least he hadn't found a dog's body or the remnants of it. I was glad I'd decided not to contact the owner of the missing collie, Breezy.

"Was the barn still locked?" I asked.

He nodded.

"That barn. I wish I knew what was inside."

"Probably just old straw and mice," he said. "Locking it keeps out vagrants."

"That beautiful old house sitting vacant would attract them, too."

"I checked it," he said. "It's locked up tight as a drum."

I leaned back in the rocker, drank my own coffee, and summed up my recent experiences. The possibly supernatural ones, that is. "I saw a blue door, a lightning flash in the shape of dog—a collie, of course—and today I heard the crying. I wonder what it all means."

A child crying because her ghost collie had run through a blue door and disappeared.

"You'll figure it out," Crane said, "and it seems harmless."

Which, in Crane's view, made it an acceptable adventure for me to have. With or without his approval, I'd gone too far to walk away from the mystery.

I smiled. "It'll be perfectly safe. I just wish…"

I broke off to savor the picture my fair-haired husband made in civilian clothes with the two black collies, Halley and Raven, lying at his feet.

"What do you wish?"

"That you could join us for the Easter brunch at the Inn," I said

"Someone has to keep the county safe," he reminded me. "I'll let Fowler have the honor of escorting you ladies. He'll enjoy that."

"You and I will celebrate Easter together later," I said. "I'll have a festive dinner waiting for you when you come home, and we'll have a jelly roll for dessert, courtesy of Camille. She's making fancy desserts for the Rescue League sale."

"I have an Easter surprise for you, too," he said. "Something in a basket."

"What is it?"

"You'll have to wait until Easter night."

"You're not buying me a rabbit or a chick, I hope."

"No more animals," he promised. "We have enough. But I was thinking of getting a pair of bunny ears for Misty to wear."

I knew he wasn't serious. We both disapproved of dressing dogs in any kind of costume and, worse, giving living creatures as presents.

"Make them rawhide ears, and you'll have a happy puppy," I said.

Speaking of Misty… I heard a suspicious rustle of paper in the kitchen. Candy was gone too. Something fell to the floor with an ominous bang.

I couldn't have been more comfortable in the rocker and hated to get up for anything, but any untoward racket had to be investigated before it turned into a calamity.

Oh, well, we both needed coffee refills.

~ * ~

The last day before Easter vacation was an enjoyable, easy day. Easy? It was downright euphoric. Principal Grimsley had gone out of town on some mysterious school business. The entire building seemed to sigh in relief. The weather was deliciously warm, and all day a steady stream of students filed out of the school to begin their vacations early with a first stop at the Igloo Palace for ice cream cones and popsicles.

Instead of continuing the short story survey in American Literature, I found an Easter poem, and we studied that. Denver Armstrong had failed to appear for fourth hour class, providing the icing on the cake.

The day passed with no trauma, and before long the last bell rang.

As Leonora entered the freeway for the long commute to Foxglove Corners, the spirit of adventure seemed to travel with us. Days of leisure and fun beckoned, and we didn't have to leave home to find it.

"I'm surprised you don't have any travel plans this Easter," I said.

"I feel like staying home. I'm decorating my sewing room."

That puzzled me. "Do you sew that much?"

"I would if I had a cheery place to keep my materials and fabric. It's that small room on the second floor with a view of the woods."

"The one you use as an extra closet?"

She nodded. "I painted the walls red and found a pair of vintage prints of old-time ladies embroidering. My next project will be curtains. I'd like to make them."

She passed a car that was driving much slower than the posted speed limit. That was unusual. Usually drivers passed us.

"Red walls?" I said.

"Bright cherry red. That's the happiest color I can think of. Then there's the Rescue League meeting tomorrow, and sometime I thought we could investigate your door mystery."

That sounded like fun to me—all except the curtain making. I had done that one summer and found it tedious.

"Don't forget we have to pick up the bakery order tonight," I said.

That was the last item on my list. I'd given the living and dining rooms a superficial cleaning yesterday but still hadn't decided where to keep the dogs.

Now that the meeting was imminent, I allowed myself to feel a little nervous. Old insecurities reared their heads. I knew very few of the League members, and the one I knew best, Sue Appleton, was still sick. Wouldn't it be like facing a new group of students? What if no one listened to me?

Well, then I'd be out of the running for president, which would please me. I wanted to stay out of the limelight and simply rescue collies.

So I told myself not to obsess about a little gathering of like-minded individuals. I had Sue's notes and agenda, and it was the least I could do for the collies. Still, all the way home, I wondered what could go wrong.

~ * ~

I reached for the last plate of cookies on the mahogany credenza that had replaced my old buffet, the beloved antique that had been destroyed in the winter's strange fire. With luck, the refreshments would last as long as the meeting.

Eight people had showed up, all strangers with the exception of Liz, Louanne Barnett, Emma Brock, and Laurence DeVille. They'd gobbled up cookies and nut bread at an alarming rate. Fortunately I had two loaves of banana bread in the freezer. But after that? After that, a hostess' worse nightmare.

And I thought I was well-prepared.

In the kitchen, Misty was whining in her crate, even though Sky, Halley, and Candy kept her company. Raven, as if discerning my dilemma, had gone outside to sleep in her house, taking Gemmy with her.

I sat in my favorite chair which should have given me confidence, wishing I could remember all the names of the people in front of me. I needed a seating chart

"Maybe we'd better start the meeting." I glanced at Leonora who had followed me into the living room with a dish of fresh orange and lemon slices. She gave me an encouraging smile.

Louanne leaned forward in her chair. "Before we do, I have an important announcement to make."

She was an attractive young woman whose red hair looked freshly washed and not quite dry. I remembered seeing her on Terra's porch when we'd gathered for the meeting that hadn't taken place. According to Sue Appleton, she was a new member.

Unlike in a classroom, the others fell silent and looked at her expectantly.

I nodded, "Go ahead, Louanne."

"It's Shadow," she said. "They've found her."

Fourteen

Shadow. Terra's collie.

Everyone began to talk at once. I raised my voice, wishing I had a gavel to bang. "Tell us what happened, Louanne."

Louanne set her empty iced tea glass on a Lassie coaster. "I got a call from a friend of mine at a shelter in Maple Creek. They had a nice tri female someone had found wandering on the outskirts of town. I drove over to pick her up, and she looked like Terra's dog, so I called her Shadow."

"What happened?"

"She responded. She knew her name."

Liz said, "That means there's hope for Terra. She'll be the next to turn up. Mark my words."

I wondered. If Terra and her collie had become separated, it might mean the opposite, but Liz' observation had electrified the group. They'd been waiting a long time for some encouraging news. So had I, but I'd learned to be cautious.

If Shadow had ended up loose on a country road, something terrible must have happened to Terra. At least we had a location now. Maple Creek wasn't too far from Foxglove Corners.

"Where is Shadow now?" I asked.

"At my house," Louanne said.

"What was her condition when she was brought to the shelter?"

"Not too bad. She was wearing her collar but couldn't get enough to eat."

That told us she'd been separated from Terra for a while, but little else.

I had seen Shadow at Terra's Christmas party but hadn't interacted with her, hadn't really looked at her. All I remembered was a pretty black collie who loved people. That could describe any tricolor collie, even Halley and Candy, which reminded me. The collies in the kitchen were quiet. Even Misty. I needn't have worried about them running amuck.

"Terra adopted Shadow from a shelter," Liz said. "The poor dog. To find herself without a home again."

"That's what happens to our dogs when we die," Laurence DeVille said. "It's the glue factory."

What a dismal observation. I directed a question to the gathering. "Would anyone here know for certain this tri is Shadow?"

Louanne said, "I have a picture of Terra with Shadow. I'm pretty sure she's Terra's dog."

"Pictures can be deceiving, and Shadow is a common name for a black dog."

As Louanne bristled at my observations, Liz said, "I'd know Shadow anywhere. If it's all right with you, Louanne, I could stop by your house after the meeting."

The meeting! I'd let it slip out of my control and ramble off in a dozen different directions, all leading to speculation on what had happened to Terra and her present whereabouts.

Mr. DeVille predicted that Terra would be found dead in a ditch someday, but the women were more optimistic. Shadow's turning up—if indeed the tricolor in question was Shadow—was a good omen, a sign that Terra was not far behind.

People believe what they want to believe, and perhaps we were on the verge of having a breakthrough in the case. But I had one of my bad feelings about Terra. It had appeared suddenly and refused to go away. I only hoped that this particular premonition wouldn't amount to anything dire.

I tried once more to gain control of the group. These grown-ups were more talkative than my freshmen and weren't about to be intimidated.

"Even if Terra comes home, she may not feel like running the sale," I said. "Sue Appleton asked me to form committees, so let's get that done. Who'd like to price the merchandise?"

"Me," Mr. DeVille said. "I used to work in retail, and I can transport the stuff in my van."

In the end, everyone volunteered for something. In the ensuing lull, I made notes and took time to enjoy a piece of nut bread and a glass of iced tea. I'd managed to turn the tide, but as soon as the items on Sue's agenda were dealt with, conversation drifted back to Shadow and Terra again.

Let it, I told myself.

The business part of the meeting was over, and I must have done something right. There were still plenty of cookies and nut bread left, and the coffee pot was full. I might be an effective leader after all.

~ * ~

The dog from the Maple Creek shelter proved to be Shadow, but Terra wasn't the next to come home.

If only Shadow could tell us how she'd gone from Terra's home to a road on the outskirts of Maple Creek. If she could just assure us that Laurence DeVille's grim prophecy had no merit. This wasn't the first time I lamented the fact that dogs can't talk.

There was no news of Terra, and nothing more anyone could do to find her. Louanne, who had no collie at present, vowed that Shadow wouldn't want for anything. Except her true owner, of course. At my suggestion, she notified the police that Shadow had turned up.

Then, suddenly, it was Easter Sunday morning. I looked out the kitchen window at a perfect spring day. The sky couldn't have been bluer or the sun brighter. The graceful white lily plant on the kitchen table filled the room with the sweet scent only a lily possesses.

After I'd tended to the collies and Crane left for the day, I dressed in a mint green suit, purchased especially for the Easter brunch, and waited for Brent. We were all going to the Spirit Lamp Inn together. Afterward I planned to ask Brent to stop at the Haver property, wondering if the ghosts would respect the holy day.

~ * ~

Shortly afterward, as Brent parked the car, Lucy said, "There didn't used to be an inn here. It was a plain brown farmhouse, and this parking lot was covered with spruce trees. Too bad. They were so pretty."

"That's why I didn't recognize the name," Brent said.

Annica patted down a red strand that had come loose from her sophisticated upswept hairdo. "I read an article about the inn. It opened this spring. The food has a five-star rating, and they specialize in pies. Good thing I'm famished."

"Wait!" I said.

Something didn't add up. "When I bought the tickets, the hostess mentioned the popularity of the Easter Egg hunt. It sounded like a tradition, not the first of its kind. Are you sure of your facts, Annica?"

"Positive. I may still have the paper at home."

"That's strange." I resolved to get to the bottom of the mystery. This one should be easy enough to solve. But later. For the moment, I set the matter aside.

Red, pink, and yellow balloons tied to porch posts sailed to and fro in a light wind, and a tall person in a white bunny costume stood in the doorway, waving us in. Although the sun was bright, the windows were outlined in tiny clear lights and decorated with spring wreaths.

"This is so different from our first glimpse of the place," I said. "Leonora and I were the only guests for lunch that day. It was storming out, and we just saw one person the whole time we were here."

"Jennet was sure the inn was haunted," Leonora added.

"Well, it looked pretty spooky," I said. "Leonora was the one who wanted to eat and run, but..." I broke off as I noticed Brent scratching absently at his right hand.

"Isn't it too early for mosquitoes?" I asked.

"You'd think so. This is some kind of bite. I don't know where I got it." He frowned. "Anything could have bitten me. I'm outside more than in."

"Not a spider, I hope," Lucy said.

I studied his hand as it rested against the doorframe, illuminated by the lights. It was marred by a small raised bump, red but without the usual white circle. Not the work of a mosquito, in other words.

"Put some anti-itch ointment on it," I said.

"Naah. That's for sissies. It'll go away."

I shrugged. "It's your hand, but you don't want it to get infected."

The bunny held the door open for us, nodding and smiling as he did. His costume was white and fluffy. It had floppy ears lined with velvety pink linings and a bouquet of *faux* carrots sewed to the waistline. "Come on in, ladies and gentleman," he said.

Inside, I handed our tickets to the hostess, who was dressed as an old-fashioned farm maid, and gazed at a dining room decorated to resemble a flower garden. There was music, too, a lilting tune that I recognized but couldn't identify.

"Oh, how beautiful everything is!" Lucy said.

"And look at that buffet! I'm *so* hungry." That was Annica, suddenly at the head of our little party.

Brent said, "What are we waiting for? Let's eat."

I knew we were entering a dining room cleverly decorated for an Easter brunch, but for just a moment, my imagination slipped into overdrive. It seemed that the double doors led to another world.

Fifteen

The message on the chalkboard had changed: *Easter Egg Hunt in the south garden. Find a dozen eggs. Win a prize.*

I handed our tickets to the hostess who dropped them into a basket. She was a petite woman with an elaborate silver hairstyle that complemented her gray dress and pearl necklace.

"Enjoy the brunch," she said. "Daisy will show you to your table. Daisy!"

"Is Daisy a bunny?" Brent asked in his booming voice.

"I doubt it," Annica said as a young girl in a demure blue gingham jumper and frilly white blouse materialized at his side.

"We're the Ferguson party," I said.

"Over here." She led us to a table for five, conveniently placed in front of a window with a view of the garden. "You can take the favors home," she said.

They were Easter bunnies reclining on nests of jelly beans.

"Chocolate!" Annica said.

I touched one pointed ear. "They're imitation. Just realistic decorations."

The dining room was crowded, and the majority of the guests were young children, for the most part well-behaved, or at least well-supervised. Now that the room was filled to capacity, the white rabbit had abandoned his post by the door. Carrying a rustic gathering basket, he hopped his way to the tables, dispensing carnations to all the ladies in his path and chocolate eggs to the children.

Annica, Leonora, and Brent already stood in the buffet line. I joined them, and, while waiting, looked for our first waitress among the girls in their blue gingham jumpers. I didn't see her. I'd have to ask the hostess how long the Spirit Lamp Inn had been in business, while making it seem casual but like the rabbit, she was constantly on the move, impossible to catch.

Beside me, Lucy froze, a graceful statue in a long blue dress, as if listening to faraway sounds only she could hear. "I have the strangest feeling about this place."

"Strange? In what way?" I asked.

"Like it's two places existing side by side, one just beyond our ken."

I was familiar with Lucy's unusual utterances. "Like an alternate universe?"

Leonora overheard our exchange. "That doesn't make sense."

"Sometimes feelings don't," Lucy said.

Leonora transferred slices of ham to her plate. "I just see an ordinary restaurant. A little fancier than most."

"Well, let's enjoy the food in this universe," I said.

Lucy eyed the rack of crisp golden French toast. "Just what I need to counteract this feeling. An overload of sugar."

"That's a good way of looking at it," Brent said. "For myself I'm trying one of everything."

"Just one?" Annica asked with a brief teasing smile.

"Or two. Those quiches are the size of quarters."

He was exaggerating, of course, but they *were* small. I set one on my plate, added ham, scrambled eggs, and a grapefruit. With hot tea, that was all I wanted. Or so I thought until I saw the selection of pastries.

As we sampled the Inn's offerings, I thought about what Lucy had said and recalled my initial reaction to the inn. Gloomy. Mysterious. Even with the sunny flower garden theme and the make-believe bunny mingling with the littlest guests, it seemed to be a place of secrets. That was odd because all I'd seen of the house was the reception area, the vast dining room, and the exterior.

To be sure, it was steeped in Easter charm today, but what about another day when the sky darkened, rain poured down, and the rooms filled with shadows?

I was beginning to understand Lucy's impression of two rooms.

Midway through the meal, Leonora said, "I'd love to watch the little kids hunt for Easter eggs. Could we do that, Brent?"

"Sure. I'd like some eggs myself."

"You'll never pass for a child," I said.

Lucy poured more hot water into her teacup. "I wonder how the Spirit Lamp Inn got its name," she said. "It might be important."

～ * ～

After most of the Easter eggs had been liberated from their not-so-subtle hiding places, Leonora said, "This has been so much fun. I hate to see it end."

"It doesn't have to," I said. "Can we stop at the haunted Haver house, Brent? It's just down the road."

"I don't see why not. Isn't that the place where you saw the blue door?"

"It was painted on the barn," I said. "The house has a reputation for being haunted."

"Well then, *that* explains the door."

"I suppose it does."

"Do you know the story behind the haunting?" Lucy asked.

"Not yet. I'd hoped to find out today."

"This may not be the best time for inquiries," Leonora pointed out. "Ghosts and Easter bunnies don't mix well. We can come back another day," she added.

"In the meantime, let's check out the Haver house," Brent said.

A little later, he parked at the side of Deer Leap Trail and we walked across the field to the barn, trying not to trample the wildflowers. This was difficult to do as the plants grew close together, creating great splashes of red, yellow, blue and white. Even the borders of Queen Anne's Lace were thicker than they'd been on my last visit. Surely Mother Nature had blessed the seeds. I'd never seen such an extravagant display.

There was no blue door on the barn today.

Annica said, "I'm going to pick some flowers. They'll go nicely with the carnations the Bunny gave us at the Inn." She bent down to pinch a red bloom with her nail. "Yikes! Blood. It's bleeding."

I looked over her shoulder. "Don't get carried away. That's plant sap."

Brent was at the side of the barn, examining the space I'd indicated. "It's smooth, Jennet. There never was a door here. You must have imagined it." He walked around to the front. "Locked."

Once again Lucy stood still, in listening mode.

"What do you think?" I asked her.

"Something sad happened here. Something bad. The remnants of the occurrence—for want of a better word—hang over the whole area like a low-lying cloud that will never float away. I can almost see it. But not quite," she added.

I didn't know what to say. Remembering the lightning flash collie and the sound of weeping in the wildflower field, I believed her.

Anything was possible. All I had to do was find the blue door again, and I'd know the answer to every mystery.

"So that's the haunted house," Brent said. "I should have brought my camera."

Annica, who often surprised me with her keen insight, nodded. "It looks like it's trying to get away from the flowers."

We walked closer to the porch, trying not to crush the magnificent floral carpet.

Brent said, "It's a fine old house with classic lines. All it needs is a little TLC and some tamer landscaping. You say it's for sale, Jennet?"

"So I heard."

In my mind, I could see the house transformed, or rather returned to its former state. All the windows open, curtains blowing in the breeze, and a glider on the porch. Wicker tables, a pitcher of lemonade. A dog lying at the top of the stairs. A collie, of course.

But I couldn't see any people.

Annica glanced down at the wildflowers she'd gathered that resembled a sumptuous farmers' market bouquet. "I don't know why, but I feel like crying," she said.

Leonora said, "Somehow we have to learn the story behind the house. There must be someone we can ask."

Brent scoffed. "You girls are too much. This is just an old farmhouse left to deteriorate. Have you seen enough?"

With a last wistful glance at the barn, I said, "For today."

Sixteen

The rest of the day was as peaceful as a holiday could be. I baked my ham and assembled side dishes for Easter dinner. Then I watched *Ben-Hur* and visited with Camille who brought over a strawberry-filled jelly roll for dessert. By the time Crane came home, I was hungry again.

Throughout the day an elusive element of wrongness nagged at me. It wasn't the haunted Haver house, and it wasn't Lucy's unsettling impression of the Spirit Lamp Inn. Not entirely.

Something else chimed a warning note, but it was too far away for me to hear it clearly. I trusted in time I would be able to decipher it.

Meanwhile, I busied myself in setting the table, moving the vase filled with Annica's wildflowers and my yellow carnation from the Easter bunny to its center, and lighting the candles in the heirloom candleholders. Outside, the sky grew dark, and it began to rain, ending the day's perfection.

At this point, inclement weather didn't matter. The house was festive enough for a late celebration, and Crane was home.

As he divested himself of his gun and gave Candy and Misty the attention they demanded, I said, "Was it a quiet day?"

"A long one. It's good to be home."

"Maybe one day we'll be able to have a whole holiday together," I said.

"You never know."

"We're going to go back to the Inn for Easter brunch next year."

While we ate, I told him about the brunch, the white bunny, and the mystery of the egg hunt—whether it was a tradition or a first-time event. But I didn't mention our brief stop at the Haver property. That would be too serious a subject for our dinner table, especially on a holiday.

Afterward when I came back from the kitchen holding the jelly roll out of Candy's reach, I found a small Easter basket where my dinner plate had been. In it an object wrapped in sparkly tissue paper sat on a nest of green Easter grass.

"What's this?" I asked.

"Your surprise," he said.

"From the Easter Bunny?"

"No," he said. "From me."

I unwrapped it to find a small crystal rabbit with tiny black stones for eyes. The candlelight flickered and set it to sparkling. Candy thrust her face in my lap, eyes gleaming at the sight of the unfamiliar ornament.

"It's beautiful," I said. "Where did you find it?"

"At your favorite shop, the Green House of Antiques."

"So it's an antique."

It looked like a figurine recently made and intended only for me. I'd have to start a new collection, a whole shelf of crystal creations sparkling in the sunlight.

"I'll have to keep the dogs away from it," I said as Candy licked her chops. "On the mantel, maybe?"

It really belonged in a place where the sun could reach it. I would decide on a permanent home later. This was the second rabbit that had crossed my path today. I chose to think of it as a good omen.

I set the crystal rabbit high on the mantel; then I kissed Crane. His unexpected gift was the true highlight of Easter. The gift and the fact that he knew me so well and that he cared.

~ * ~

A good omen for me was a bad omen for Terra, although she was beyond caring about portents and had been for days. Monday's *Banner* carried the story on the front page. Terra's body had been found in a heavily wooded area by a group of young friends on a spring nature hike. The exact cause of death had yet to be determined, but strangulation was a possibility and she had a head injury.

The wooded area was east of Deer Leap Trail.

I remembered Laurence DeVille's remark about Terra's body lying in a ditch. Did he know something about the murder or was he just making a failed attempt to lighten the mood?

I sat in a booth at Clovers over a doughnut and coffee staring at Terra's picture. She had her arm around a collie, not Shadow because the dog was a sable. As I re-read the article, the doughnut turned to dried paste in my mouth and the strawberry jelly spilling out on the white plate looked like blood. Doughnuts usually made me happy. Not this morning.

Annica dropped into the seat next to me with a sigh too heavy for the early hour. "So this is how it ends," she said.

Leaving too many questions unanswered. "It didn't look good, but we all hoped for a happy outcome," I said.

I had pictured Terra hosting a special gathering of the League members to explain the inexplicable as she took up the reins of leadership. In my mind, she still looked the same with no head wound and no marks of strangulation.

"That's the road we were on yesterday," Annica said.

"Deer Leap Trail." Near the haunted house and the Spirit Lamp Inn.

Could there possibly be a connection? There had to be. Of all the roads in Foxglove Corners, why would Terra's body be found on this one so close to the Haver house and barn?

"To think we drove past her body," Annica said. "She was there all the time in the woods while we were laughing and talking about ham and Easter eggs."

"It's a miracle they found her at all. Only hunters and nature buffs go tramping through those woods. And someone found Shadow outside Maple Creek. How did she get there?"

"Maybe she walked. Like Lassie?"

"Lassie came home," I reminded her. "Shadow didn't live in Maple Creek."

Still, there were several ways Shadow could have traveled from the crime scene to another town. Most of them ominous. Also, the wooded area might not have been the crime scene, only the place where the killer dumped Terra's body.

"Uh, Miss?" a voice called out. "More coffee over here, please? And could we see a menu again?"

"Drat," Annica said. "I have to go to work. Talk to you later."

I felt bereft, as if I had lost a member of my family. Terra had been an important force in so many lives, both human and canine. Like Caroline Meilland, the slain animal activist, she could never be replaced, but the number of collies in need would continue to increase, and the Lakeville Collie Rescue League couldn't simply fold up its tents and steal away.

We'd have to elect a new president now. Certainly we'd be calling one another, hoping someone had more details.

Since Terra's disappearance had turned into a homicide, Crane would have access to information that wouldn't be in the news. The method of murder, for instance, or other details surrounding it, like the possibility of suspects.

The arrangements. I almost choked on my coffee. They would perform an autopsy, of course. The mere thought of an instrument ravaging Terra's body made me ill.

Her soul isn't bound to her body anymore, I thought, reminding myself how every time I walked through the rooms of the Foxglove Corners Animal Shelter, I sensed Caroline's spirit alongside me, whispering words of praise for our efforts to help the beleaguered animals.

I left the rest of the doughnut, an unappetizing mess of soggy dough and seeping jelly, and finished my coffee which had grown cool.

Caroline's killer had been apprehended and had paid for his crime. Could we do less for Terra?

Seventeen

"Morning, Jennet. Are you coming or going?" Brent Fowler towered over me, eyeing the doughnut mess on my plate.

Absently I crumpled my napkin. "Going. I just read about Terra Roman's murder. It didn't quite sink in yet."

He nodded and dropped into the seat across from me. "It's terrible. I didn't know Terra, but by all accounts she made a big difference in the lives of dogs. That's good enough for me."

"I can't imagine who killed her. It must have been an enemy she made in her work."

"Terra got in somebody's way; that's for sure. Have a cup of coffee with me," he said. "Or is there some place you have to be?"

"Only home. I took the dogs for their walk already. I have the week off, but finding out what happened to Terra zapped me right out of vacation mode."

"Hi, Brent," Annica said, with a saucy clinking of her seashell earrings. "What can I get for you this morning?"

"Breakfast, please," he said. "Ham, eggs over easy, hash browns, biscuits, grapefruit juice, and coffee, black. Another cup for Jennet. She's going to stay and keep me company."

Obviously devastating news didn't affect Brent's appetite. For me, the realization that Terra was gone from the earth and in such an appalling way was too new, too raw.

"Coming up." Annica looked a trifle disappointed that this initial encounter was over so quickly. Moreover, a party of five had just come through the front door. She was going to be too busy to chat with him.

"I still can't believe Terra was murdered," I said. "It seems unreal. Like something that happens to a stranger."

"Unfortunately the trail is probably cold by now."

"Shadow could tell us."

"If dogs could talk. I take it Shadow didn't meet up with the same fate."

"No, somehow she ended up in a Maple Creek shelter."

"What will happen to her now?"

"One of the League members has her. She'll probably stay there."

"If she needs a home, I'll take her," he said. "I have lots of room."

"I'll let you know."

Brent's generous offer made me feel like crying. I bit my lip and willed myself to keep the tears inside. I couldn't possibly cry in a public place. Still... From Shadow, my thoughts drifted to Halley and all the collies I'd taken into my home. Of the transiency of life.

I focused my attention on the ruined doughnut on my plate and thought about sunshine and fresh air and the subtle scent of spring flowers and the wind blowing away the debris of tragedy.

"Don't be sad, Jennet," Brent said. "It's part of life."

Sometimes Brent amazed me with his sensitivity, but he was only half right. Murder was never an acceptable part of life.

"I won't," I said. "I'm all right. See? I'm back to normal."

In public anyway.

Annica returned to pour the coffee, and Brent wrapped his hand around the cup. I noticed the red bite on his hand. It looked inflamed, almost angry. Was it larger too?

"Did you put anything on that bite?" I asked.

"A little ointment, but it wears off. It's hard to keep anything on your hand."

"Because it doesn't look good," I said. "Maybe you'd better see a doctor."

"For a bug bite?" He scoffed. "It wasn't a snake that bit me. It'll go away eventually."

I took a sip of coffee. "It's just that I don't want to lose another friend."

"That's not going to happen," he said. "Not until we go for our hot air balloon ride anyway. You and me and Annica."

I looked at him, feeling a tinge of apprehension I thought I'd banished. What odd phrasing.

"And that'll be your swan song?" I asked. "A flight over Foxglove Corners and then the curtain falls?"

My remark, intended to be humorous, fell flat.

"Gad, Jennet, are you always this dramatic in the morning?" he demanded.

Instead of answering, I smiled, which seemed to satisfy him. "It was your choice of words and the way you strung them together in a sentence. Remember I'm an English teacher."

Annica brought Brent's great farmer's breakfast. The portions were giant-sized. Even the plate was different from Clovers' regular china, larger with six corners. She wasn't above giving Brent special treatment.

I drank my coffee and watched Brent demolish his ham and eggs. He saved the hash browns and biscuits for last. Every now and then my gaze strayed to his hand. It seemed to be swelling. If that were my bite, I'd be a lot more concerned.

~ * ~

Even before Terra's body was released to her sister, Tina, for burial, Sue Appleton planned a memorial for her. She stopped by on her way home from Lakeville, made a fuss over the collies, and accepted my offer of tea and jelly roll. We sat in the kitchen talking somberly while the dogs begged for handouts.

"It'll be in Saint Perpetua's church tomorrow at seven," she said. "I expect a crowd, so you might want to come early."

"Do you know when the funeral will be?" I asked.

"There isn't going to be one. Terra wanted to be cremated. She was always terrified of being buried in the ground."

So was I, whenever I re-read one of Poe's stories about being buried alive.

"She told Tina once that she wanted her ashes scattered over Lake Huron," Sue added. "Tina is going to do that as soon as... Well, as soon as it's possible."

"I'm afraid of fire," I said. "Crane insisted we make out a will, so we did, but I don't think about death until I have to. Like now."

Now I remembered all the times in the past when I had practically courted death, had stepped blithely into danger. Never again, I always said. Until the next time.

Was that what Terra had done? Courted death?

"Instead of flowers, Tina requested donations to the Lakeville Collie Rescue League and the Foxglove Corners Animal Shelter," Sue said.

"But there should be flowers."

To die in the spring of the year... In a time of rebirth. To lie in the woods with wildflowers in bloom all around you...

"There will be," Sue said. "People make up their own minds about memorials. I thought we'd send one from all of us in the Rescue League. I'll order them."

I forced myself to pay attention to what Sue was saying. She had leaped from funeral flowers to business.

"We have to meet again and hold an election. We just lost another member. If this keeps up, we'll dwindle away to a couple of people and there'll be no collies to offer potential owners who come to our site."

"Don't you think it's too soon?" I asked. "Terra isn't even buried yet. That is, I mean, she isn't cremated."

"We can wait a while, but not too long. The best way to honor Terra's memory is to continue her work."

"And to find her killer," I said.

Eighteen

On the second morning of my vacation week, I sat alone at the oak table in the kitchen drinking hot tea, for once without a muffin or doughnut to accompany it. I'd taken the collies out for an extra-long walk this morning which should have invigorated me, but I felt tired and listless, completely without ambition at nine o'clock.

All of the dogs except Misty were snoozing in their favorite corners. Misty had found her toy goat and lay at my feet, eyes sparkling in a blatant invitation to play. She knew no one could resist her.

I tossed the toy into the dining room. She dashed after it and didn't come back. How could we play Fetch this way?

"Misty," I called. "Bring it back."

She appeared, wagging her tail, but without the toy. Well, maybe I'd inadvertently thrown it onto a high surface. But if that were the case, wouldn't she have barked?

She lay down again and stared at me, resting her head on her crossed paws. Oh, no! My malaise was affecting her. My lively, happy puppy.

I took another sip of the tea. It was still the way I liked it: hot but not too hot to drink. The kitchen was clean, everything in its place, everything I'd added over the years still possessing its ability to charm and soothe. The sun streamed through the window, bathing my tulips in light, issuing another blatant invitation.

Did I really want to waste a glorious spring morning drinking tea in my own kitchen as if I'd aged thirty years overnight? All too soon I'd be back in the classroom struggling to control and teach groups of noisy teenagers while longing for the infinite peace and tranquility of the Foxglove Corners by-roads.

So get up. Move. Do something.

I poured the rest of the tea down the drain, lured Misty into her crate with a treat from the Lassie tin, and set out for a solitary drive on those roads, destination the Haver property.

Ever since Easter when our party had descended on those acres, I'd wanted to return alone on another day to see if anything untoward would happen. By untoward, I meant the materialization of a blue door or a collie in the form of a lightning flash, or a sound of weeping from an invisible source.

If only there were even a hint of fog, but the air was clear and the sun was so bright it seemed as if nothing could hide from its reach.

A flutter of yellow crime scene tape in the distance caught my attention as I drove down Deer Leap Trail, and as I came closer, I saw yellow ribbons tied to the trees that lined the road. Yellow ribbons for remembrance. For Terra. The people of the Rescue League must have been here. I wished someone had asked me to join them.

Feeling newly bereft, I continued on my way and soon reached the haunted house and the mysterious barn.

You'd think a place wouldn't change in two days, but the wildflowers had spread unchecked across every free inch of the area. What would happen when they ran out of space?

The border of Queen Anne's Lace had lost its shape and looked like a white pond shining alongside the barn. It was impossible to walk without tramping on some unfortunate stem. But I did my best.

And of course there was no blue door. The barn was locked. Nothing stirred, not even a restless bird overhead or an insect in the weeds. Still, as I stood in the surround of flowers, the air seemed to thicken and fill with a heaviness that was almost palpable. It told of loss and sadness and the fragility of life. And tears.

I tried to breathe and was surprised that I could.

Was that a sound of weeping over where the meadow flowers flowed into the woods?

No, it was still silent, but something, a weight, seemed to be closing in on me, squeezing, pushing me back.

Get out of here! It's growing stronger. It—whatever it is.

I reached out to touch the barn door, a stable pillar in a wavering world, and heard the intrusive hum of a motor. A door slammed. It was an angry sound.

Alarmed, I whirled around. A car was parked in front of the Haver house, a dark station wagon that crushed the flowers under powerful black tires. A woman strode resolutely toward me. She didn't look very happy.

The woman was tall and slender, and her red shirtwaist dress had the shimmer of silk. She wore a shade of bright red lipstick. Glittering barrettes held back dark hair with auburn lights in the sun. Sunglasses hid her eyes, but I assumed they were as fiery as her voice.

"What the hell do you think you're doing here?" she demanded.

I felt like running away, but I stood my ground, trying desperately to think of an explanation for being on private property with my hand pressed against a structure on that property. Any explanation, even if it wasn't plausible, would do.

I'm following a wounded collie. Somebody shot her. I'd say that.

"I'm looking for a collie," I said. "She headed this way. She had a gunshot wound and was bleeding."

All true, and I could sense some of the woman's anger evaporating. But not the suspicion.

"Did you think you'd find this dog in a locked barn?"

"I just noticed the lock," I said. "You know sick or wounded dogs will find a quiet place to die."

I'd better stop rambling as I was tempting fate and not furthering my cause. I tried to read the woman's expression. She might not believe me, but there was a possibility the wounded dog was real. She was going to give me the benefit of a doubt.

Anyway, what could I possibly want in an empty barn?

"My name is Jennet Ferguson," I added. "I live on Jonquil Lane." Inspiration struck. "I belong to the Lakeville Collie Rescue League, but even if I didn't, I'd stop to help a dog in need."

That information seemed to turn the tide.

"Well, my family has been bothered by vagrants before," she said. "They've done a lot of damage. You don't look like one, though."

"I'm not." I decided to embroider my story. A mixture of truth and half-truth might convince her.

"I've been here before and thought I saw a collie rounding the barn. It happened so fast, there and gone in a flash. I couldn't be sure that what I saw was real and haven't been able to stop thinking about it."

"You saw a collie?" she said.

"Like I said, I'm pretty sure I did for a split second. But then it was gone. And I heard something out in the meadow that sounded like someone or something crying."

I felt that she believed me.

"But there was nothing there?" she asked. "Nothing tangible?"

"Not that I saw. I know collies can be crafty. If they don't want to be found you'll never see them."

"I thought that was cats."

"Maybe. I never had a cat."

"Then this didn't just happen today?" she asked.

"It happened a few days ago. I'm still looking for the dog."

She paused, gazing across the meadow at the dark woods and the shadows that lay on the wildflowers. The color had drained from her face. She looked older, her vivid lipstick more pronounced. As she removed the sunglasses, I saw a glimmer of tears in her eyes.

"My name is Linnea," she said. "Linnea Haver."

Nineteen

Linnea Haver. Of course. The homeowner. Who else would take such a proprietary stance?

"Well," I said, "obviously there's no collie here today. I'd better be on my way."

"Wait!" Ms. Haver took a step forward. "Before you go, would you tell me your story again? Don't leave anything out."

While I hesitated, she said, "We can sit in the house where it's more comfortable. I just drove out to check that everything was okay. I do that once a month."

I almost asked her why she wanted to hear about my experiences again but decided not to antagonize her. Here was a chance to see the inside of a haunted house at the invitation of the owner. How could I pass up that opportunity?

We walked up to the house, tramping on the rampant wildflowers. There was no way to avoid them.

"Look at this mess," Linnea said.

"The wildflowers?"

"I'll have to get someone to mow them down."

"Don't do that," I said. "They're so beautiful. They're like a picture in a magazine."

She looked at me as if I'd said something nonsensical. "They're invasive. Those pink spirals." She yanked one out of the ground. "They look like loosestrife."

I said, "I didn't leave any details out of my story. I don't know who shot the collie."

"I'll bet I do. That crazy kid, Lyle Bradshaw, who lives down the road. He shoots at anything that moves."

She pulled a large cloth purse out of the front seat of the station wagon, found her key, and we climbed the steps to the porch. She unlocked the door, and we stepped into a small vestibule. The air in the house was close and musty. Once again I took a deep breath, surprised that it was possible.

The living room, smaller than I'd thought from the outside, was sparsely furnished with sheets covering shapes easily identifiable as chairs and tables. The place had the eerie atmosphere of a house too long deprived of human occupants. It felt dead, and it was so quiet that our voices bounced back to us as echoes.

"The electricity's been turned off or I'd turn on the air," Linnea said.

She crossed to one of the windows, high heels tapping on the bare hardwood floor, and pushed it open. Dust particles drifted from the fraying beige curtains. She sneezed, and fumbled in her purse for a tissue.

"That'll get more fresh air in here," she said.

"Is the house for sale?" I asked.

"It was, for three years. It didn't sell, and we took it off the market."

"I heard a rumor that it was haunted."

She smiled, a bitter twisting of her too-red lips. "Talk like that is inevitable when a house is vacant for a long period of time. That's probably why it hasn't sold. Let's go back to the kitchen," she added quickly.

She led me to a spacious country kitchen with dated gold appliances and antique yellow chairs arranged around a wood table. Flowerpots lined the sunlit windowsill, all colorful, all empty. This might have been a cheery room once, could be pleasant again, but at the moment it was clammy and uninviting.

"I wish I could offer you a cup of coffee or a soft drink," Linnea said, "but we cleaned out the cupboards."

"That's okay."

Which wasn't true. My throat felt scratchy, probably because of the dust flying around or maybe from the overwhelming crop of wildflowers. The very thought of those allergens set me to coughing.

"There's bottled water if you don't have to have it cold," she added. "I never got used to tap water. Would you like a drink?"

"That sounds good," I said.

She opened a liter of Michigan Pure for herself and one for me. "Now please tell me your story again. Start at the beginning."

I'd told it countless times, but it was still immediate, as if it had happened yesterday, still heart-wrenching.

"I was bringing my dog home from the vet one morning and found myself driving in a thick fog," I said. "I heard a gunshot. Moments later I saw a collie lying near the road."

I re-created the experience for her, downplaying the appearance of the blue door as an illusion borne of the fog. I also omitted the impromptu visit we'd made on Easter Sunday, and there was no point, as I saw it at that moment, of telling her about the murder of Terra Roman.

What I left out made a whole separate story. Maybe I was wrong, but I had to follow my instincts. I'd just met Linnea Haver, and she hadn't yet explained her interest in the affair, except that the events had taken place on her property. Perhaps that was reason enough for her desire to know what I'd experienced.

"I can't bear the thought of that poor collie still in the vicinity," I said. "That's why I came back, in case she's still here."

"The dog could have run away into the woods," Linnea pointed out.

"Yes, that's possible, and I can hardly go hiking through them."

"And she might be dead. But you said you saw a collie and heard weeping."

"That's what I thought," I said, "but I wouldn't swear to it. This is an extremely atmospheric piece of land. It plays on the imagination."

Linnea took a long swallow of water. "Even this tastes wrong," she said. "It must be me, or maybe it's this place."

I thought it tasted good. Cool but not ice cold because it hadn't been refrigerated.

There was a silence that went on so long it grew uncomfortable. Finally Linnea broke it.

"I believe you saw the collie," she said. "I've seen it too and once I heard weeping in the meadow. Two people aren't going to have the same illusion."

Which collie? As I absorbed that unanticipated revelation, I realized it was important to be clear.

"I may have given you the wrong impression," I said. "The collie I saw wasn't the one who had been shot."

"I don't understand."

"The wounded collie ran away from me into the meadow. I don't know how far she could have gotten. On another day I saw…" I paused, searching for the right words. If you talk about inexplicable occurrences to strangers, they think you're deranged. On the other hand, hadn't Linnea just said she had seen a dog and heard weeping?

"It moved so quickly all I had was a brief impression of light in the shape of a collie," I said. "I don't know how else to explain it. It's like something you see out of the corner of your eye. Then you look again and nothing is there, not even a speck. Call it a phenomenon."

"That's it exactly!" Linnea cried. "That's what I saw! There's something here." She found another tissue and dabbed at her eyes. "No one ever believed me. After a while, I started to doubt myself."

Linnea obviously didn't have my history of seeing things that weren't there. I searched for something appropriate to say. All I could come up with was, "Where does that leave us?"

"I have a story of my own to tell you," Linnea said. "Three years ago my younger sister, Grace, disappeared in that meadow and her dog with her. Callie was a collie."

The words hung in the thick air, giving rise to a thought that echoed in my mind like the reverberations of our voices in the untenanted house.

Like Terra Roman disappearing with her collie, Shadow, into the thin air that hangs over certain sections of Foxglove Corners.

"She was planting the meadow with wildflowers that morning. She had a wheelbarrow filled with those bags of mulch and dirt or whatever, mixed with seed. It was an experiment because there was no way she could keep them watered. She'd just throw handfuls of that stuff wherever it fell."

"What happened?" I asked.

"Grace never came back to the house. Neither did Callie. I never saw either one of them again."

Or their bodies.

She didn't say that but implied it.

"You said you couldn't tramp through the woods looking for your wounded collie," Linnea said. "Well, I did. The neighbors helped. We never found a sign of her. The wheelbarrow stood alone in the meadow with two packages of *Sow and Reap* still unopened. It's out there now, rusting away."

"I didn't see it."

"You would in the winter. Now Grace's flowers are hiding it."

She continued. "Then one day I heard weeping. Grace never cried. Not even when she was a little girl and hurt herself or broke her doll. She just didn't."

"Maybe it wasn't Grace you heard then."

"I felt it was, deep down. And once I thought I saw the dog. What you saw."

Linnea was crying now, tears streaming down her cheeks, unmindful that they were smudging her mascara and the rosy blush.

"We moved away soon after that. This place didn't want us here. We didn't want to be here."

Even if Grace's spirit remained behind? I thought of asking her that, then thought the better of it. It was close and stuffy in the kitchen, approaching the unbearable. I took a drink of water. It didn't help.

"So this is a haunted place," I said.

"Yes, I believe that. Little do those rumormongers know. What they're saying about the house, it's all true."

Twenty

The house was quiet. It seemed to me to be at rest, at peace. You could hear the proverbial pin drop. I found myself listening for it. Perhaps it was only the surrounding land that was haunted—the meadow where a lost soul wept and the barn near which the lightning flash collie had appeared.

"What are you going to do now, Ms. Haver?" I asked.

"Nothing different," she said. "I'll check on the house every month or so, same as always, and leave it off the market. It's unlikely the property would sell anyway, and we're not going to give it away. I can't sit around and wait for a ghost to come along."

"That seems sensible."

"Even though I'd love to see my sister again. Just to know what happened that day."

I didn't understand why she wished to have the wildflowers destroyed, though, especially since she had no immediate plans to sell the house. Wouldn't she want to keep them nourished in memory of Grace? In her place, I would.

I decided to ask her and risk being thought insensitive.

"They were the cause of whatever happened to Grace," she said. "If she'd never had the idea to turn the meadow into a field of flowers, she'd still be with me. I always intended to store the wheelbarrow in the barn. It's all rusty and has a flat tire. But I never got around to it. If Grace ever comes back, she'll be surprised to see it."

If she came back.

After three years, I thought that was unlikely. Like Terra she might be lying in a pond or a secluded wooded area uninvestigated by the searchers.

Or what was left of her.

After all this time, after the changing seasons, Grace would be bones and scraps of clothing. If she was dead.

The clock on the kitchen wall had frozen at five o'clock. I glanced at my watch, surprised to discover that an hour had passed. I became aware of the drifting dust and the stuffiness and the tomb-like silence of the Haver house and found myself craving a breath of fresh spring air.

"I'd better go," I said. "I never meant to stay so long."

Linnea smiled, that slight twisting of her lips. "Neither did I, but this has been a productive encounter. I'm glad I came by when I did."

She took our bottles of water, both empty, and set them on the counter. "Feel free to stop by anytime," she said. "And I hope you find the dog. The one with the gunshot wound, that is. You won't find her in the barn, though. It's empty."

The barn!

I'd almost forgotten. "One time when I stopped to look for the dog, the barn was open," I said.

Linnea frowned. "That's impossible. I never left the barn unlocked or the house either. That would be inviting vagrants or vandals."

"I only know what I saw," I said. "Does anyone else have a key?"

"Just my father, and he rarely leaves home."

"It's a mystery then."

"I think I may drive out here more often," Linnea said. "All this is going on, and I didn't have a clue."

And I hadn't even told her about the blue door. Or about Terra's body being discovered on the woods along Deer Leap Trail.

Neither one of us mentioned that other dog who appeared as a flash of lightning. The ghost dog. The dog Linnea must think was the spirit of Grace's collie, Callie.

~ * ~

On the way home, I reviewed the story of Grace Haver and the wildflowers. It added a layer to the strange happenings on the Haver property but didn't point the way to any answers. It did serve to convince Linnea that she hadn't been imagining the sound of weeping and the lightning flash collie. As for myself, I'd never been in doubt.

Perhaps because the grim finality of Terra Roman's death was still very much with me, I thought Grace Haver might be dead as well. Or she might have been kidnapped. Lured away. Leaving her wildflower project unfinished and the wheelbarrow and her bags of seeds out in the open? It was possible. But there was little traffic on Deer Leap Trail. The idea of an abductor driving down a country road in search of a victim was far-fetched. Someone who had already chosen Grace as his victim, then.

I would have to know more about Grace. For example, whether she might have arranged her disappearance. Whether she was buried in the same meadow from which she'd vanished.

I recalled Annica picking a flower and crying out that it was bleeding. I'd told her what she thought was blood was only sap. Then I remembered Lucy saying that something bad had happened here.

At the time, I thought she'd been referring to the wounded collie. That was bad enough. Possibly there was more. Lucy's impressions were usually on track.

I wanted to talk to Linnea Haver again, but at present, that seemed unlikely. She hadn't suggested another meeting. We'd probably never be at the Haver house at the same time again.

So what could I do?

Find someone else to talk to, maybe someone who had listened to or even started the rumor that the Haver house was haunted. Someone at the Spirit Lamp Inn?

Why not? I was free all week, and both Annica and Leonora would be eager to help me solve a mystery. Making plans for the next step, I soon found myself in familiar territory. Jonquil Lane lay ahead, bathed in a springtime haze, and the yellow brick road of daffodils was guiding me home.

~ * ~

Brent sat on the front porch playing ball with Misty and Candy while the other dogs wandered around the front yard, enjoying the myriad new scents that had appeared since their last foray.

Abruptly he changed the game, tossing Misty's puppy-sized Frisbee over the grass. It came to rest in our own wildflower meadow where a white blossoming tree had almost lost its flowers. The tree had sprung up one day from a wind-borne seed, or so I assumed. Crane claimed he knew nothing about it.

Misty bounded after the flying disk, but Candy was too fast for her. She raced back to Brent, Frisbee firmly in her mouth, with the puppy loping in her wake. Brent threw it again, farther and watched the two collies scamper after it.

"This is the life," Crane said, settling into the wicker rocker with a can of beer. "Country living and good friends."

I smiled at them, my handsome fair-haired husband in his civilian clothes—he usually wore blue—and Brent in red plaid. The men had not always been friends. Once they had been rivals with me as the prize, although Crane always had the first claim on my heart. Now Brent was a faithful family friend who often joined us for holidays and dinners. He had helped me with many a mysterious matter that came my way unbidden.

Brent had a keen interest in the story of Grace Haver's disappearance. "The sound in the meadow. Could it be Grace crying because she's dead?"

"I vote for a bird or a small animal," Crane said. "Just because you didn't see it doesn't mean it wasn't there."

"I never heard an animal make a sound like a human weeping," I said. "And don't forget the dog. And the door."

Candy dropped the Frisbee at Brent's feet. He tossed it into the air again, and both dogs dashed after it.

"I don't see how the blue door fits into the puzzle," Brent said.

"Annica and Lucy think it's a door to another dimension. The crying lady and the dog ran through it and can't find their way back."

"That's fine, if you believe science-fiction is real," Crane said.

"At this point, I don't know what I believe." To change the subject, I commented on Brent's bite. I'd noticed that it hadn't changed. It was still large and an angry shade of red. From time to time, he scratched it.

"Are you sure you weren't bitten by a snake?" I asked.

Brent glanced at his hand. "Pretty sure. I'm still living. Anyway, I've got other troubles."

This was the first time he'd mentioned any ripple in his usually smooth life, aside from the insect bite which he insisted on minimizing.

"Such as?" I said.

"Napoleon is sick," he said. "It looks like I may lose him."

Twenty-one

Napoleon was Brent's trusty guard dog, a large gentle canine who resembled the cartoon character, Marmaduke. Brent had rescued him from a shelter, and he repaid Brent with unlimited loyalty.

"The vet doesn't know what's wrong with him," Brent said. "She ran every test in the book."

"I'm sorry to hear that. What are his symptoms?"

"He's lethargic and off his feed. He just wants to sleep, and he whines for no reason. He's never done that."

The lack of interest in food caught my attention. When a dog stops eating, it's time to worry about him.

"You took him to Doctor Foster at the animal hospital, I assume," I said. "What does Alice think?"

"She doesn't know. Napoleon doesn't seem to be in pain. I could tell."

"But you said he was whining. If only dogs could talk."

"How long has Napoleon been sick?" Crane asked.

"A couple of weeks. About the time I noticed the bite on my hand." He stared at his hand. The bite mark was still there, still red. It looked as if he'd just gotten it.

A connection slipped into place. Brent's bite and Napoleon's illness. "Maybe whatever bit you took a chunk out of Napoleon, too," I said.

"I don't see any wound on him, but he has a thick coat. I could have missed it."

"Alice would have noticed something," I said. "She's pretty thorough with her hands-on exam. How is Chance?"

"Chance seems fine, but he's slowed down too," Brent said. "To keep Napoleon company, I think. He lies beside Napoleon during the day. Before they used to go running together."

Unlike Napoleon, Brent's collie, Chance, had been purchased from a breeder. To my knowledge, he'd never been sick. Because he'd been a rescue, Napoleon's life before the shelter was a mystery.

"Could Napoleon have eaten something like a rabbit or a deer carcass?" I asked.

Chance and Napoleon had the run of Brent's stable and the land surrounding his mansion. Both locations were rural, which encouraged dogs to become hunters.

"It's possible," Brent said. "How could I know for sure?"

"What if someone poisoned him?" Crane asked.

"I hadn't considered that." Brent's face was drawn, the dark red hair more pronounced. He was baffled and concerned. When your dog is ailing, nothing in your world is right.

I was loath to abandon the connection. "Something's working against him and you," I said.

Suddenly I had it. The haunted painting known as *Ada's Litter*, a present from my sister, Julia, last Christmas. It had turned out to be as lethal as any poison.

No one, not even the artist, Aura Lee Larkin, could explain it, but the sentimental painting of a girl with collies had a long history of bringing misfortune to its owners. In some way, that cursed painting had started a fire that destroyed my heirloom buffet and its contents. It could have claimed our lives if Candy hadn't alerted us to danger.

Brent had scoffed at the painting's so-called power, declared that he was a match for it, and moved it from our house to his.

"Do you still have *Ada's Litter*?" I asked.

"Sure do. It's hanging in my study."

"Get rid of it," I said.

"You don't seriously think the painting is making Napoleon sick."

"I do."

"Well, I don't. *Ada's Litter* is just a canvas covered in oil. It has no magical power. We've been through this before."

"You know the story behind the painting," I said. "All those people who experienced serious setbacks in their lives. Have you forgotten what happened to me? The fire?"

"All that could have a rational explanation."

"I've never come up with one. You have a bite that should be long gone by now and a sick dog. What's next? When you took possession of the painting, it transferred its power to you."

Crane said, "I was unhappy when Jennet told me you took the painting, Fowler. We care about you. Listen to Jennet. Get rid of it."

"I didn't expect superstitious claptrap from you, Sheriff," Brent said.

"I like to keep an open mind about things."

"Remember the writing on the back of the painting: *Evil RIP*," I said. "I love Napoleon and don't want to see him suffer or worse. And I don't want anything to happen to you or your animals."

"You've given me something to think about," Brent said. "But I don't believe a painting made Napoleon sick. Something else is going on."

And he changed the subject.

~ * ~

The spacious room in St. Perpetua's church served as a gathering place for funeral luncheons and memorials and other happier activities. Tonight it was filled with flowers sent in spite of Tina Roman's request for donations to the Rescue League and the Animal Shelter. Candleholders placed at intervals cast sinister shadows on the ivory walls.

Those floral scents that were pleasant out of doors underwent a change when they vied for air in a room with poor ventilation. Trying not to be overwhelmed by the cloying mixture of fragrances, I searched the crowd for the familiar faces of the League members.

Sue Appleton beckoned to me from a seat near an enormous memorial collage of photographs featuring Terra with dogs she'd owned and rescued over the years.

"I didn't think you'd make it," she said, moving her cardigan and purse from the chair next to her. "I saved you a seat."

"I ran into road work."

With five minutes to spare, I didn't consider myself late. I sank into the chair, glad I'd arrived safely but wishing the smell of funeral flowers weren't so strong. Didn't it bother anyone else?

It's just that you don't want to be here, I told myself. *Not in this crowded room. Terra should be memorialized in the open air with flowers still in the ground.*

In a place like the wildflower meadow on the Haver acres.

At least there was no coffin, no body frozen in death, dressed in an outfit chosen by another, her lifeless hands resting forever on a rosary.

I resolved to remember Terra the way she'd been when I'd last seen her. If only I could remember that last time.

"Excuse me." Laurence DeVille made his way awkwardly down the row and plopped into the chair on the other side of Sue. "Did they start yet?"

His tone reminded me of Brent, who was often loud and irreverent in a situation that called for solemnity.

"Any minute now," Sue said.

Tina Roman, all in black, had come to the podium and stood shuffling through papers. Beside the podium an easel decorated with black ribbons held a picture of Terra. It was a studio portrait, and Shadow was part of it, sitting sedately at her side. I felt the sting of tears. Sue brought a tissue out of her purse.

"Hell of a thing," Laurence said. "A good woman like Terra cut down in her prime. What is this world coming to? Did they catch the killer yet?"

"Not that I've heard," I said.

"How about we all pitch in and collect money for a reward?"

"We all?" Sue asked.

"The Rescue League."

"We could do that," I said. "But we're a small group. How much could we hope to collect?"

"We can use the money in the treasury."

Sue couldn't control her outrage. "That's for the collies. For food and vet care and medicine."

"It's not like we have any collies to rescue," DeVille pointed out.

"But we will. Terra wouldn't want the League's money spent on a reward."

"She's out of the picture. Besides, do you think the group is going to survive without Terra?" he asked.

"Of course it will," Sue countered. "We'll elect a new president and attract new members, and if we don't have any collies now, that'll change."

"Shhh," someone said.

At the podium, Tina set her papers down and looked down at the mourners.

"Good evening, ladies and gentlemen," she said. "Thank you for coming. I'm inviting anyone who has a special memory of Terra to share it with us. I'll begin."

Twenty-two

After a while, my mind began to wander. Voices droned on and on, sharing memories and tributes. The mixed scents of the funeral arrangements intensified, and it seemed as if the candle flames increased the heat in the room.

All imagination; still uncomfortable.

The homespun anecdotes rolled on. The time Terra had been bitten by a protective collie mother. When she had rescued a scrawny puppy from a burning house. The tornado that had swept a lovely blue merle girl away from her home. Another blue merle found scavenging for food behind a restaurant after the same tornado.

Some tragedies, some triumphs. Terra was always on the scene when a collie needed rescuing.

I stirred in my seat and thought of meadows filled with wildflowers soaking up the sunlight. In my mind, I pictured the Haver acres and planned my next trip to the property. Wisps of fog would rise from the ground. In the distance I'd see a blue door ajar and beckoning. Like Alice's rabbit hole.

All I had to do was step over that threshold to find myself in the company of Grace Haver, her dog, Callie, and the wounded collie whose name was Breezy…

All the lost ones found again. But first, I had to find the door.

..."and that's how Terra rescued her first collie. Initially she enlisted the aid of a few like-minded friends, myself included, and by the end of the year, the Lakeville Collie Rescue League had fifteen members. Today we number twenty, and in the wake of the tragedy, we have pledged to carry on Terra's work."

Sue Appleton stood at the podium wrapping up her tribute. When she had left her seat at my side, I had no idea; but she was coming back. I rose to let her pass more easily, and the next moment others were rising, too. The memorial service was over. At last.

Louanne caught up to me as I headed for the exit. Her eyes were red and bleary, her black mascara smeared. She managed a weak smile.

"How is Shadow?" I asked.

"She's adjusting to my home. Collies do that, although they never forget their previous owner. Yesterday she wagged her tail."

"Poor Shadow. Are you going to keep her?"

"If no one objects, and why would they? Tina approves. She's grateful that Terra's dog has a new home."

"Shadow was lucky to be rescued twice," I said.

"Luckier than Terra. I wonder if we'll ever know what happened to separate the two of them and who killed Terra."

"The police will find out."

"You hope. They don't always solve their cases."

That was true, but I believed in the importance of being optimistic, while it was possible. "Well, no, and this one won't be easy. But you know what they say. Murder will out."

"What does that mean?" Louanne asked.

"Sooner or later they'll find the killer, or he'll be overcome by a guilty conscience and give himself away."

Even if we had to wait years. In Terra's case, there were simply no clues. No suspects, no motive. No confession.

Not yet.

Louanne stopped to talk to a friend, and I went through the open doors and took a grateful breath of the air I'd been craving. There was still plenty of daylight left, and a light breeze stirred the new plantings in front of the church. I had a short walk to my car, then a short drive, then home.

"Jennet! Wait up!"

Sue Appleton reached my side, panting and red-faced. "We're getting together on Friday at seven for an emergency election and to regroup. It's at my place. Can you make it?"

"Sure," I said. "Would you like me to bring something?"

"One of your banana nut breads, if you don't mind. They're so good."

"I'll bring two."

I'd once thought it was too soon to replace Terra, but the memorial had been an ending of sorts. Next Terra's body would be released, then cremated. Who knew how long that would take? In the meantime, we had to move on.

"I can't let that DeVille creature think our group is going to fall apart," Sue said. "He's a first class jerk, if you want my opinion. The king of the pessimists."

I had to agree with her. He'd had Terra dead in a ditch before the hikers had found her body in the woods.

"And he's not getting his paws on the League's money," Sue added. "Oh, I know what his game is."

"But the idea of offering a reward is a good one," I said. "It may encourage informants who wouldn't get involved otherwise. I've always thought someone must have seen Terra in her neighborhood or somewhere else."

Sue nodded. "Money talks. We'll come up with a reward through private donations. Let's talk about it at the meeting."

~ * ~

I had more vacation days and a burning desire to return to the Haver acres. Linnea's story had given me proof that something strange was going on in that place of beauty and mystery.

This time I also planned to visit the Spirit Lamp Inn and needed a lunch companion. Leonora or Annica? Or two companions?

Leonora took the decision out of my hands. She and Jake were planning a day trip to Maple Falls.

"That sounds serious," I said.

"It's just a little excursion. For once Jake and I are free at the same time."

"What's the attraction in Maple Falls?" I asked.

"Scenery. They still have snow up there."

"Ugh. I'm tired of snow. It's blossom time."

"We'll do something together later in the week," she said.

Fortunately Annica had an afternoon off and an evening class. I arranged to meet her at Clovers and in the interval took the dogs for a walk on Squill Lane down to the horse farm. We saw horses enjoying the warm weather but there was no sign of Sue. I came home, changed into a green rayon dress, and drove to Clovers.

Annica was ready, like me, dressed for lunch in an elegant place, which meant that neither of us would go tramping through the wildflower meadow. On the way I told her about my encounter with Linnea Haver.

"Another disappearance," she murmured. "They must be connected."

"Not necessarily," I said, "but possibly. Remember, three years separate the incidents."

Moreover, people disappear every day, I reminded myself. Quite often the missing were children and young women. But not always. Especially in Foxglove Corners. Especially on that mysterious road known as Brandymere that, according to local legend, led to World's End. When wayfarers reached that point, they dropped off the planet.

A fantastic story to tell around the campfire and at Halloween parties. It didn't seem to keep people from traveling on Brandymere Road, though.

Now, with the discovery of Terra's body and the mysteries surrounding the Haver house, Deer Leap Trail was well on the way to inspiring another chilling legend.

The crime scene tape still fluttered around Terra's woodland resting place and yellow ribbons for remembrance decorated the trees. Such a happy bright hue to be a color of mourning.

We passed the Haver property, vibrant with unearthly color, stopped at the crossroads, and soon reached the Spirit Lamp Inn. It no longer looked like the spooky place I'd first seen with Leonora. Today the parking lot was crowded, and large pots of pansies flanked the entrance.

"It's busy," Annica said. "I hope we won't need a reservation."

"It's past one. I'm sure they'll find a place for us."

"But no one will have time to talk to us."

"Then we'll have to come back another day," I said. "In the meantime I'm starved."

At present, food took precedent over mystery.

Twenty-three

The Inn had different entrées on the menu board this day and a spirit lamp sketched along the side.

One-half Barbecued Chicken

One-half Steak Sandwich with Cup of Beef Noodle Soup

Stuffed Cabbages with Rice

Vegetable Lasagna

Annica tossed her head and set her silver bell earrings jingling. "Clovers has a better menu. We give our customers more specials to choose from. The barbecued chicken sounds good, though," she added.

"Everything does," I said and smiled at the hostess. The employees seemed to be in a constant state of flux. This was a young woman with a scattering of freckles on her nose and a sleek dark pageboy with bangs. Her floral patterned skirt swept the floor. Fortunately the skirt's background was navy blue, almost black.

"Two for lunch?" she asked with a bright smile.

"We'd like a table by the window, if you have it," I said.

She led us to a table near the one we'd had for the Easter brunch with its spectacular view of the Inn's garden.

"You're right," Annica said as she set her straw bag on an extra chair. "This *is* a strange place."

"I agree, but why do you say that?"

"From all the cars parked outside, I thought the dining room would be packed, but it isn't, not really."

I glanced around, estimating about twenty diners, some of them obvious family groups. Why didn't I notice that? I was the senior detective in our mystery-solving enterprise.

"So where are all the people who belong to the cars?" she asked.

"The Inn has rooms to rent," I said. "Maybe they're sleeping in."

"On such a beautiful day? Who does that? It's unlikely they'd go anywhere on foot. You need a car to get around this part of the state."

"Then I don't know."

Still it was, as Annica said, strange. We ordered barbecued chicken dinners from another hitherto unseen waitress, this one named Kay, and sipped iced tea in tall, frosty glasses. Remembering the oddities associated with the Spirit Lamp Inn, I'd just decided to ask the waitress how long it had been in business when I chanced to look out the window.

In the shade of a pink flowering cherry tree, a dark sable collie lay sleeping on its side. The sun reached through lacy treetops and touched the rich mahogany in the dog's thick coat. Sunlight made the full white collar sparkle.

"Look!" I said. "A collie!"

Annica followed my gaze. "You find them wherever we go. It's uncanny."

"This one looks comfortable here."

"So it does. Could he be the Inn's watchdog? If so, he's sleeping on the job."

"The young woman who waited on Leonora and me claimed she hadn't seen a collie. I was looking for the wounded collie then. She said they didn't encourage dogs to hang around the restaurant."

"He looks right at home," Annica said.

"Either their policy changed or she was lying. If she was lying, the question is, why?"

When Kay served dinner, I said, "That's a beautiful collie. Does he belong to the Inn?"

"To a guest, I think."

"It'd make a pretty picture," Annica said. "I wish I'd brought my camera."

"Oh, no one is allowed to take pictures at the Inn."

"Why not? I asked.

She flushed, and the freckles on her nose almost disappeared. "It disturbs the ghosts. It's silly, but that's one of the Inn's ironclad rules." So saying, she went on her way, apparently with no thought to the effect her announcement had on us.

"Did she say guests or ghosts?" Annica asked.

"Ghosts, I'm sure."

"Well, there you are, Jennet. You thought the Inn was haunted. Or did you say it had a haunting name? Or was it a haunting air? Maybe the dog is the ghost."

"The dog I saw at the Haver barn, or whatever I saw, wasn't completely formed. It resembled a flash of lightning. This is a real dog, although he's lying so still he might be deep in an enchanted sleep."

"Or dead."

Even as we speculated, the dog, instantly awake, leaped up, jaws snapping, eyes following the progress of a small flying creature.

"He sees a bee or a wasp," Annica said.

"And he's trying to catch it. I've seen my dogs do that."

I could barely discern a speck of black zooming far out of the dog's reach, even though it was quite large.

"I've never seen a bee fly that high," Annica said.

"Usually when we see them, they're buzzing around flowers."

"I'm glad it got away."

"I should say so. If the dog caught it, he'd be very sorry."

The collie had given up on the flying insect and also, apparently on his nap. Prey forgotten, he nibbled at the grass.

"Excitement over," Annica said. "Just in time. Here comes our dinner."

After we'd eaten and finished a dessert of strawberry shortcake, I went ahead with my plan to ask our waitress to tell us about the ghosts. As she thanked us, took our money and appeared to be on the verge of leaving, I said, "Did you mean the Spirit Lamp Inn is haunted?"

"So they say. Personally I've never seen a ghost and don't believe in them anyway."

"What supposedly haunts the Inn?" I asked.

"The lady in the blue raincoat." She rolled her eyes. "She supposedly lost her traveling companion at the Inn and keeps coming back to look for her. That's the version I heard. This happened way back in nineteen fifty-five."

"A long time ago. I thought the Inn was a new business."

"Oh, no, it's been around forever. It had a different owner, though, and a different name—and a low profile. The Inn started the new year under new management."

"Who has seen this lady in the blue raincoat?" Annica asked.

"No one I know." She lowered her voice. "The owner likes to keep the story alive. It's good for business. She had a ghost hunter here one year."

"You said 'ghosts,' though," I reminded her. "Who else?"

"The lost companion, I guess. No one ever found out what happened to her."

Like Grace, I thought. Although we might still learn about Grace's fate.

"That sounds interesting," I said when she'd left. "If only we knew more details."

Annia nodded. "Aren't there books about Foxglove Corners hauntings?" she asked.

"In the Foxglove Corners Public Library. I consulted them when I was doing research on the library's secret room."

"Aren't we getting away from the mysteries at hand?" she asked. "The blue door, the phantom dog, Grace Haver's disappearance?"

"In a way, but what if they're all connected?"

"How likely is that?"

"Not very, but 'You never know' is my motto," I said.

Twenty-four

We left the Spirit Lamp Inn and ten minutes later reached the Haver house. Afternoon sunlight bathed the wildflower meadow in golden light, and a deep silence lay on the acreage.

"It's beautiful," Annica said. "Like a painting. So many colors all together. The house is okay. It fits, but that old brown barn totally spoils the effect."

"It has character," I said.

I slowed down, looking for Linnea's vehicle beyond the trees that lined the trail and provided a measure of privacy from the infrequent motorists. At Annica's urging, I brought the car to a stop on the trail's verge.

"No one's here today," I said. "It's quiet."

"The weeping ghost must be asleep. Where is the lightning dog, I wonder?"

And where is the blue door?

As time passed, I could easily believe I'd imagined that door. I needed to see it again to keep my faith in it alive.

"There's no sense in getting out of the car," I said. "I suspect the supernatural show waits for me to visit alone."

"That's okay. We're not dressed for exploring anyway. We could hardly go out to lunch in jeans and hiking boots."

"So we chose to dress up and have a nice lunch over roughing it." I took the car out of park. "This is one of those rare perfect days. I've observed that ghostly apparitions prefer unusual weather conditions."

"Like thunderstorms," Annica said. "With lots of thunder and lightning."

"I was thinking of dense fog. Ghosts like shadowy places to hide, but it was a perfectly normal day when I saw the lightning collie and heard the crying in the meadow."

"So they can come anytime."

"I'm not an authority on the spirit world," I said. "What I wonder is if Grace is the crying ghost. And did she ever leave this meadow?"

I took another look at the property before starting the car. Something was definitely here, altering reality, sending mournful sounds into the atmosphere—calling to me. But it wasn't necessarily Grace Haver.

Who then?

I drove down Deer Leap Trail, sparing a glance at the fluttering yellow ribbons that marked Terra's temporary grave. It felt as if I were drowning in mysteries. Did I really need another one? Or, as I had intimated to Annica, were they all part of the same ever-expanding puzzle?

"I'm going to see if I can find out anything about the Inn's ghost at the library," I said. Then I remembered. "The waitress said at one time the Inn had a different name. I should have asked her what it was."

"Just look for a story about a specter in a blue raincoat," Annica said. "That should be easy to find."

"It would be even easier if we knew her name."

~ * ~

I dropped Annica off at her home and drove to the Corners. It really was a corners, with the post office, the fire and police departments, Zoller's General Store, an ice cream parlor with a candy cane striped awning, the Hometown Bakery where I stopped to buy a dozen doughnuts, and the Foxglove Corners Public Library, an old white Victorian and my favorite place to visit. All were in easy walking distance.

Miss Elizabeth Eidt had donated her family home to the town for a library several years earlier and remained as the lone librarian. She still thought of the house as her own. No matter what the season, she lavished care and expense on maintaining the grounds and keeping the interior pleasant and welcoming.

Tulips in red, yellow, apricot and purple bloomed along the foundation, and the beds were raked clean of any twig or dried leaf that dared to fall in this immaculate spot. "Woe betide anyone who picks one of my flowers," she often said.

Miss Eidt's cat, Blackberry, reclined on one of the porch's wicker chairs, cozily nestled on a plump yellow pillow. The feline and I were old friends. Once Blackberry had saved my life. She regarded me with a hard jewel-eyed stare.

"How are you today, Blackberry?" I asked.

She hissed at me.

"That bad? Well, maybe your day will improve."

Wondering if Miss Eidt knew the kind of welcome her pet gave the library's patrons, I pushed open the door. It was properly quiet inside. A few people sat at tables with books and magazines open and a few browsed in the New Arrivals.

Dressed in her usual outfit—a pastel suit, soft lavender today, and pearls—Miss Eidt sat at her desk, idly flipping through the pages of a large coffee table book. Her face brightened when she saw me.

"Good afternoon, Jennet," she said. "It's been months since you've visited us. I have a stack of Gothic novels set aside for you." She measured a vague two feet with her hand.

"Why thank you, Miss Eidt. And here's something for you."

I gave her the box from the Hometown Bakery. Like an excited child, she removed the string. "Cream horns! My absolute favorite. Would you believe I was just thinking about them?"

I smiled. "Not unless you're reading a cookbook."

"Actually it's about travel. I'm dreaming of faraway places." She closed the book. "You'll join me for tea, won't you?"

"After I do what I came for. I need to research ghosts."

Her eyes sparkled. "Again? How exciting!" Then the sparkle faded as she glanced at a colorful poster along the back wall. It was illustrated with a bright yellow arrow: *This way to the Secret Room of Eidt House.*

The room, discovered after decades when no one was aware of its existence, had held a secret and hosted a genuine ghost. It had become a minor tourist attraction in Foxglove Corners.

"Your new ghost doesn't have anything to do with the library, does it?" she asked.

"No, but you're close. I'm looking for a lady in a blue raincoat who hangs out at the Spirit Lamp Inn."

"Never heard of her. Does she have a name?"

"That's what I'm hoping to find out."

"Well you know the way to our haunted section," she said. "Now where did I put those Gothics?"

I made my way through the stacks to a suitably dim row. Here books about the supernatural filled the shelves. Several of the volumes dealt with Michigan apparitions and, more specifically, those in and around Foxglove Corners.

Anyone would think there couldn't be that many books in existence on the subject in a small town, but I gathered five of them, ranging from a new book with a glossy graveyard scene on the cover to another so old it looked as if it had been in the collection for decades.

I took the books to a table near the window and began reading. Soon I was so engrossed in tales of the strange and terrifying that I almost forgot what I was supposed to be looking for.

Finally I found it in the fragile vintage volume—a section devoted to unexplained disappearances. The first chapter, titled 'An Incident at the Oaken Bucket Inn,' drew my attention. With the first sentence, I knew I had found the lady in the blue raincoat, the spirit who haunted the inn on Deer Leap Trail.

Her name was Rachel Carroll, and as I read her story, I was uncomfortably reminded of myself and my adventure-seeking companions. Annica and, in pre-Jake days, Leonora.

Twenty-five

The author had included a black and white picture, supposedly of the Inn's ghost. To me it looked like a trick of the lighting. I reread the account quickly, not wanting to miss any crucial fact.

On a stormy August evening, Rachel Carroll and her friend, Cynthia Lauren, were on their way home from a vacation in Michigan's Upper Peninsula. They stopped for the night in the Oaken Bucket Inn. At that time the Inn, although located in an isolated wooded area, as it still was, had acquired a reputation for chicken dinners and picturesque rooms.

The young women were given a double room—213. Cynthia, who had a headache, decided to take a nap, while Rachel went downstairs to have dinner. When Rachel returned to the room, she found it empty. Cynthia had vanished. She had left her suitcase open and toilet articles and makeup strewn on the dresser. A still-folded nightgown lay across one of the beds.

No one with the exception of Rachel had seen Cynthia after the girls checked in. In spite of an exhaustive search of the Inn, the grounds and the woods, Cynthia was never seen again. For a brief time, Rachel was suspected of dispatching her companion, but she had no apparent motive for doing so and no opportunity.

Another woman who disappeared in Foxglove Corners, I thought. *Another strange happening on Deer Leap Trail.*

Rachel went home reluctantly but returned to the Inn every August hoping to find some trace of her friend, some clue, anything relevant. She never did. Then one year she didn't come. A visitor to the Inn brought news of her death.

Time went by, years apparently. One summer evening, a maid reported seeing a woman in a blue raincoat drifting down the hall toward Room 213. Half a woman, actually.

"From the waist down, there was nothing but a bluish haze," the maid said later. "She was wearing a light blue raincoat with a hood. Her hair was black and sort of untidy. Like she'd just come in from the rain."

It wasn't raining that evening. In fact it was hot and humid. Nobody was wearing coats.

The ghost had walked away from the maid. "It wasn't exactly a walk. More of a glide." When she reached the end of the hall, she vanished, along with the haze.

Over the years, the lady in the blue raincoat had been seen, often in August on the anniversary of Cynthia's disappearance. Presumably she still hoped to find her lost companion, perhaps hidden in one of the Inn's little-used rooms. It was said that Rachel couldn't rest in peace until she found out what had happened to Cynthia.

I closed the book, chilled by the haunting tale. In truth, there were two stories in one: Cynthia's disappearance and Rachel's haunting. I remembered once reading a similar story that had taken place in a European city in the nineteenth century. Perhaps it was a true account. That one had an ending with an explanation of sorts. The kind one can chose to believe or disbelieve. I couldn't remember the details.

Still searching through my sources, I found another version of Rachel's and Cynthia's story. Essentially the two accounts were the same.

Sunlight streamed through the library window. It found the volumes spread out in front of me on the table and shone a spotlight on them. A voice seemed to say, *This is no story written to entertain a reader. It happened. We've been forgotten for so long. Please remember us.*

Was that all Rachel wanted? Remembrance? And Cynthia? Wouldn't she want people to know what had happened to her, no matter how many years had gone by? But there was only one ghost. Rachel had long black hair; Cynthia was a blonde. And the Inn kept its secret. Neither mystery had ever been solved.

Today the girls' story had become a colorful tale kept alive to lure the curious to the newly christened inn.

I stacked the books, and my thoughts turned to tea with Miss Eidt in her office. Maybe she could point me toward a more recent account, perhaps a newspaper clipping of the ghost hunter's experience.

Rachel and Cynthia had indeed reminded me of myself and Annica, intrepid girl sleuths of the twenty-first century. How many mysteries had we undertaken to solve in stormy weather? How often had we made sense out of the inexplicable? Or not.

The next time I went to the Spirit Lamp Inn, I intended to ask if I could have Room 213.

~*~

In the morning I went to Clovers for breakfast, hoping to find Annica working. She was, filling the dessert carousel with pies for the luncheon crowd. The charms on her bracelet jingled as she moved her hands. When she took her break, I told her in between bites of pancake what I'd learned about the haunting at the Inn.

Annica said, "This is beginning to sound like science-fiction. Suppose beyond the blue door, these women are waiting to be liberated. Cynthia, Grace, and Terra. Maybe they have the collies with them. You know. Blue door, blue mist."

Trust Annica to make a bizarre story even more frightening.

"We certainly won't find Terra there," I said. "The morgue still has her body. Or maybe she's already been cremated."

"You have a point. When we go back to the Haver house, we'd better stay close together or at least in sight of each other. People don't usually disappear in pairs."

That wasn't true. I'd recently read of an entire family of four who disappeared while on vacation in South America. Had they ever been found? I didn't recall reading a follow-up.

"Sure they could," I said, "but there should be someone to sound the alarm and initiate a search."

"You're thinking of fiction. Not real life."

The bells on the door rang out their cheery notes, and Annica's expression underwent a startling change. "It's Brent, Jennet! He's out and about early this morning."

"And he looks upset. Something's wrong."

As he walked toward us, Annica jumped to her feet. "Good morning, Brent. What'll you have? A nice scrumptious country breakfast?"

"Just coffee today," he said and sank into the chair she had vacated.

"Did you eat already?" she asked.

"I'm not hungry."

"One coffee coming up then. Sugar, no cream. I can't wait till we go up in your hot air balloon," she added.

The first of May would be here in two days. Between Terra's murder and ghostly matters, I had forgotten to worry about my commitment. Was it too late to back out?

Brent *did* look upset. I glanced at his hand. The bite mark was still there, still red, and the swelling in his hand hadn't gone down."

"What's the matter?" I asked.

Without preamble he said, "The *Sky Dancer* exploded yesterday. Mike is in the hospital. I just came from there."

"My God! Is he going to be all right?"

"I hope so."

"I'm so sorry, Brent. How did it happen?"

"We don't know yet. I knew the risks. So did Mike. They were minimal. Hot air balloons fly all the time with no problem. I never expected anything like this to happen."

Annica set a mug of coffee in front of Brent. "What happened?" she asked.

I answered for him. "The *Sky Dancer* exploded. Brent's employee, Mike, has been hurt."

"For real?" She sat, not seeming to hear the voice calling her from a nearby table.

"Mike's in the hospital," Brent said. "He's hurt. His passengers walked away with minor injuries, but Mike… We just don't know."

Annica's vibrant face was pale; her eyes were enormous. "We were going up in the *Sky Dancer*. You and me and Jennet."

Not anymore, I thought, remembering the fears I'd attempted to banish. Thunderous noise and fire and death rushing up to gather us in its arms. Or perhaps we'd be dead before hitting the ground. All imagination on my part. Reality for the *Sky Dancer* and its people.

"That's up in the air," he said. Then, "Guess I could have said that in a different way."

Steam rose from Brent's cup. Still he took a long gulp of his coffee. "Well, the *Sky Dancer* is no more. Thanks, Annica. I needed that."

I broke a piece of pancake with my fork and decided I didn't want it. If I put it in my mouth, I thought I'd choke on it.

"I don't know how this happened, Brent," I said. "But I know why."

Twenty-six

"And I know what you're going to say," Brent said. "The painting caused my balloon to crash."

"Think about it, Brent. The *Sky Dancer* explodes. You have a bite that won't heal, and Napoleon is sick. Your life has been going downhill ever since you hung *Ada's Litter* on your wall. That's more than I did."

When I had owned the painting, I'd kept it on the buffet mostly to humor Julia and later in the basement. Out of sight, out of danger, I'd thought. It didn't work that way.

"Mike didn't have anything to do with the painting," Brent said.

"Neither did Annica. Yet both of us could have died in the fire at my house. Annica and Mike were innocent bystanders."

Brent wasn't ready to accept my explanation. In a sense, I couldn't blame him. It *did* sound far-fetched, but he'd never been dogged by bad luck until he took possession of that accursed painting.

"I don't see how that's possible," he said. "If I get rid of the painting, does that mean this damned bite will go away, Napoleon will get well, Mike will be miraculously healed, and the *Sky Dancer* will reassemble itself?"

"Well, no, but it'll be insurance for you that nothing worse will happen."

"I'd be afraid to touch it," Annica said with a shudder. "It's evil. Margaret was evil."

I hadn't set eyes on *Ada's Litter* for months, but I could see it clearly in my mind, every detail. The golden-haired girl, Margaret, the tumble of collie puppies, their proud mother, and the green grass and flowers of a summer day. It was hard to accept that such a happy, innocent scene could be touched with evil. But Margaret had done a wicked deed. The painting's subsequent owners had suffered setbacks of various kinds. Someone had even written *Evil RIP* on the back.

It reveled in fire, ever since Margaret had set her own house ablaze, killing family members. The artist Aura Lee Larkin, its creator, had urged me to burn it.

If only I had.

Brent finished his coffee and stared at the empty cup as if willing it to refill itself. "I'm not saying I believe an inanimate object can have that kind of power, but I'll give it some thought. Later. I have too much on my mind right now."

"Let me know how I can help," I said. "Stop over anytime. We'll see what Crane thinks."

Annica rose, finally remembering her other customers. She cast a practiced glance over the restaurant. A young man beckoned to her.

"Let me fix you something to eat, Brent," she said. "An omelet, maybe. Everything looks more manageable when you have some food in your stomach."

He smiled at her. "All right. An omelet and more coffee. Then I'm heading back to the hospital."

"And I have to go home," I said.

I hated to leave Brent sitting alone at the table staring into his cup but had no doubt he'd soon be appearing on our doorstep. Crane and I were his good friends. Everyone needs friends, especially in times of adversity.

I'd never seen him defeated. Not by man, nor beast, nor force of nature. But he was close to the edge now. One more stroke of bad luck and he'd be over that edge. Then maybe he'd take my advice and get rid of the painting.

~ * ~

The next day I drove the short distance to Sue Appleton's horse farm on Squill Lane to attend the emergency meeting she had called. Twenty of us showed up. That was more people than I'd ever seen at a Rescue League gathering. A few of them I'd never met at all. The new people.

It was a pleasure to sit in Sue's spacious ranch house surrounded by equine décor and forget about ghosts and a rogue painting for a few hours.

Until I remembered Terra and the reason for the meeting.

"Has anyone heard anything about Terra's killer?" Sue asked.

Liz Melbourne said, "Not a word. The cremation has taken place. Terra's sister is going to spread her ashes over Lake Huron." She stumbled over the word, 'cremation.' "I'm afraid the trail is getting gold."

"Humph." Laurence DeVille shook his head. "It's frozen over. The cops aren't doing their jobs."

"Could you do better?" Sue asked, a bite in her voice.

"You bet I could."

"Too bad you're not on the Force then," she countered.

"That's neither here nor there," Liz said. "I'd like to report that we have almost two thousand dollars in the treasury and all debts paid. We're in great shape."

"Wow!" someone said.

"We had a few memorial donations. Most went to the animal shelter."

"But where are the dogs we're supposed to be saving?" Laurence asked.

"I assume no collies need rescuing at present," Sue said. "That's good news."

"It won't last."

Mr. Laurence Negativity. Unfortunately in this case he was right, and one collie's vet bills could easily gobble up a chunk of the League's money.

Sue ignored him. "I was hoping we wouldn't have to do this, but it's time to face facts. We need a new president. I nominate Jennet Ferguson. You all know Jennet. She has six collies. All but one is a rescue. Jennet's a natural for the job."

I snapped to attention. Sue was talking about me. My face grew warm as nineteen pairs of eyes turned in my direction.

Say something.

"I second the motion." That was DeVille of all people.

"Thank you, but I couldn't possibly accept," I said. "My classes keep me busy. I teach high school English," I added for the benefit of those who didn't know me well. "I think Sue Appleton would be a much better choice. I nominate Sue."

I suspected Sue wanted the position of president, but she could hardly nominate herself. I relaxed a little as some of the attention shifted toward Sue.

Please, I thought. *Someone second my nomination.*

I only wanted to keep on rescuing collies. Breezy, if it were still possible, and some future collie doomed to be surrendered, or one rendered helpless by a gunshot wound or malnutrition. The leader of the Rescue League should be someone who truly wanted the position with all its administrative detail.

"I second it," Laurence DeVille said. "Sue Appleton for president."

"Well, if you're sure, Jennet," Sue said.

"I'm very sure."

"Then I'd be honored to serve as president."

"Let's vote," Liz said. "Sue Appleton for president. A show of hands will do."

Every hand in the room went up, excluding Sue's, including mine.

I sighed in relief, realizing I'd dodged a major bullet. Now all the future collies who came to the Rescue League would be in good hands.

Twenty-seven

Rain fell, hitting the windows with hail force and turning the slightest depression on Jonquil Lane into a miniature lake. I gazed out the bay windows and refused to let inclement weather dampen my spirits.

Dogs know what the sound of rain means. After a brief trip outdoors, they were happy to go back to sleep while their coats dried. I had loftier ambitions and loads of energy.

Time was passing. Vacation days are always shorter than school days.

In the mid-morning, I donned a raincoat, took an umbrella, and drove through ever-increasing puddles to Lucy Hazen's house, Dark Gables. Lucy had asked me to visit her during Easter break. I hadn't been to her house for ages, so I'd called and invited myself over.

Dark Gables, located on Spruce Road, hid behind a small forest of towering evergreens and hardwoods that lined a long shadowy drive. Her home in its wooded setting provided her with the solitude she required for her writing.

I parked under a dripping oak tree, and Sky, her collie, greeted me with raucous barking from the shelter of the front porch. Moments later, Lucy opened the door and waved to me. Her long black shawl fluttered in a sudden wind gust.

I hurried up to the porch and leaned my umbrella against a post to dry. Sky sniffed at it curiously but rushed to slip inside between Lucy and me. We went to the back of the house where Lucy's sunroom made a valiant attempt to live up to its name. Here she planned and wrote her stories. I glanced at her desk and the stack of papers about two inches high under a crystal paperweight. Another book was progressing nicely.

"I've been thinking about Brent all morning," Lucy said. "And about poor Mike too. He's not out of the woods yet."

I nodded. "I dreamed about hot air balloons last night. Thankfully none of them exploded." I sat on the wicker love seat. Sky jumped up and settled herself beside me. Lucy put water on to boil for tea in the adjoining kitchen and set a plate of chocolate wafers on the table along with her plain white teacups.

I knew what that meant. She was going to read our tea leaves. To be accurate, she was going to read mine. She'd once told me that she couldn't tell her own fortune in the leaves.

"Do you think that painting, *Ada's Litter*, is the cause of Brent's run of bad luck?" I asked

"It's more than likely. I almost convinced him to get rid of it."

"How did you do that?"

"By advising him to look on it as an experiment. He doesn't have to believe in its power. Just take it out of the house and see what happens. Then if his bad luck continues, it isn't the painting's fault. It's life."

"That was clever," I said. "He wouldn't listen to me. Then the explosion shook him out of his stubbornness."

"We'll have to see if he follows through. It's a matter of pride with him."

"So was his fleet of hot air balloons. You remember I almost went up in the *Sky Dancer*. Annica and I were scheduled to go on the first of May."

"That's tomorrow," Lucy murmured.

"But I was afraid. I kept wanting to back out."

"Always listen to those inner voices," Lucy said. "I do."

The teakettle's whistle drew her to the kitchen. As she poured boiling water over the leaves, I brought her up to date on the haunting of the Spirit Lamp Inn.

"That story reminds me of another one," she said. "The woman had contracted Bubonic plague. She was spirited away to avoid starting a panic. It was all an elaborate conspiracy."

"I wonder if something like that happened to Rachel's friend," I said.

"Most real life ghost stories don't have neatly tied-up endings," Lucy reminded me.

I went back to inner voices. "That same voice keeps telling me to go back to Deer Leap Trail. The answer to every mystery can be found at the Haver property and the Inn."

"I sensed evil in the Haver meadow," Lucy said. "It's still alive, still waiting. It's a trap of sorts."

Lucy always seemed to be trying out spooky phraseology for her future work. I was used to her way of talking. Still, her words had an adverse effect on me. If the wildflower meadow was a trap waiting to be sprung, I didn't want to stumble into it. On the other hand, I knew I wouldn't be able to stay away.

When we finished our tea, I drained the excess liquid, turned the cup toward me three times, which formed the patterns, and made my wish. The ritual never varied.

I handed Lucy the cup and waited while she peered into it. I was watching her face so I was aware of the exact moment when her expression changed. She seemed paler, the color fading from her face.

"What is it?" I asked.

"Oh, your wish will be granted," she said brightly. "You're going to receive an unexpected present and an offer. A new dog will enter your life."

"A collie?"

"It looks like a collie, yes." She pointed to a long leaf that had come to rest near the cup's handle.

This was one fortune I didn't believe. Except the part about the collie. Collies, like enemies, were always part of my life.

"Why don't you tell me the rest?" I asked.

"The rest?"

"The bad stuff. You always did before."

The color came back to Lucy's face with a vengeance. "You know me too well, Jennet," she said.

"Well?"

"If you insist. I see danger. It's very strong. Very powerful. You might not be able to hold your own against this Force. Not this time."

She set the cup down on the coffee table. Sky tilted her head in that endearing way collies have.

"Don't stop there," I said. "What can I do?"

"I don't know. This foretelling isn't written in stone. It could happen. Maybe it won't. In the end it's going to be up to you. All I can do is advise you not to take chances."

"Like going up in a hot air balloon."

"Like that."

"And listen to the inner voices."

She smiled. "Listen carefully. Sometimes it isn't easy to hear them over the noise of every day."

I stroked Sky's head, trying to regain a measure of calm. I told myself that I didn't really believe Lucy could look at pictures formed by loose leaves in my teacup by and see future happenings in my life.

Didn't I?

Reading tealeaves was only an amusing pastime akin to a parlor game and not to be taken seriously. It was different from her psychic talents.

But in the past, certain of Lucy's predictions had come true. Not always in the way she had described them, but often I was able to look back in the aftermath of a harrowing event and realize that Lucy had anticipated it.

I couldn't ignore a warning. An early alert to an enemy. Lucy was always seeing enemies in my cup, always issuing warnings.

She gathered cups and saucers and spoons and set them on a tray. "Maybe this wasn't a good idea, Jennet. I didn't mean to upset you."

"Not at all," I said. "I'm glad we did it. Forewarned is forearmed."

~ * ~

By the time I left Dark Gables, the rain had spent itself. As I turned on Spruce Road, I beheld a watery landscape glittering in weak sunshine and a fragile rainbow arcing across the sky. The day could be salvaged. I could go anywhere I pleased, but I knew my destination would be home. With a short detour to Deer Leap Trail.

Lucy's advice echoed in my mind. I didn't intend to take any chances. Not today. Not ever. I merely wanted to keep an eye on the haunted Haver acres and perhaps have a bowl of hot soup at the Spirit Lamp Inn.

But, as I'd told Lucy in parting, that didn't mean I was going to walk away from an intriguing mystery.

"Just be careful," she'd said. "Promise?"

The wildflower meadow would be radiant after the rain Perhaps the rainbow would last until I reached the Haver House. My plan made sense. After all, next week I'd be teaching my afternoon classes at this time. My free hours would dwindle down to minutes.

The yellow ribbons near Terra's temporary grave looked as fresh and crisp as if they'd just been hung. This was an illusion, I knew. If I stopped to touch them, they'd be soggy.

Was everything on this seldom-traveled trail an illusion?

In the distance, the Haver place shimmered amidst splashes of color. I could gather another bouquet for tonight's dinner table.

And bring the evil into our home?

No. Besides, now that I'd met Linnea Haver, I knew I'd be stealing. But she wouldn't mind. She'd talked about having the wildflowers mowed down. The weeping spirit, whatever or whoever mourned in the meadow, wouldn't like that.

I glanced behind me to make sure I was alone on the road and steered onto the verge. Drawn by the mesmerizing color, I gazed at the acres.

And saw a blue door on the side of the barn. It was there, undeniable there, on a day that couldn't be clearer. It couldn't possibly be an illusion.

Willing the door not to disintegrate, I got out of the car and hurried to the barn, for once unmindful of the hapless flowers in my path.

Twenty-eight

The door was cornflower blue. Seen on a clear day without wisps of fog obscuring the barn, it was obviously painted on like the one I'd seen before. Still, the brass doorknob appeared so real and bright in the sun that I almost reached out to turn it.

The artist had talent but was sloppy. Splatters of paint glistened on the white Queen Anne's Lace that grew up to the barn's wall. In fact... I touched the door lightly with my fingertip. The surface looked wet. It was dry, of course. It couldn't have been painted this morning in the rain.

Yesterday, then, or the day before. I glanced down at the ground. The flowers that grew near the barn had been trampled into pulp. Why hadn't I noticed similar destruction when I'd first seen the door? Well... The flowers hadn't spread up to the barn yet, mere days ago.

Incidentally, how had the previous blue door been covered up?

That was obvious. With paint chosen or mixed to blend in with the rest of the barn, a dull, drab greyish-brown. The answer was so simple I marveled that I hadn't realized it before.

However a question remained. Why would anyone paint doors on a barn? Why not paint the entire barn? Here was another. Did

Linnea Haver know that someone had defaced her property? Maybe defaced was the wrong word. The blue door improved the appearance of the structure and enhanced the eerie beauty of the wildflower meadow. It was unique—and eye-catching.

However, the owner should be the one to alter her property. Possibly Linnea liked the weathered look in barns.

Belatedly, I glanced toward the farmhouse. There was no car in sight, no sign that anyone had entered the house since the day Linnea had discovered me at the barn.

I walked around to the entrance, treading on flowers that had been crushed under the heels of a previous visitor. It was still locked. Still silent. I was willing to bet there was nothing inside. Nothing living, at any rate. Certainly not the evil Lucy had described.

Everything that surrounded me was silent but not still. A light wind stirred the wildflowers. Out in the meadow they swept down to the woods, and dark trees shadowed those growing close to the woods' edge. The sun blazed in a cloudless sky the color of the painted door, strong enough to chase the otherworldly elements away. No one mourned in the meadow today.

This wasn't a supernatural mystery. No whimsical spirit had painted a door on a dilapidated barn. The artist was a human whose motive was a genuine puzzle. A person trespassing with paint can and brush, treating the barn as if he owned it.

I had to tell Linnea about this liberty the unknown painter had taken with her property. But how could I notify her? I didn't even know her present address.

You'll figure it out, I told myself.

But not here. Not in this haunted place, even though the haunt was asleep today.

~ * ~

I was no longer in the mood to stop at the Spirit Lamp Inn. I had soup at home and six collies waiting for my return. And dinner to make. I couldn't forget dinner.

As soon as I reached home, I took the dogs for a long walk. The rain had left a fresh-washed landscape and hundreds of tantalizing smells in its wake. We progressed more slowly than usual up the lane, past the unfinished construction, that place of mystery, all the way to Squill Lane. On an impulse, I turned left, and we headed in the direction of the cottage at Lane's End. It was in so isolated a location that I tended to forget it existed.

The charming yellow cottage was still untenanted. It had acquired a ghostly look, and the scarecrow in the cornfield with its tattered clothing glowered pure menace at us. Sky and little Misty moved closer to me.

The only life we encountered was wild, a deer leaping across the lane and vanishing into thick brush. The sight drove Candy into a frenzy. She tugged on her leash, desiring above all to give chase. I held on tight, unwilling to deal with a runaway dog, and eventually she surrendered to the inevitable.

After the deer sighting, we continued on our leisurely way home, which gave me a chance to think about the morning's discovery.

I could look for Linnea Haver's address and phone number in the Lakeville Directory. If she wasn't listened, then I had an even better source: search engines on my computer.

She should be informed about the blue door, and I was the only one who could do it. Perhaps when she knew about the uninvited painter, she'd visit the property.

What would that accomplish? At the moment I didn't know enough about the goings on at the Haver place to hazard a guess. But an appearance by the owner would give me another opportunity to talk to her and might lead to a clue.

~ * ~

I found Linnea Haver's name on *People Finder*. Ironically she lived in Oakpoint, my home town before the tornado that changed my life. Sycamore Boulevard was a quiet neighborhood of stately old houses and equally old trees. Her phone number was unlisted, but I could visit her next week when I was back in school. In the meantime, the blue door wouldn't be going anywhere.

Or so I assumed.

I told Crane about it that evening after dinner. The next day, as soon as he stepped through the door, he informed me that he'd driven past the Haver house but hadn't seen a blue door painted on the side of the barn. This time I didn't question my sanity.

"Someone painted over the door again," I said. "What's going on there?"

"Maybe there's a juvenile artist in the area who thinks everything on the planet belongs to him?"

"Or whoever painted the door wasn't satisfied with the finished product. He wanted to try again. And again."

"Your interpretation makes sense, but I don't think that's the explanation."

I turned the oven off and began to mix a salad. Seeing I was working with greens and vegetables, Candy turned her attention back to Crane.

"Annica will be disappointed," I said. "She thought the door led to another world."

He smiled. "Annica—and Lucy and Jennet. Over on Spruce Road there's a waterfall scene painted on a garage door," he added. "It looks nice and cool when you're passing by on a hot day."

"Well I'm going to get to the bottom of the mystery, and I'm going to do it this week while I'm on vacation."

"Did you forget about the wounded collie?" he asked.

"Of course not, but I couldn't find her and can only assume her name is Breezy and she's gone."

Assumptions again. They'd take me to a dead end. I needed another approach.

Still I longed to be able to call the number on the 'Lost Dog' poster and announce that a dog who was possibly Breezy had been found. That was what every rescuer hoped for.

"Maybe I'll still find her," I said.

~ * ~

Brent was his old self, confident, jovial, playing Frisbee with Misty in the house, frightening Sky with his booming voice. It was as if all his troubles had melted away. Not the bite though. I stole a glance at his hand as he tossed the Frisbee. Was it my imagination or was the wound larger and redder?

"Mike's expected to make a full recovery," he said. "And Napoleon ate a little bit of his dinner last night. Life is good."

He didn't mention the bite.

"Did you get rid of the painting?" I asked.

"No. Why should I, now that my luck's turned around?"

Sometimes Brent could be dense and infuriating. "Because of what may happen next."

"I don't look too far into the future, Jennet," he said. "Nobody knows what's in store for us. You could trip over an exposed root in the Haver meadow and break your neck."

"I'm always careful."

"I hope you are," Crane said. "If anything happened to you out in the middle of nowhere…"

I thought it best to divert his attention from that strange isolated meadow. "It won't. Besides, remember, I don't have the painting anymore. Brent does."

Twenty-nine

The fog thickened to the consistency of pudding. I couldn't see what lay in front of me or behind me or on either side, but I could feel the woods leaning precariously over the road, branches like hands stretched out to grab me.

Then I was out of the car, trudging through flowers so high they brushed against my waist. I was in the wildflower meadow at the Haver place, following the sound of weeping. It led me to a blue door half-open to reveal a barn scene, dimly-lit and shadowy with straw and tools arranged neatly on a shelf. A dark sable and white collie lay across the threshold.

The dog fixed me with a plaintive stare but didn't move. Was it real or a life-sized statue carved of stone? If the dog were real, wouldn't she be on her feet barking, or lunging at me with teeth bared?

I opened my eyes, wide awake and unsettled by the memory of the fog and the rapacious woods. The collie had looked familiar. Like the picture on Breezy's 'Lost Dog' poster. Like the wounded collie who had disappeared into the meadow. Who was Breezy. Or so I'd convinced myself.

What could the dream be telling me? That the barn was haunted by Breezy's spirit?

I remembered the lightning flash collie. Was that Breezy—the way she looked now?

Well, nothing would be gained by dwelling on a dream made up of jumbled images from my subconscious.

Let it go.

It was still dark outside but time to get up. Crane was asleep, and I wanted him to stay that way a little longer while I made his breakfast. I turned on the bedside lamp whose sixty watt bulb wouldn't disturb him until the alarm went off.

Halley lay in the doorway watching me. She reminded me of the collie in the dream. They had the same soulful stare. She rose and stretched and padded along behind me as I descended the stairs.

Disturbing images crowded my mind: Lucy setting my teacup down on the coffee table, her forebodings of danger and doom ringing in my ears. Brent's picture of me tripping over a root in the wildflower meadow and presumably staying there, undiscovered, until I died of exposure. My friends, however well-meaning, were detrimental to my peace of mind.

Halley followed me to the kitchen where the other dogs had gathered in a prancing, whimpering group to wait for their breakfast biscuits. I fed them, then gathered ingredients and began mixing batter for pancakes. The last vestiges of the dream drifted away as practical matters claimed my attention.

The griddle. Squeezing oranges for juice. Making coffee. Marking another vacation day off the calendar.

By the time Crane joined me, freshly shaven and resplendent in his uniform, I had his breakfast ready for him and had decided on an agenda: shopping for summer clothes at the Maplewood Mall and lunch, preferably with Leonora. If she had other plans, I'd go alone.

I needed a brief respite from the mysteries that swirled around me.

~ * ~

Leonora was nursing a cold. "I have to get well for school," she'd said. She didn't need or want anything. "Only to go back to bed."

Knowing Annica would be working at Clovers, I set out for the mall alone.

Shopping without a companion is no fun, but I traveled more quickly from one store to another and soon had a shopping bag crammed with shorts and bright summery tops. A solitary lunch wouldn't be fun either, but I'd eaten out alone before. When I decided I'd spent more than enough money, I drove to the Spirit Lamp Inn.

She travels the fastest who travels alone.

The parking lot was half-full, and the hostess was new. Rather she was someone I hadn't seen before. The Inn must have a revolving door through which the wait staff came and went, which was odd for an off-the-beaten-path country inn. Or maybe not, if the employees lived some distance away and grew tired of commuting.

I glanced quickly at the menu board and saw that the club sandwich and chicken pot pie were among the day's specials, together with cream of asparagus soup.

"Good afternoon," the hostess said. "Just one today?"

"Yes."

I followed her to a small table with a window view. I hadn't noticed before, but the entire room seemed to consist of windows. As I sat, I spied the collie out in the yard. It looked like the one we'd seen before, napping in the shade. It had the same gorgeous dark sable coat and snowy markings. Yes, it must be the same collie. Breezy?

I frowned, recalling conflicting stories. Supposedly dogs weren't allowed at the Spirit Lamp Inn. Later, from another source, the dog belonged to one of the guests.

When the waitress handed me a menu and I commented on the pleasing picture the sleeping collie made, I received a third version. "That's Lassie. She belongs to the cook. Lassie comes to work with her."

Well, all right. No mystery then. But wait! A cook taking her dog to work?

This is the Spirit Lamp Inn, I told myself, *where stranger things have happened.*

I was finishing my sandwich when Laurence DeVille entered the dining room. I hoped he wouldn't notice me, but my luck had run out. With an ingratiating smile that reminded me of Principal Grimsley, he waved the waitress away. "I'll be joining my friend at her table."

I heard him from across the room. So did the people sitting near me.

With a quarter of a sandwich on my plate and an almost full glass of iced tea, I had no choice but to smile back.

"Jennet," he said. "What a nice surprise to see you here. I thought this place was my little secret."

Glancing at the other tables, rapidly being filled, I said, "I'm sure everybody has heard of the Spirit Lamp Inn."

"Mind if I join you?" he asked.

I did mind. "I'm almost done."

Then at his crestfallen look, I realized how rude that sounded. After all, Laurence and I were both members of the Collie Rescue League. Someday we might find ourselves working together. So what if I didn't like him? That shouldn't matter.

"But sit down, if you like," I said and added, "Please."

"Shouldn't you be in school?" he asked. "Or are you playing hooky?"

"This is spring break," I said.

He accepted a glass of water and a menu but instead of studying it, he said, "Are you working at the sale tomorrow?"

It took me a minute to realize he must mean the Rescue League's yard sale at Liz's house in Lakeville. I'd almost forgotten about it.

"I haven't been asked to work, but I'll stop by," I said. "I'm always interested in collie art and books."

"And memorabilia. Ask me. I trucked in most of it. There's a lot of breakable items like figurines. Someone should be on hand to see that they're not broken."

"I could do that," I said.

"Terra shouldn't have accepted some of that stuff. It's tacky. Anything with a collie on it or in it, even if it's ugly."

Even this mild criticism of Terra annoyed me. Who was Laurence DeVille to judge what was appropriate for the sale? I was sure Terra had worked hard to collect collie merchandise, and she hadn't lived long enough to enjoy the fruits of her labor.

"Beauty is in the eye of the beholder," I said. "I'm sure there's a buyer for everything."

"A collie clock? A hideous collie tie?"

"Why not?"

He fell silent, but I didn't like the way he looked at me, the way his lips curved into a wolfish smile. No, that wasn't right. I liked wolves. A Cheshire cat smile then. To break the ensuing awkwardness, I said, "How about you? Do you work?"

"I was laid off when my company downsized. I'm always looking, but jobs aren't plentiful."

"That's too bad," I said.

"Not really. I have my unemployment checks to fall back on."

I knew I shouldn't make assumptions based on appearances, but DeVille didn't look as if he was needy. His jacket was expertly tailored and his watch looked expensive. When the waitress stopped at the table the second time to ask if he was ready to order, he selected the priciest item on the menu—the prime rib dinner—along with a costly bottle of wine.

Let him spend his funds as he saw fit. Probably he'd owned nice clothes and the watch before he lost his job. It wasn't my business. It was just that I didn't like anything about him. In the interest of freeing myself from his company and his bold stares as soon as possible, I decided to forego dessert.

Thirty

In spite of a forecast for afternoon thunderstorms, the weather cooperated for the Rescue League yard sale. Except for the humidity. I found a parking place halfway down the block and walked to Liz' house, feeling as if I hadn't thoroughly dried myself after my shower. My pink cotton shirtwaist dress, supposed to be wrinkle free, was already crumpled.

Well, that was the Michigan summer—although technically it was still spring.

Balloons tied to trees in the front yard tried to flutter in welcome but instead hung motionless in the air. Practically every inch of grass was covered with tables of collie memorabilia, much of it breakable as DeVille had claimed. Two teenaged girls in skimpy attire manned a lemonade stand.

I made a mental note to give them my business as soon as I looked around.

Liz was sheltered from the sun under a rainbow-striped beach umbrella, the cashbox in front of her, while Sue Appleton wandered through makeshift aisles, answering questions and reciting set pieces designed to make a customer feel as if he were getting a bargain.

The sale had drawn quite a crowd, about twenty people with customers constantly arriving and leaving. I saw Louanne and Emma Brock but not Laurence DeVille. That was just as well. Maybe he thought he'd made his contribution by hauling items to Liz' yard.

"Isn't this a lovely figurine?" Holding it gingerly as if to discourage the would-be buyer from touching it, Sue addressed the question to a gray-haired matron who had squeezed her plump body into a pair of denim shorts and a low cut top.

I peered over her shoulder. The little statue wasn't particularly lovely. It looked more like a zebra than a dog.

"It's a border collie, made in Michigan and inspired by the artist's own dog," Sue said. "But it's still a collie, and it's only thirty dollars."

The woman shook her head. "Too much money."

I agreed with her. Giving Sue a brief smile, I gravitated toward the books and felt instantly at home. Collie-themed paperbacks with smudged covers, old Albert Payson Terhune hardcovers, even a mystery, *The Clue of the Howling Collie*. I grabbed it and was busy perusing the other titles when Liz came up to me. Louanne sat in her place, elbow on the cash box.

"Do you need any help?" I asked.

"Thanks, but we have it covered. My nieces are here." She gestured toward the girls at the lemonade stand. "Lord, but it's hot."

With a moderately long line, they seemed to be enjoying more business than any of the dusty memorabilia on the tables. Not that any of the wares were dusty. Someone, Liz probably, had cleaned them until they had a shine in the sun.

"Don't you have anything without dogs on it?" the woman asked.

"What were you interested in?"

"Oh, jewelry, clothes, wigs, tools…"

Wigs? Tools?

"We have men's ties and women's apparel, but they all have collie images on them," she said." You understand, this is a Collie Rescue League yard sale. The people who donated items are collie lovers."

"You should have advertised it that way then," she said. "Save everybody time and gas."

We had, of course. Undaunted, Sue said, "Why don't you look around? You might find something for a gift."

"I don't like dogs," the woman said.

I would have said, "You're wasting your time here then."

Sue was more diplomatic. "Do you know someone who does? We have mugs. Everybody can use those. And we have the darlingest collie teapot. I've never seen one like it. Best of all, you'd be helping an abandoned dog get food or medicine."

Crash!

All eyes turned to the source of the ominous noise, a grubby red-headed urchin perhaps four or five, running free in the yard. He'd dropped the zebra collie on the concrete walkway. On the grass, it might have survived the fall.

"Oh no!" Liz was on her feet instantly. "Where's this kid's mother?"

Apparently no one wanted to claim him. Then a lady said, "He lives down the street. I think his mother dropped him off."

"For us to babysit? What nerve!" Sue was livid. "Andrea…" She beckoned to one of the lemonade girls. "Will you please find out where this little boy belongs? And take him away."

167

Andrea came forward. The little boy's face had turned red at Sue's scathing tone. He started to cry. I was angry at his parent who had turned him loose on a mission of destruction and angry that the figurine had been broken. In pieces, the collie looked less like a zebra. Somebody would have loved it.

I bent to pick up the shattered figurine. It was in two pieces, and the tail was missing, not with the other body parts, almost impossible to find in the shadows cast by the tables and the grass.

"Maybe we can glue it together," Sue said, taking the pieces from me. "We can sell it at a reduced price. Say a dollar."

"A dog without a tail? It's a lost cause," I said, but at that moment spied the missing piece under a table. "Who's going to pay even a dollar for a patched together figurine?"

"I hate to just throw it away. That miserable kid." Sue pressed her hand against her right eye. "I'm getting a migraine. Whose idea was it to have a yard sale anyway?"

"Terra's?"

"Oh, yes."

"To raise money for the rescues," I reminded her. "If you want to take a break, I'll cover for you," I said.

"That's sweet of you, Jennet, but I have headache pills in my pocket. I'll just take them with a glass of lemonade."

My offer rejected, I checked out the artwork, most of which was uninspired, and returned to the books. Did I still have every Terhune book? Not *The Way of a Dog*. This could well be a collector's item, and it was priced at only five dollars. And here was *Bruce*. My own childhood copy, with the same orange cover, had disappeared over the years.

With everything apparently under control, I paid for my books, bought a glass of lemonade, and left. The yard sale was packed, but the stacks of tee shirts and ties and collie mugs hadn't gone down much. What was selling, I wondered, aside from the lemonade?

Well, the day was young.

I walked back to the car carrying my treasures and headed to Clovers for lunch.

~ * ~

"I really, really want to go on a ghost hunt," Annica said as she joined me in the booth. Her long seashell earrings clinked merrily against each other. She was once again ready for adventure.

I unwrapped the utensils from a white napkin covered with green clovers. "Which ghost?" I asked.

"Either one. The lady in the blue raincoat, or the spirit who cries in the meadow."

"Don't forget the lightning collie," I said.

"I'd rather catch a human ghost than an animal."

"I don't think ghost hunters actually catch ghosts," I said. "They look for signs of spirit life and try to capture them on film."

I spread mustard on my corned beef sandwich. I wasn't so much trying to convince Annica as myself.

"No one has seen the lady in the blue raincoat for years, and I only heard the sound of weeping once," I said. "It's not like the Inn and the Haver place are crawling with ghosts."

Annica refused to be discouraged. "Let's concentrate on the meadow then. You saw the blue door again."

"But it was painted on. I saw paint spatters on the flowers. There's nothing supernatural about that."

"Then let's figure out who's going around painting on people's doors."

"We could do that," I said. "The first day you're free. Next week it'll have to after school though."

"That's better than nothing."

The many-faceted mystery was on hold until I made contact with Linnea Haver. I no longer thought I'd have any answers by the time school started. Maybe not even after that.

"But I don't know when we'll be able to do it," Annica added. "Did you look at the week's forecast? We're supposed to be getting rain every single day."

"Good," I said. "That's the best ghost hunting weather."

Thirty-one

The storm crashed through Foxglove Corners that evening, putting on a spectacular show with thunder and lightning and for about five minutes a bombardment of hail.

Crane was safe at home and the collies were all with us, even Raven who forsook her palatial dog house on nights like this. Sky had crawled under the dining room table where she trembled at each new thunderclap, and Misty had joined her, convinced that Sky knew all the house's safe places. The other collies took the storm in their stride.

I tried to concentrate on *The Clue of the Howling Collie*, but my mind kept wandering back to my discussion with Annica. To be sure a stormy night was ideal ghost hunting weather, but the haunted meadow would turn to a lake of floating flowers if this deluge continued. We wouldn't be able to visit the Haver house until the countryside dried out.

I imagined the wildflower meadow growing less and less hospitable with every passing moment. The ghosts wouldn't feel the pelting rain or hail. Lightning would hold no terror for them. Nor would thunder, I thought, as a peal exploded directly overhead. Misty crept out from under the table and put her front paws imploringly on my lap. I set the book aside and lifted her up.

"Did you remember to buy batteries for the flashlights?" Crane asked suddenly.

He'd asked me to do this last week. With all the time in the world to shop and do errands, I'd forgotten.

"I'll do it tomorrow," I promised. "If we lose power, we'll light candles."

One was burning already on the mantel, mostly for atmosphere. The radio needed a fresh battery too.

"Don't forget," Crane said as he rifled through the *Banner* looking for the business section.

With a sigh, I returned to my book. There was a storm in it with lightning and thunder, similar to the one we were experiencing. Aside from that, the plot had yet to catch fire.

My thoughts drifted away to the yard sale. I hoped Liz and Sue had been able to move all the collie collectibles inside before the storm started. They'd had plenty of warning. I couldn't understand why I felt a vague apprehension creeping into the cozy room. It was probably my contemplation of the soggy meadow.

~ * ~

Liz called early the next morning. I could tell she was upset by the tremor in her voice when she asked if we'd had any storm damage.

"Just trees down in the woods," I said. "How about you?"

"A lot of branches in the yard. Did you hear that a tornado touched down west of Maple Creek? No one was hurt, but roofs were blown off and windows broken."

"That's close to home." Considering my past experiences, I should have been worried about tornadoes last night instead of haunted meadows. I had a curious certainty that I was safe as long as Crane was near.

"Something's wrong, Liz," I said. "What is it?"

"We had a theft at the sale yesterday. The cashbox disappeared."

Ah! The cause of my apprehension surfaced. Hadn't something whispered to me that all was not well? "Wasn't someone always watching it?"

"Oh sure, until the storm broke. Then it was pure chaos. We were all scrambling to move everything inside and somehow..." She took a deep breath. "Well, suddenly the cashbox wasn't there. Did you notice anybody suspicious loitering around the yard?"

Hordes of bargain seekers, some sloppily dressed, some careless as they handled the merchandise. Some eagle eyed looking for a treasure in disguise, others obvious browsers. But no obvious criminal types.

"I wasn't there long," I said. "And there were so many people."

"Too many to watch all the time. That kid came back after Andrea took him home. I was going to give his mother a piece of my mind. Then the storm came and the cashbox went missing."

"I wish I could help," I said. "How much was stolen?"

"Eight hundred dollars, give or take. It was all for nothing."

That would have bought a lot of dog food and treats and toys. Maybe it would pay a vet bill or two. Some homeless collie had been robbed. It wasn't right.

"I called the police," Liz said. "But I'm afraid the money is gone for good. It was either one of the shoppers...or one of our own."

"Surely not a League member?"

"I guess not. More likely someone passing through who seized his opportunity. Just before the storm, that kid's mother, Mrs. Sinclair, came back all upset and yelling because we made her little lamb cry."

"Did you charge her for the broken figurine?" I asked.

"I tried to. She said she'd sue us for child abuse."

"She can't do that. She was bluffing."

"The League can't pay for a lawyer," Liz said. "We can't afford a lawsuit."

"It won't come to that. You could tell her you'll take her to small claims court."

"For a thirty dollar statue?"

"You weren't going to get thirty dollars for it," I said. "You won't really do it. Just threaten to."

"I'll probably never see her again. In the meantime, we're still drowning in collie stuff. I don't have the heart to arrange another sale."

"Maybe next year?"

"I'll pack the leftover items away. Someone else can put on the next one."

"Try not to worry about it, Liz," I said. "It was no one's fault."

A thought occurred to me as I closed my cell phone. It might be far-fetched, but maybe the angry mother had stolen the cashbox. I could only imagine the chaotic scene, not having been there, but Mrs. Sinclair was at the sale at the right time. She was belligerent and possibly in need of money. Weren't most people nowadays?

All I knew for certain was that things had started going wrong for the Rescue League from the time Terra had disappeared. What would happen next?

~ * ~

Lightning Strikes Stable, Twenty Horses Saved from Fire.

I couldn't believe what I was reading. That was Brent's barn.

Everyone and all the animals were safe, thanks to the heroic collie, Chance, and Brent's two employees who lived on the premises. I couldn't find a mention of the owner.

Then he must be all right. But both his land line and cell phone went straight to voicemail.

He must be busy. There would be a dozens of details to take care of. And if the barn was destroyed, as the article indicated, he'd have to find temporary stabling for the horses. Not all of them belonged to Brent.

He was already coping with the fallout from the explosion of the *Sky Dancer*...

It had happened again. More bad luck, another fire! That accursed painting wasn't through with him.

But lightning can strike anywhere, I told myself. It can kill instantly. You don't have to own a haunted painting to be its target.

Still, bad luck had been dogging Brent even, I suspected, before the mysterious bite. I recalled thinking that something was troubling him when he insisted that all was well.

I took my empty coffee cup to the sink and rinsed it. I had another free day with no particular plans. Should I drive out to Brent's barn or would I be in the way? I wanted to know if he had taken Lucy's advice and rid himself of the source of ill fortune. If he had, then the lightning strike was a coincidence. Unless destroying *Ada's Litter* wasn't good enough.

What if the bad luck effect lingered? If that were true, what if it lingered for me?

I wanted desperately to connect with Brent, but decided to wait until he sought us out, and he would.

Perhaps tonight.

Thirty-two

"I couldn't throw the painting away," Brent said the next night. "Every now and then we have a bonfire at the stable to burn trash. We had one last week. I thought about what Lucy said and decided to take it down from the wall, but..." He paused, his hand frozen on Misty's soft head. She looked up at him as if to ask what was the matter.

I refilled his glass from the bottle of wine he'd brought and exchanged a worried glance with Crane. Brent had never seemed so vulnerable. Much of his signature bluster had left him.

"In the end I couldn't do it," he said.

I nodded. "The painting wouldn't let you. It doesn't want to be destroyed."

"Jennet," Crane said, "think about what you're saying. *Ada's Litter* is an inanimate object. It doesn't have a will of its own."

"You might say that. I thought you agreed that the painting was dangerous."

"I do, but there's a limit."

It seemed to have grown cold in our cozy living room. I recalled the time the painting had rested on my antique buffet—that priceless heirloom now destroyed by fire. It had leaned against the wall for days while I slowly became aware of its power. It hadn't raised any objection when I'd moved it to the basement.

In the end, that hadn't made any difference. *Ada's Litter* could work its dark magic from any place in the house, even from Crane's work bench in the lowest level.

"So it was still hanging on the wall when the storm came," Brent said.

"That storm caused widespread damage," Crane pointed out. "I saw most of it."

"But no other lightning strike."

"Thank goodness no horses were killed," I said.

"It was a close call, but we got them out in time. The stable's gone, though."

"Where are you going to keep the horses?" I asked.

"Sue Appleton took some of them. A few owners found other homes for them. Now I'm worried about Chance. He was all right during the fire, a real hero, but now he's moping around the house. You'd think he blames himself for what happened."

"Collies are a sensitive breed," I said.

He sighed. "First Napoleon, now Chance. My dogs."

"Is Napoleon still ailing?"

"He's no worse. Guess I should be grateful for that."

I took a sip of wine. It was good but I really wanted hot tea. In a moment I'd get up and put the water on to boil.

"You're going to rebuild the stable, aren't you?" I asked.

"We already took the first steps. Lined up a contractor. Ordered the lumber."

"And you're going to get rid of *Ada's Litter* once and for all."

"If I can."

"Of course you can. Why couldn't you?"

He shrugged. "I'll have to find a way to do it."

"For heaven's sake," I said. "I'll do it for you. We can have another bonfire and roast hot dogs to celebrate."

Hearing a word she knew, Candy looked hopefully in my direction.

"I don't think you should go near that painting, Jennet," Crane said.

Occasionally to my chagrin, Brent sided with Crane. "Neither do I. Don't worry, Sheriff. I won't let her through the door."

Brent set the wine glass down on the coffee table. It was empty again. As he reached for a brownie, I noticed the bite on his hand. It looked the same: red, angry, no larger. It should have gone away long ago.

I thought about *Ada's Litter* still hanging on Brent's wall, still in possession of its demented power, planning its next move.

When would this madness end?

~ * ~

On the first day after spring vacation, Marston High School offered a different kind of madness. It was unseasonably warm. The students were still in holiday mode—and dress. Keeping their attention was a gargantuan task. Worst of all, Principal Grimsley patrolled the halls, artificial smile pasted on a newly-tanned face. He was looking for troublemakers, determined to find them.

I didn't have time to think about the mysteries or to worry about Brent's ongoing problems.

At lunch Leonora and I hurriedly ate our sandwiches and lamented the loss of a leisurely mid-day meal: lunches at Clovers, or brunch at the Spirit Lamp Inn.

"Easter was late this year," she said. "It won't be long until June. Do you have any vacation plans?"

"Crane and I talked about going to Tennessee to see his family, but we've talked about it before. Something always comes up to prevent it. What about you?"

"I'll probably rent a cottage up north."

"Alone?" I asked.

"Me and Wafer. Jake may join us. It's sort of tentative, but I found a nice cabin on a lake. It's free in July."

That sounded serious. I longed to hear more details but knew Leonora wouldn't take the bait. Lately she'd been secretive about her romance with Deputy Sheriff Jake Brown, possibly because she suspected my sister, Julia, might still be interested in him.

"We didn't get a chance to hang out last week," Leonora said. "I had that cold. But we can go out for lunch some weekend."

"Don't forget after school we're going to visit Linnea Haver."

Rather than drive her own car to Marston and back, Leonora had decided to accompany me. I'd wanted to call Linnea first but her number was unlisted, so I didn't know if we'd be able to contact her. Still, nothing ventured, nothing gained. We'd leave as soon as the last bell rang.

~ * ~

The street where Linnea lived was, as I remembered it, about a mile long with shady trees on either side of an avenue. The houses were all different, built in the years before and after World War II, I'd guess, although a stately Victorian had been recently erected on a previously wooded double lot.

Linnea's house was a yellow frame whose front porch contained a glider and a profusion of hanging plants that gave the place an illusion of privacy. There was no garage and no car in the driveway. 'No Parking' signs preserved the street's air of privacy. Curiously the house reminded me of the Haver farmhouse. Silent, stately, and untenanted.

"She isn't home," Leonora said.

"It doesn't look that way, but I'm going to ring the doorbell."

We got out of the car. I rang the bell and listened to the notes chiming deep in the house. No one came to the door.

"What do we do now?" Leonora asked.

"Go on home and write her a letter. I should have done that as soon as I knew the address."

"You could leave her a note. Tuck it in the storm door."

"A letter will be safer."

The stop had only taken fifteen minutes but had failed to yield any new information. Feeling frustrated once again, I found the nearest freeway entrance and started the long drive home.

Thirty-three

I mailed my letter to Linnea Haver the next morning and imagined that I'd hear from her soon. In the meantime I drove by the Haver farmhouse on Deer Leap Trail one day after school. The blue door was gone again, painted over.

Would Linnea believe me or dismiss my claim as the rambling of a busybody? She had appeared to believe me before when we'd exchanged stories about the anomalies on her property. Or was she just humoring me?

I considered. The splatters of paint would still be on the flowers. There was my proof. This, at least, had a natural cause.

Just to be certain of my facts, I parked on the verge and walked toward the barn. Every time I visited the Haver house, I was struck anew by the profusion of wildflowers, the riot of color that overwhelmed the landscape. The flowers always seemed more numerous, more vibrant, even taller than they had been the last time I'd seen them. How could any plant possibly grow so fast and luxuriant without a steady diet of some super plant food like Miracle Gro?

A person could get lost in the meadow. Lost never to be seen again.

I listened, trying to hear a muffled sob in the soft wind, perhaps a plaintive whine from a canine throat, but the silence was absolute.

Except for the sigh of the wind. Finally I checked the barn's real door. The lock and chain were still in place, but around the entrance more flowers had been trampled down. A trail of crushed petals and leaves and torn stems led to the road.

It wasn't difficult to figure out what had happened. Someone had trespassed on the property as far as the barn and back to the road. Stashing or transporting cargo, I thought. Stolen merchandise?

That's it!

A band of thieves hid their loot in this nondescript out-of-the way structure where it would be safe until it could be moved to another location. The blue door was a signal to the confederate to collect the goods.

Watch for the painted door to tell you when the barn is full. Transport the goods by the light of the moon.

Now, of course, the barn would be empty, all traces of the door covered with a coat of brown paint.

It made sense. The one time I'd seen the interior, someone had slipped up and left the barn door open, but by then there was nothing to see.

So I had a simple, logical answer to one of the mysteries. I was sure it was the right one. All I needed was proof, but that might present an insurmountable obstacle.

"You could be right," Crane said that evening. "Do you think the woman who owns the place is in on it?"

"Probably not. She doesn't live there. She doesn't even visit often."

Leonora and I had driven by the house in Oakpoint three more times. Linnea was never home. Curiously, she never had any mail in the mailbox, or newspapers lying in front of the door. The plants on the porch were flourishing, however. Someone must be watering them.

"Now that I think of it, I'm not sure where she lives," I said.

Four days had passed. If Linnea lived at the Oakpoint address, she should have received my letter by now, but she hadn't responded to it, hadn't called.

Maybe she'd received it but didn't want to contact me, in which case there was nothing I could do.

"You can't leave property unattended," Crane said. "There's always someone ready to vandalize it or steal whatever can be sold. People have been known to move right in to a vacant house."

"There aren't any neighbors close by," I said, "and I doubt if Deer Leap Trail sees much traffic. So can you do anything, Crane?"

"With what you have, nothing. My guess is the barn's empty. Who knows when the blue door will reappear?"

"Be painted on again," I corrected. "You can keep an eye on the place, though, can't you?"

"Sure, but what are the odds that something will be going on when I drive by?"

"Not great, I guess. If only Linnea would get in touch with me."

"Maybe she's out of town."

"That's probably it. With the newspapers stopped and someone to pick up her mail. We could swing by her house in Oakpoint again," I said.

"Or wait a few more days."

I sighed. "It's not like I don't have anything to do. I should be reading my story for school now."

I glanced at the textbooks on my desk, the set I kept at home. Tomorrow's story was *The Dog of Pompeii*, a short tearjerker that should appeal to my rowdy freshman class. Maybe, maybe not. With teenagers, you never could tell.

I should read the story now and decide on a relevant composition topic. After all, teaching was my job, not delving into the mysteries of the wildflower meadow. Still I hated to leave any project hanging in mid-air. That was the location of the Blue Door Mystery. As far out of reach as one of Brent's hot air balloons.

~ * ~

Brent planned to sell Skyway Tours, his hot air balloon business. "As soon as I find a buyer," he said.

He made the announcement over dinner that night. Since I'd expected him, there were two roasted chickens and extra mashed potatoes on the table. He'd brought a blueberry pie from the Hometown Bakery for dessert. It was a cozy, relaxed get together, and up to this point, Brent had seemed his old self.

"Are you afraid to go flying again?" I asked as I passed him the potatoes.

"It's not that. The explosion took the fun out of it. I'm going to concentrate on rebuilding the stable. It'll be bigger and more modern. Then I want the horses home again, all in one place."

"Is Mike recovering from his injuries?" Crane asked.

"He's making slow progress. I sent him to Florida for the summer for a little R and R. In the fall I'll find work for him if he's up to it."

"That's generous," I said.

But Brent was good to his employees and friends. I'd always known that.

I glanced around the table, making sure that Crane and Brent had a helping of each dish on their plates. Then I asked the most important question. "Did you get rid of *Ada's Litter?*"

"I moved it to a storage shed behind the barn. Where the barn used to be, that is. It can't do any more harm there."

"That isn't good enough, Brent. Remember on the night of the fire, the painting was in the basement."

"Technically it was still in your home."

"Now it's still on your property."

"If you have another bonfire, we have some stuff to burn," Crane said.

I looked at him. "We do? What?"

"That old bookcase that was in the basement when you moved in."

"We can always use a spare bookcase," I said.

He returned my look. "We can afford to buy a new one." His tone indicated that the discussion was over. Belatedly I realized he was trying to encourage Brent to take the final step in ridding the world of the painting. As its creator had once advised me, "Burn it." Then it couldn't cause another fire.

Brent had already caught on. "Don't worry about me," he said. "I finally have a handle on things. Only…"

He paused to take a bite of his drumstick.

"Only what?"

"I hate caving into something I don't really believe in."

"It's best to be on the safe side," I said. "You don't have to believe."

"That what Lucy tells me. Still, it doesn't set well. Lightning can strike anywhere. Hot air balloons can blow up. Dogs get sick."

And you have a mysterious bite on your hand that won't go away.

I didn't say that. There was no point in reminding Brent of something he knew.

Instead I found myself thinking about *Ada's Litter*, that beautiful, accursed painting, stashed in a dark, airless shed where no one could gaze on it in admiration, marveling at the realistic depiction of the collie puppies, their proud mother, and the lovely golden-haired Margaret who was evil incarnate.

The girl, Margaret, lived on the painted canvas, on a mission to destroy the lives of her owners. She wouldn't be happy shut away from the rest of the world.

Thirty-four

The Dog of Pompeii was a surprising success with my freshmen. It was different enough to appeal to a wide range of youthful readers: the sentimental, the adventurous, the aspiring archaeologist, and the ones who preferred a shorter length. It even inspired a few tears.

I found myself answering questions that also intrigued me. Did excavators really find the skeleton of a dog in the ruins of Pompeii? Did this happen or was it a made-up story? Where was Pompeii anyway? And could that happen here?

I had explained the background briefly before we read the story, but sensing greater interest, went over it again, adding more detail. Not every lesson proved to be so popular with my rowdy bunch, and I couldn't resist bragging a little to Leonora as we ate our lunch, uninspired fare from the cafeteria today.

Leonora was accustomed to classroom successes. She possessed that enviable touch of magic I lacked.

"Kids love dog stories," she said. "That one is a charmer."

"I only wish the stories in the American Lit book were that good," I added. "Most children like dogs. Who doesn't?"

The last time I'd been in Lakeville I'd noticed that fresh 'Lost Dog' posters with a different picture of Breezy had replaced the old weathered ones. The reward had increased by two hundred dollars. Breezy's owners were still hoping for her return.

Again I debated the wisdom of contacting them. But what could I tell them at this late date?

I'd never set eyes on the wounded collie—if indeed she was Breezy—after she stumbled off into the wildflower meadow. The lightning flash collie didn't count, as that one might have been a figment of my imagination. At any rate, I'd never seen it again. Or I should say, almost seen it.

As for the collie at the Spirit Lamp Inn who resembled Breezy? She belonged to the cook.

"Speaking of dogs, are we going to have a League meeting in the near future?" Leonora asked.

"I haven't heard, but we should, especially now that we have a new president. I'll check with Sue Appleton when I get a chance."

"I guess no one has any collies to save," she said.

"That'll be the day."

Still, it was strange. To my knowledge, no new reports of abandoned collies had come in lately. When Terra had been alive, it seemed that people were always rescuing collies, always looking for foster homes for them and finally forever homes.

"You don't suppose the League is just going to die out, do you?" Leonora asked.

"Sue will never let that happen."

It would take time, but eventually the Lakeville Collie Rescue League would be reorganized and running smoothly again. If not, we'd start another group. The lost and castaway collies needed humans in their corner.

~ * ~

Whenever possible, Crane and I liked to celebrate special occasions with an out-of-the-ordinary activity. When he asked me what I'd like to do for my birthday, I suggested dinner out at the Spirit Lamp Inn. I'd had Easter brunch and lunch there but never an evening meal. There would be a more elaborate menu and loads of atmosphere—dim lights and shadows.

I'll admit the place still intrigued me, mainly because of the ghost story associated with it. Not that I thought a ghost would appear to me as a special birthday present, but I always hoped to learn more. I sensed the Inn had further secrets to reveal.

So we went to the Spirit Lamp Inn that Saturday night as a couple. I had a new dress, blue silk, and the pearl pendant Crane had given me, along with the dozen yellow roses on the dining room table. In civilian clothes, Crane looked incredibly handsome.

As I'd suspected, the hostess was someone I'd never seen, a very young woman with auburn hair arranged in a fifties style page boy. Her black sweater sparkled with sewn-on sequins suitable for glamorous evenings.

I was right about the menu—the specials were prime rib and filet mignon—and I was right about the atmosphere. The dining room had a ghostly ambience, full of shadows and flickering candlelight and subdued voices that sounded like whispers. I felt as if we'd taken a step back in time to the year the woman in the blue raincoat and her friend stopped at the Inn on their way home from up north.

Because I hadn't seen our waitress, Amy, on previous visits, I'd pretend this was our first time at the Inn. Well, Crane had never been here.

"We came to see the ghost," I said.

Amy almost dropped the water pitcher. "I beg your pardon?"

"The lady in the blue raincoat who haunts the Inn."

"Oh." Quickly she regained her composure and poured the water, her eyes riveted on the tall glasses. "That's just an old story. There's no truth to it. None at all."

Was she protesting too much? Definitely.

"But I heard…" I changed direction. "I read about the haunting in a book of unusual happenings."

"I wouldn't know about that," she said firmly. "Are you ready to order or do you need a minute?"

"Is prime rib okay?" Crane asked.

I nodded. "With leftovers for the dogs."

"I've arranged for a special dessert," he said to Amy. "The name is Ferguson."

"Sure thing, Mr. Ferguson. It's ready."

"What dessert?" I asked.

"You'll see," he promised.

I leaned back in my seat, nibbled on a hot roll from the bread basket, and watched the candlelight bring out the frosty flecks in Crane's gray eyes and the silver streaks in his blond hair. We hadn't been out together for ages, it seemed. I wouldn't have to cook tonight, and the dogs would have a feast of their own. Our dining room would be filled with the fragrance of roses. Maybe I'd leave my new necklace on…

A scream shattered the romantic scenario I was creating and that sedate, elegant ambience. It seemed to originate from deep within the Inn, from the first floor, I'd guess, toward the back. A single terrified cry. Then silence.

"What was that?" Crane, instantly alert and on his feet, rushed toward the kitchen.

The diners moved restlessly in their chairs, shocked voices raised, seeking the source of the sound. One man left his table and hurried toward the reception area.

As Crane reached the kitchen, the auburn-haired woman materialized in the doorway, sequins glittering on her sweater.

"What happened?" Crane demanded, moving toward the entrance.

"Just a minor mishap."

"It didn't sound minor to me."

She shrugged and tossed him a knowing smile. "Young people tend to be dramatic." Turning to the diners, she said, "We're sorry for the disturbance. Please go on with your dinners. It's nothing. Just a little cooking accident."

The sounds of alarm gradually subsided. The man returned to his companions, and Crane returned to me. "I guess no one got killed tonight," he said.

The next instant Amy swept by her bearing a tray: Thick slices of prime rib decorated with sprigs of parsley. A baked potato on a separate plate. String beans on still another plate.

"Would you like sour cream for your potatoes?" she asked as she set our dinners in front of us.

"I would," I said.

"None for me." Crane fixed Amy with a frosty look. "Is everything all right in the kitchen?"

"Perfectly. It was just a—uh spill."

To cause that piercing scream? I doubted it.

I cut a small piece of meat, thinking that the collies were in luck. The prime rib took up the entire plate. When Amy was out of earshot, I said, "Do you believe her?"

"I have no reason not to."

"Come now, Crane. That scream was loaded with terror. The kind you'd expect from someone who was being murdered. They're a little too anxious to minimize it."

"If something were really wrong, they'd send people hightailing it out of here. It's to their advantage to avoid panic."

"So they're covering up something."

"Or the chef grabbed a hot handle."

"Cooks know better."

Crane looked up. A merry glint in his eyes proclaimed that he knew exactly what I was thinking and going to say next. I could never surprise him.

"It sounded to me like someone saw a ghost," I said.

Thirty-five

The surprise dessert was a chocolate layer cake decorated with long-stemmed yellow sugar roses and candles. Luckily I had eaten sparingly of the main course because, based on the high swirls of frosting, the cake looked as if it would be out of this world. Strange that I described it that way.

After admiring it and making a fuss over Crane's thoughtfulness, I made a wish and blew out the candles while Amy hovered over us with a cake server and dessert plates.

"The cook outdid herself," Amy said.

I'd wished for a quick solution to the many mysteries that had plagued the spring. One of them was the scream at the Inn. I didn't accept Crane's hot handle explanation. That was too prosaic and no fun.

After the initial disturbance, the ghostly ambience had returned to the dining room. People departed, others took their places, and I suspected those who were gone had already forgotten that somewhere tonight a woman had screamed once in terror.

Tomorrow we'll read in the paper that a guest had been stabbed in a dark hall. The assailant escaped into the garden, leaving the murder weapon embedded in the body.

"A penny for your thoughts," Crane asked.

"I'm thinking about my handsome husband," I said.

"You were a thousand miles away."

"Yes, I was on Cloud Nine."

"Seriously."

I scraped a yellow rose from the frosted top of my slice. The cake was truly out-of-this world, and since it was my birthday, I could have another piece without even thinking about added pounds.

"I was also wondering if something nefarious is going on at the Inn," I said.

"Because we heard a scream?"

"Well sure, but consider. The hostesses and waitresses keep changing. They tell different stories. There's a resident collie who looks a lot like Breezy, and the Inn is reputed to be haunted."

"That sounds like one of those old paperbacks you read."

Exactly. From the beginning, when Leonora and I took refuge from the storm in the spooky old inn, we'd entered the world of a Gothic novel.

"I have a strange feeling about this place," I said.

"I don't know about feelings, but they serve a great prime rib."

Crane's plate was empty. The dogs' hand-outs would come from mine.

"And a fantastic cake," I said. "This has been a perfect birthday."

Subconsciously I touched my new necklace. I was fortunate to have this keepsake of my perfect night. Just in case it was the last time Crane and I would share a celebratory dinner.

The last time?

The thought appalled me. Where had it come from and why would it surface on this happy occasion? Unbidden and unwelcome, it lay heavily on my heart, shutting out the euphoria.

My life with Crane couldn't have been happier, but life could change in an instant. Crane's job was dangerous. Leonora and I risked our lives every school day on the freeway. A few times in the past, I'd found myself at the mercy of a killer and twice in the path of a tornado.

Across the country the weather had been unpredictable with storms that claimed lives. Always other people's lives, but you couldn't trust Mother Nature. She was far too capricious.

I had grasped the pendant in my hand as one would a talisman.

Upset with myself for this unwarranted mood swing, I pushed the doomsday images away. All anyone could do was enjoy the present and refuse to worry about the future. And always, always be careful.

~ * ~

"Something's wrong in the League," Sue Appleton said. "And I'm afraid to delve too deeply into it."

She'd appeared unannounced at the door in an excitable state, alluding vaguely to an alarming discovery. Now we sat on the porch drinking lemonade while she appeared to summon her courage to speak.

I remembered Leonora's fear that the Collie Rescue League might die out. Could that be what troubled Sue?

Deciding to help her along, I said, "Why?"

"I'm afraid of what I might find."

"Just tell me what the problem is."

"We're missing a lot of money."

"The cashbox from the sale? I know about that."

"That's a drop in the bucket. All the money Liz said we had in the treasury, it's mostly gone. There's only fifteen dollars and a tiny bit of interest left."

I never expected this development. "How could that happen?" I asked.

"Liz kept the books, but she didn't handle the cash. Mostly the donation money went to Terra. She kept it in a special account with her sister's name on it. When they went to close it and open another one, they found a grand total of fifteen dollars. There were withdrawals in five hundred dollar increments over time, supposedly made by Terra."

"Are you saying that Terra stole the Rescue League's money?"

"It looks that way."

"How about her sister?"

"She swears she didn't touch it. Her name was just on the account in case of emergency."

"I don't believe Terra would dip into the League's funds for her own use," I said.

"Can you think of another explanation?" Sue asked. "Anything?

"Offhand, no. Unless she took out money to pay for her Christmas party."

"A thousand dollar social event?"

"I guess not." I stared out at the woods across the lane as if hoping to find inspiration there. Corruption in organizations wasn't unheard of. In the dismal economy, sums of unattended money could be a temptation.

I recalled the theft of the cashbox during the sale. But Terra was dead by then, and I suspected the mother of the destructive little boy. In any event, thefts at yard sales weren't unusual. Siphoning money from an account set aside for a specific purpose was another matter.

But this was the Lakeville Collie Rescue League, for heaven's sake. This was our Terra. This was the collies' money. Donations and the profits from countless fundraisers were needed to cover veterinary care and grooming and so much more. I could see why Sue was troubled. This theft affected us all.

"Who else knows about this?" I asked

"Well, Liz, of course, and Terra's sister. Now you. I don't think it should become general knowledge among the members until we find the guilty party. And if by chance we learn that Terra was keeping the money for herself...I don't know what to do then."

"Haven't there been vet bills and medicine to cover over the past months?" I asked. "And spaying and neutering? What if all of these expenses were paid for but just not recorded?"

"I suppose that's one answer," Sue said.

"That money could go in no time. I don't think we have to jump to the conclusion that Terra was in any way dishonest."

On the other hand, it was unlike Terra to be careless about keeping track of expenditures.

"We can start from scratch," Sue said. "From fifteen dollars, that is. Liz and I will keep the books together. We'll write down every single penny we spend."

I nodded. "A new beginning. I think we should have another yard sale. We have enough merchandise."

"Liz and I will put our heads together and come up with some other fundraisers."

It wasn't ideal, but it was certainly preferable to besmirching Terra's name. What bothered me was that we were allowing the thief—no, two thieves—to get away with robbing the Rescue League.

That wasn't right.

Thirty-six

"I think you should call another League meeting," I said. "Do something special so that everybody shows up. Maybe combine it with a barbeque."

"That's brilliant." Sue set her empty glass down on the nearest wicker table. "But weren't we going to keep the missing money a secret?"

"We will. Just skip the treasurer's report. I'd like to have all the members together. Maybe I can develop a list of suspects."

Warming to the idea, Sue said, "I'll tell people we decided to hold another yard sale and need to organize helpers into groups. That'll be the truth."

She picked the empty glass up again and turned it around and around. "We have a few new members. Terra approved their applications. I don't know them well. That doesn't mean they're guilty, of course," she added.

"It'll be a start."

"Wouldn't it be wonderful if we could get our money back? Do you think you can find out who stole it?"

"I'm going to try. If there's a thief in the Rescue League, we have to know who it is to prevent something similar from happening again."

"It won't. We're alerted now. I told you Liz and I are going to keep track of incoming money and expenses."

"And during the next yard sale, whoever's in charge of the cashbox can't let it out of her sight."

Sue hazarded a smile. "She'll chain it to her wrist." She set the glass down again. "I feel better now that we've talked. I'll try to get everyone together for a barbeque next Friday. If we wait, people will be going on vacation."

"One of them with the collies' money," I said.

We couldn't let that happen.

"And we're keeping this a secret, okay?"

"For now only the four of us will know."

That meant I wouldn't be discussing the theft with Leonora or even Crane. Let no one suspect that all was not well with the League's finances. And if a collie came into Rescue needing surgery or costly treatment, we'd find the money somehow.

~ * ~

Time does pass, even when school days seem to drag. The summery weather continued. Student dress grew more casual, senior excitement rose with the temperatures, and not even the prospect of final exams could stem the euphoria that gripped the school.

One day when Leonora drove her own car to Marston, I stopped at Clovers on the way home for take-out dinners and found Annica listlessly rearranging the desserts in the carousel to make the offerings look less skimpy.

"I'm so bored," she said. "No one's eating out today."

That was an exaggeration as half of the tables were filled.

"Can you take a break?" I asked. "I'll order take-out later."

"Sure can. Mary Jeanne went home early, and Marcy has it covered. I'll treat us to lemon pie." There were only two pieces left.

She signaled to Marcy, who acknowledged her unspoken request with a nod, and poured coffee for us. When we were settled in a booth, I told her about the scream that had briefly interrupted my birthday dinner at the Spirit Lamp Inn. "Something's going on there."

"Besides the ghost?"

"I think so. The lady in the blue raincoat may be just a distraction."

"Why would anyone want to create a distraction?"

"I don't know yet."

"What are we going to do?" she asked.

"Continue to patronize the place at different times. Sooner or later we may come across someone who's willing to talk to us."

"That's pretty haphazard."

"If you have a better idea, let me know."

"Not just now. Let me think about it."

"I wish I knew who screamed and why," I said. "There was nothing in the paper about any trouble at the Inn. Well, I guess there wouldn't be."

"Maybe it's something simple like a waitress seeing a mouse or a rat."

"Ugh. Perish the thought."

"I'm not working Saturday," Annica said. "We could drop by for lunch and look around. We'll stroll in the garden with our magnifying glasses like real sleuths."

"And ask to see the room the ghost girl had."

I said that last with a smile. I was willing to bet the haunted room was no longer in use and also that whatever was going on at the Inn had nothing to do with ghosts. Our plan was indeed haphazard, like searching for an unknown entity without a map. If nothing else, it would be a diversion.

~ * ~

I knew immediately that our lunch at the Spirit Lamp Inn was going to be more than a diversion. Our waitress, Penny, was a veritable fount of information, bubbling over with bits and pieces of the Inn's history, all inspired by Annica's casual reference to the place's unique charm.

We finally learned how the Inn had acquired its name.

"The first owner had a collection of spirit lamps," Penny said. "There used to be a gift shop where you could buy all sorts of lamps, real antiques and neat reproductions."

There was nothing mysterious about the Inn's name then.

Penny knew all about the lady in the blue raincoat. "She's the reason I wanted to work here this summer. I'm dying to see a ghost."

"Have you seen her?" I asked.

"Not yet, but it's only June."

"I'm interested in the Haver property," I said, taking the menu she offered me. "It's the most beautiful stretch of land I've ever seen."

She wrinkled her nose. "It's too flowery for my taste. I couldn't breathe in that meadow. Linnea Haver would never have let it get so overgrown."

But she had. To be sure, she'd spoken of having the wildflowers mowed down, but she'd never done anything about them. Then she'd as good as disappeared like her sister. At least I'd never been able to contact her.

You're missing something, I told myself. *Backtrack.*

Annica closed her menu. "I'll have the corned beef sandwich. No Swiss cheese, no horseradish. Just a dill pickle. Brown mustard on the side."

"Maybe she'll get around to neatening up the property one of these days," I said.

Penny stared at me, a bemused smile on her face. "That'll never happen."

"How do you know?"

"Well, she can't, can she? Not from Roseridge Cemetery."

"She's dead?" Annica said.

"Dead as a doornail. Oh, you didn't know? I thought everybody did."

But she couldn't be. I'd talked to Linnea Haver a few weeks ago. She'd opened the door of the Haver House and offered me bottled water. She'd told me that eerie story of her sister's disappearance, said she'd also heard weeping in the wildflower meadow.

She had a house in Oakpoint. Where mail and newspapers weren't delivered.

"Miss Haver was killed in an accident on Deer Leap Road," Penny said. "She and her sister died at the scene. It was a hit-and-run. They never found the other driver."

"Who owns the property then?" Annica asked.

"Some relative. The girls' uncle, I think. It was for sale at one time."

I scanned the column of sandwich offerings, couldn't still my thoughts long enough to make a choice. If Linnea Haver was dead, who had invited me into the farmhouse on Deer Leap Road?

I could think of only one answer. Linnea's ghost. The most lifelike ghost I'd ever encountered.

Thirty-seven

"This is one ghost too many," Annica said when Penny left to fill our order.

The mourner in the meadow. The lightning flash collie. The lady in the blue raincoat. And now Linnea Haver.

"It's like a gathering of the clan for Midsummer's Eve," she added. "Or a bad horror movie."

"It *does* seem excessive," I said. "Penny mentioned a cemetery—Roseridge. That isn't too far out of our way. After lunch we can drive over and see if the sisters are buried there."

"We could do that," Annica said. "But how would we know for sure that Linnea Haver is actually in her plot?"

"We assume the cemetery doesn't make mistakes."

"It would be better and quicker to find their obituaries on the Internet. If there was a hit and run on Deer Leap Trail, it'd have been in the paper. Besides it's too hot out to go tramping through a graveyard."

"That makes sense," I said. "The woman I saw didn't exhibit any ghost-like behavior. She was as real as you or Penny or any one of these people here in the dining room."

"Then Penny was lying," Annica said. "But why would she lie?"

"Or the woman I encountered at the Haver farmhouse deceived me. I'll ask the same question. Why?"

The woman who had identified herself as Linnea Haver had a key to the farmhouse. She was familiar with the contents of the cupboards. She'd spoken with emotion about her sister's disappearance and her own glimpse into the other world. Could everything she said be an elaborate ruse?

"It's hard to solve a mystery when you can't trust what people say," Annica said.

That was true, but I was beginning to see an upside to the puzzle. "If some Haver relative owns the property, I won't worry about trespassing."

"When did you ever worry about that?" Annica asked. "But it's still a dangerous place and a haunted one. It must be the real Linnea or her sister you heard crying in the meadow."

Trapped by death. So close to home, yet separated from it by acres of wildflowers, forever held in thrall by rapacious, unnatural stems. What a nightmare scenario!

"At this point I don't know what's true and what's fabrication," I said. "I only know what I saw, and I'm more curious than ever."

"We'll just have to separate the wheat from the chaff. Did I say that right?"

"I guess."

We fell silent, Annica gulping her ice water and I remembering our drive to the Inn. When we'd passed the Haver place, there had been no discernible change in the meadow. Wildflowers encroached on the man-made structures. In the meadow, jumbles of brilliant color marched off to disappear into the shadows of the dark woods. There was no blue door on the side of the barn.

Before that we'd driven by Terra's makeshift temporary grave in the woods. The crime scene tape had been removed, but the yellow ribbons tied to trees still clung to their branches. They looked limp and washed out, as if to symbolize the slowly fading memory of the murdered woman.

With the talk of the Inn's resident ghost and the new information about the Haver sisters, I'd almost forgotten our own tragedy. Terra was gone, her legacy tarnished by an opportunistic thief. I'd promised Sue Appleton I'd try to find the traitor in our midst.

Why did I always promise to do the near impossible?

You have the here-and-now to deal with, I told myself. *For the present, forget the spirit world.*

~ * ~

Away from the heat of the sun, I sat in the air-conditioned comfort of my home and searched the Internet for an account of the hit and run accident that had taken the lives of Linnea Haver and her sister, Grace.

So much for the tale of Grace's thin air disappearance while planting the wildflower meadow. The abandoned wheelbarrow must be a work of fiction added to give the story a poignant touch. The Haver woman—I had to stop calling her that—counted on the unlikelihood of my combing the fields for it.

It was relatively easy to find the story. The accident had occurred a year ago at the crossroads on Deer Leap Trail. It was surmised that a vehicle had come out of the fog and struck Linnea Haver's Jeep broadside as she crossed to the other side.

Being familiar with that area, I could visualize the scene: a stop sign hidden from view. Thick walls of fog on either side. Deep country silence. Except for the hum of a motor, the sound muffled. The hit and run car must have been traveling too fast for weather conditions, an invitation to disaster in the fog.

There, on this isolated stretch of roadway, a passing motorist discovered the sisters in their smashed vehicle. Both were dead. Not surprisingly, the driver of the other car had never been found. He or she had driven off into the fog and obscurity.

How many hit and run drivers returned to the scene of the crime? Especially if there were no witnesses.

So Linnea Haver was dead. The evidence was undeniable. Who then was the imposter who had stolen her identity?

I stared at the screen, trying to figure out how the unknown woman had acquired a key to the farmhouse. An obvious answer presented itself. She could be the relative who had inherited the property, one who bore a slight resemblance to the real Linnea Haver. Of course. Then she'd know there was bottled water in the cupboard but no coffee or tea. She'd have a key.

But wait! One of the waitresses at the Spirit Lamp Inn said the heir was supposed to be an uncle.

In any event, why the subterfuge? That was what I had to discover.

~ * ~

Almost all of the League members showed up at Sue Appleton's farmhouse for the barbeque and meeting. Some brought covered dishes. Liz was there, looking worried, and I saw Laurence DeVille, who was the first to seat himself at the long picnic table. Leonora was one who couldn't attend the meeting, having a prior commitment as co-sponsor of the Drama Club at Marston.

The meeting was held on the patio. It was an informal affair with cold drinks and a variety of snacks. Liz apologized for being unable to give her treasurer's report and promised to have an updated one at the next gathering.

Sue explained the advantages of holding another yard sale while the good weather held, and no one reminded her that it was only

June. Quickly and efficiently, she organized volunteers into groups, then announced that dinner would be ready in a few minutes.

All this time I had been glancing surreptitiously at my fellow collie rescuers. No one looked suspicious. Well, what had I expected? Shifty eyes and oversized handbags?

Especially interesting to me were the new people, like the woman with long red braids and a dressed-up denim outfit. I remembered her from Terra's house before we knew that Terra would never be there again.

Her name was Cathy, and she was standing alone, murmuring to one of Sue's rescue collies, a stunning blue merle named Summer. I joined her.

The enticing smell of chicken and ribs hung heavily on the air, but people were slow to exchange their cold drinks and gossip time for food.

"Nice day for a barbeque," I said, for want of a more inspired comment.

"Yes, it is. This is a wonderful farm Sue has. I've always wanted a place for horses."

"Where do you live?" I asked.

"In Lakeville. In a subdivision. A real farm like this would be heaven. I guess I'll have to keep dreaming."

"There's lots of acreage for sale in Foxglove Corners," I said.

"I can't afford to move. I can barely afford to stay where I am." She paused, looked around, and said in a low voice, "Don't you think something odd is going on in the League?"

"Not really."

"Well, I do. I have feelings, and I'm never wrong."

"That must come in handy," I said with a smile, realizing belatedly that she might think I was being sarcastic. "What do you think is wrong?"

She shrugged. "I'm not sure. I feel left out of the loop."

"You're new to Rescue. It takes a while to know everyone."

"They're all locked in their little cliques," she said. "You're the only one who's talked to me—except to say hello. I only stay in the League because of the collies."

"So that's what's bothering you? You don't feel welcome?"

"It's more than that." She started to walk to the table where salads and platters of deviled eggs were set out—food that would spoil in the heat of the afternoon if it weren't quickly devoured. Summer followed us, as hopeful as my own Candy.

I filled a paper plate with pasta salad and a hot roll and turned to another table near the grill laden with trays of chicken and ribs.

"It feels like they're all in on a secret, except me," Cathy said. "And maybe you, if you don't think anything is off."

I wasn't happy to hear that. Cathy couldn't know about the missing money. Could she? What about the stolen cash box? Had Sue and Liz been indiscreet? I hadn't told a soul the League's business, not even Leonora or Crane, but was it possible that everybody who was milling around Sue's yard was in on the secret?

It seemed, just for a minute, my friends and acquaintances in the Lakeville Collie Rescue League had donned masks.

~ * ~

"Hey, Jennet, saved you a seat."

Laurence DeVille brandished a barbequed drumstick. With his free hand, he patted the empty chair at his side.

I glanced behind me, expecting to see Cathy, but she'd stopped to talk to Sue. What happened to her claim of being snubbed by the membership? Well, I was glad for her. She needed that sense of belonging.

Unable to extricate myself gracefully from DeVille's invitation, I set my plate and lemonade down on the table.

"Great spread," he said. "We should do this for every meeting."

"I don't agree. Then the emphasis would be on food rather than rescue. I saw that happen in a book club I belonged to once. Everyone was competing to host a more elaborate dinner."

Food was certainly the star of this show. I glanced at the delicacies I'd gathered. Chicken, ambrosia salad, deviled eggs, homemade corn relish, olives. No room for anything more, except a slice of the chocolate sheet cake in the center of the table. Somewhere DeVille had found a larger plate, almost the size of a platter.

"What do you think about this second yard sale so soon after the last one?" DeVille asked.

"It's a good idea. Why hold onto saleable merchandise when the League needs money?"

"It'll be a flop, mark my words." He tossed the drumstick bone to a side of his plate. I'd never seen chicken disappear so fast. "Nobody's going to come out to see the same old stuff. They should wait till fall when the leaves change color. The ambience will be totally different. It'll attract a whole new crowd."

"Sue is planning other fundraisers," I said. "I know for sure there's going to be a puppy fun match in September."

He sighed loudly. "Guess I'm stuck hauling merchandise to Liz' house again."

"Didn't she keep the unsold items in her garage?"

"I understand there've been more donations. Collie magazines and books and a few vintage prints."

They'd go faster than figurines and miscellaneous bric-a-brac. I was looking forward to sampling them myself.

"I'll have at least five stops to make," he said.

The sun was hot on my shoulders. The barbequed chicken breast on my plate remained warm. So did the deviled eggs. As I took a sip of lemonade, I felt a brush of velvet on my leg. Summer stood at my side licking her chops. I broke off a piece of chicken for her and whispered, "Go find the grill; there's more chicken there."

"Spoiled rotten. I wonder if she came that way?" Laurence picked up a wing, one of several on a stack. "Did you hear the rumor about Terra?"

"About her killer?"

"About her surreptitious activities."

"I try not to listen to gossip," I said. "Sometimes it's unavoidable."

He ignored the hint. "They say she was stealing the League's donation money. Spouting slogans like 'Any sacrifice is worth making for the collies' while siphoning off funds right and left. Maybe that's why she was killed."

"That," I said, "is pure slander. Did 'they' offer any proof?"

"I'm trying to find out. Terra's cronies are awfully close-mouthed. I bet they're all in on it. Did you notice Liz didn't give her treasurer's report?"

"She will, at the next meeting."

"Yeah, we'll see, won't we?"

DeVille's claims disheartened me. Weren't we going to have a chance to squelch that sordid tale?

"According to the grapevine, you're supposed to be something of a detective," DeVille said. "Care to work with me? We can put our heads together and find out what's really going on."

"I don't think so," I said.

"Why?"

"I'm not a detective. If I were, I'd work alone."

"Terra used to encourage us to cooperate with one another."

"That was with dogs."

Summer nudged my hand and whined. She might as well have another handout. My food had suddenly lost its appeal. When I got home, I'd cook dinner for Crane—not chicken—and eat with him. Under DeVille's disapproving glare, I fed Summer the rest of the chicken breast.

Tired of pushing deviled egg filling around on my plate with my fork, I took in the scene. People going back for seconds. Cathy eating at one end of the picnic table, alone again. A chocolate cake rapidly disappearing. From the house, muffled barking. On the surface, normalcy, camaraderie. A small group of people united to save collies from untenable situations.

At least that was the mission.

I'd been proud to be a member of the Lakeville Collie Rescue League and sincerely thought I was making a significant contribution to our cause. Now I'd allowed a few stray bits of conversation to shake my faith in the organization. Was it all a sham?

~ * ~

"You're invited to a witch burning," Brent said that evening. "Both of you. Tomorrow afternoon at five o'clock. You can throw a piece of wood on the fire, if you like."

I took a sip of the wine he had brought. "It sounds ghastly."

"I'll be on duty," Crane said. "If you're going to burn someone, maybe I should swing by your place."

"Like I said, you're welcome. I'm torching *Ada's Litter*. Burning her down to ashes and burying the ashes deep in the ground. I've finally had enough."

"Thank heavens," I said.

Automatically my gaze traveled to his hand. The mark left by the bite had never faded. It looked like a fresh wound. After all this time.

211

"Did you ever see a doctor about that bite?" I asked.

"Yes. She said I'd never know what bit me and it'd go away one of these days."

"We knew that," I said.

"If it hasn't killed me yet, it isn't going to."

That wasn't necessarily true, but there was no point in pointing that out. Instead I said, "When that accursed painting is gone, your luck will turn around."

"It already has. I think I found the perfect buyer for Skyway Tours."

"You're really going to sell the business?"

"As soon as I can unload it."

My feelings were mixed. I knew Brent had loved his fleet of balloons. I'd never gone up in the *Sky Dancer*, never flown over the treetops and lakes of Foxglove Corners to view my home from that unique perspective. Now I never would. Of course there were other hot air balloon companies. Other seasons. I could still muster my courage and have that experience.

But it wouldn't be the same.

Thirty-eight

The sun rode high in the sky over Brent's stables, scorching my arms. My sleeveless tank top seemed to be melded to the skin on my arms, and my long denim skirt was heavier than it had a right to be. In addition, the humidity was thick without the slightest breeze to cool the air or stir the wildflowers that wilted at my feet.

Even with the heat, it was a perfect day for a bonfire. With no wind, the flames wouldn't spread. Fear of an out-of-control blaze was the reason I'd never start a bonfire on my own property.

Brent's stable helpers had gathered in the field to enjoy rare downtime, throwing a package of marshmallows to one another as if it were a beach ball. They were young men in their late teens or early twenties and a girl with a shining blonde ponytail who looked capable of holding her own among the males. Unlike some of his neighbors, Brent preferred to hire American students who loved horses…rather than migratory workers.

Chance and Napoleon danced around Brent's heels, both of them panting, although Napoleon, looking droopy, danced a little more slowly.

The stack of discards in the center of the field consisted of gnawed shelves, planks, broken stools, rakes—and one painting in an ornate frame too fine to consign to the flames, but Lucy said it was part of the painting; it could well be part of the curse.

"Still, it's a shame to burn that beautiful frame," I said.

"Better safe than sorry."

"I guess so."

But the frame was also part of Julia's Christmas present to me. I had a bittersweet memory of that Christmas when I'd first unwrapped the mysterious box and set eyes on Aura Lee Larkin's painting.

From the beginning it had fascinated me. The girl with the golden hair, Margaret, her collie, Ada, and the puppies frolicking in front of Margaret's blue Victorian porch. I didn't know their names then or anything about them, didn't know someone had written *Evil RIP* on the back of the canvas in heavy black marker. The bad times were still in the future, unimagined.

I'd seen only an oil paint depiction of a girl and dogs on a bright day in early summer with wildflowers blooming in the grass, a scene so real I could imagine myself stepping into it.

I felt a moment of panic as *Ada's Litter* became almost a sentient being.

Don't let him do this to me!

"Stop!"

Lucy glanced at me. Surely I hadn't said that out loud?

Brent tossed a small white what-not shelf on the heap. It promptly broke into pieces. I stepped back, feeling dizzy, feeling the beginning of a headache.

Lucy touched my shoulder. "Are you all right, Jennet?"

"Yes," I said. "I'm just hot. It's so hot today."

She nodded. "It feels more like August than June. There're all sorts of cold drinks set out in front of the barn. Would you like me to get one for you now?"

"I'll wait till we're finished," I said.

"Everybody, step back," Brent shouted. "I'm going to light the fire. Does anyone want to say goodbye to a haunted painting? Speak now or forever hold your peace."

The young people broke into boisterous laughter, probably not at what Brent had just said. The marshmallow package flew through the air.

Brent held his brawny arm out to the stack. It was as though the fire were already burning, casting a burnished glow on his face and his dark red hair that was the shade of a certain kind of maple leaf in fall.

"Burn it," Aura Lee had cried.

"Be careful, Brent," Lucy said.

You can't kill it, I thought.

Brent tossed a match into the heart of the pile. It was one of those safe kitchen matches with long wooden handles, the kind that would never burn your fingers.

And the first flames rose.

~ * ~

The fire burned.

My head throbbed. Was that a scream and puppies crying in agony and terror?

Save them! Don't let them die!

No! That was impossible. I didn't hear anything. It was the infernal heat. The sun. The fire hungrily devouring its offerings. My runaway imagination.

There had been a real fire in Margaret's past life, one she had set herself. That, I suspected, was what had set the curse in motion.

I ran my hands up and down my arms. The tenderness and hurting were the first stages of a sunburn. Why hadn't I brought a long sleeved blouse to throw over my shoulders?

Because the temperature had soared past ninety-five, and the thought of another layer made me feel faint.

More to the point, why had I accepted Brent's bizarre invitation? I could have gone straight home after school to my collies and an air-conditioned house and avoided being broiled alive.

Brent moved back to stand between Lucy and me. It would be over soon. I'd take a pain pill—being a teacher, I always carried them in my purse—and I'd drink bottled water and soon, very soon, feel better.

"Well, that's that." Brent glanced down at his hand. The bite mark was still there. "Good riddance," he said. "I wish I'd done that months ago."

"You weren't ready to admit the danger," Lucy said.

"I should have."

"Yes," she agreed.

The edges of the painting were charred and beginning to curl. The colors appeared to be melting. Blue, green, pink, and yellow pooling in a new color that resembled blood. The package of marshmallows landed at my feet. They were melting too.

"Sorry." One of the boys snatched the package away from my feet.

Brent swiped his hand across his forehead. "Now that's done, I want you ladies to see my new acquisition. He's in the stable."

"You have a new horse," I said.

"Imported from Germany. He's a beauty. It was so hot the day he arrived, the hottest day of the year so far. Guess what his name is."

"Firebrand," Lucy said.

"Sunrunner?"

"You're both on the wrong track. It's Eskimo. He's dapple gray and gigantic, sixteen point two hands tall with a beautiful white tail and white eyelashes."

"I can't wait to see this equine marvel," Lucy said.

"I have pictures on my cell phone, but Eskimo in the horseflesh is waiting in his stall." He started to walk toward the barn. "Let's cool down with something cold. Beer, lemonade, sweet iced tea, ginger ale... You kids keep an eye on the bonfire."

"Just cold water for me," I said.

I turned away from the fire. Unaccountably I felt a little better. Maybe I wouldn't need that pain pill after all.

~*~

Heat and the acrid smell of smoke followed us into the stable, but the structure offered protection from the sun. It had been built in record time to replace the previous one destroyed by the lightning fire.

I stood in the doorway, bottled water in hand, breathing in the fragrance of hay and horse and that wondrous new barn smell. Everything was clean and fresh and sparkling, a horse lover's paradise.

"He's back this way," Brent said, leading us past the stalls. Whinnies, restless stomping, and curious dark eyes marked our progress.

Lucy and I dodged Chance's paws, while Napoleon found a large pail and lay down in front of it, lapping water loudly. We weren't alone in the barn. Two young girls with braided hair worked on a pony tethered on each side to a stall. They were so intent on their task that they didn't look up as we passed. If only I could groom my reluctant collies that way.

I tried to imagine Candy tied to two ropes and couldn't.

"So many horses," Lucy murmured.

"They're not all mine," Brent said. "Some of them are boarders, like the girls' pony back there." He came to a stop. "And here's Eskimo. My pride and joy."

"Oh, my…" Other, more appropriate, words failed me.

With his dappled gray body, Eskimo reminded me of an Anna Lee Larkin ice sculpture. He had lively, intelligent eyes and big teeth, and he was a giant, a creature from mythology, towering over me.

"He's magnificent," Lucy said. "At a time like this, I wish I could ride."

"Why can't you?" Brent asked.

"Because I'd fall off and break every bone in my body. I lead a sedentary life. But I can admire beauty and this animal is beauty personified."

"Aura Lee should paint his portrait," I said.

And give him wings like Pegasus. Paint him flying across a cobalt blue sky into the sun. Ice in motion.

"Good God, no," Brent said. "I just got rid of one demon painting. At least I assume it's gone by now."

I rushed to Aura Lee's defense. "As far as I know, *Ada's Litter* was her only diabolical work. You have another one of her paintings. The little fox."

"Then only *Ada's Litter* is evil," he said. "I meant to say, was evil." He glanced at his watch. "By now I figure it's a pile of ashes."

I felt suddenly strange discussing the haunted painting, felt disrespectful. As if I were tempting fate. In fact I felt so strange that I quickly changed the subject.

"Eskimo has such big teeth," I said. "Will he bite?"

"Keep your hands away from his mouth," Brent said. "He loves apples and carrots and sugar cubes, but In Europe they don't feed horses treats so much, so he isn't used to it."

"So he'll bite?"

"Don't think he's like a collie who'll eat gently from your hand. My hand, now... That's a different story."

From his pocket he produced a knife and an apple. He cut the apple in half and offered the half to Eskimo. In a second it had disappeared into Eskimo's mouth, the sound of crunching loud in the silence.

"As soon as Skyway Tours sells, I'm going to concentrate on the horses," Brent said. "Eskimo represents a new beginning for me." He frowned as his gaze fell on my arms. "You're getting a sunburn, Jennet. Better put some lotion on it. I think there's a tube on the shelf over there."

"It's too late to reverse the damage," I said.

"Use cold tea bags as compresses," Lucy said. "They'll help take the pain away."

I took a swig of water. It had rested in a cooler filled with ice, but was already room temperature. Barn temperature, I corrected myself, and thought with longing of the sun tea I was making at home. I'd have six bags of Red Rose right there.

"I think I've had enough sun and fire for one day," I said. "I'm going home."

"Don't you want to stay for the burial?" Brent asked.

I shook my head. "I'll trust you to finish the job properly."

~ * ~

Crane brought the hamburgers he'd grilled inside and set them on the counter. "You're burned to a crisp, Jennet. Did you stand too near Brent's fire?"

"When you're outside, there's no escape from the sun," I said.

As soon as I'd come home, I walked the dogs a short distance, wearing a sheer beach cover-up. Even the touch of sheer had irritated my arms.

Lucy's tea bag remedy had soothed my burn for a few minutes, but the damage had been done. My arms and a bit of my chest were as red as a boiled lobster.

I cringed at the image. Never in a million years would I boil a lobster. Only my own fair skin.

But life and dinner preparations went on. I made a huge pasta salad to go with the burgers, fed the dogs, and brought the pitcher of tea out of the refrigerator. It was later than our usual dinner hour, and I realized how hungry I was.

"So *Ada's Litter* is finally gone," Crane said as we sat down to dinner. "Maybe now things will settle down for Fowler."

"He hopes so, but he still has that pesky bite, and poor Napoleon is a ghost of his former self."

"Give it time."

Our talk verged on the serious, and that wouldn't do at dinnertime. But an annoying uncertainty gripped me. Maybe, like my sunburn, irreversible damage had been done to Brent. Maybe Napoleon would never recover from his vague illness and Brent's bite would never heal.

Perhaps something of the painting's evil would live on, no matter how deep Brent buried its ashes.

I should ban distressful thoughts as well as conversation during the dinner hour, I thought as I passed Crane the pasta salad. While we ate, I told Crane about Eskimo and the League's second yard sale and the last day of school. All happy things.

When my mind sent me a picture of *Ada's Litter* reassembling itself, I refused to look at it.

Thirty-nine

With a deafening roar like that of a dam exploding or a chorus of thunderclaps, the last class of the last day ended. A semester's worth of notes rendered into confetti rose high in the air and fell to litter the dark tile floor.

Ten minutes later, silence reigned in the building. The next two days' testing sessions would be different, blessedly quiet and probably with no unwelcome drama. That master of drama, my nemesis, Denver Armstrong, had been absent for the past week. I thought it unlikely that he'd show up tomorrow for the exam. On the downside, that meant he'd fail American Literature, a course required for graduation, and be back on my class list in the fall. Unhappy thought.

Shades of next school year aside, the end of the second semester was always a happy time. I likened it to tying a bright festive ribbon around a box filled to the top with triumphs and failures and memories. In the fall I'd begin again with a new box. In the meantime, the lazy summer days beckoned. I planned to enjoy every single one.

Slinging my purse over my shoulder, which was still tender from sunburn, I grabbed my grade book and opened the sliding door to Leonora's room.

"That's over," she said with a sigh as she closed the last window. "My class went berserk toward the end."

If that were true, they'd done it quietly. I hadn't heard a sound over the din in my own classroom. But her floor, like mine, was layered with confetti, and desks were pushed out of their neat rows.

"I'm really tired today," Leonora confessed.

You'd never guess it. In her beige shirtwaist dress and orange beads she looked as fresh and crisp as she had this morning. Blondes always look fresh and crisp, I thought. I felt like a wilted plant.

"It's the heat," I said.

Only a few areas of the school were air-conditioned. The science labs and the front office, of course, where Principal Grimsley took refuge from the heat behind his desk. The rest of us sweltered.

We walked through the halls, bits of paper sliding under our feet, without seeing another soul. In the parking lot a few abandoned balloons flew free through the thick air.

"That's how I feel," Leonora said. "Wondrously free."

I watched an unlucky red balloon sail recklessly into a maple tree and get stuck. It struggled, but the branches held it fast. Poor balloon. Its flying days were over.

It reminded me of Brent's fleet of hot air balloons, of the *Sky Dancer* exploding in the air, of dreams with wings.

Sometimes free isn't all that wonderful.

~ * ~

I couldn't get away from balloons.

Dozens of them in all colors moved languidly back and forth in the breeze at the Rescue League's yard sale. They were tied to every table and the lower branches of the maple tree in front of Liz' house. The girls had set up their lemonade stand again in the same place, and new merchandise adorned the outer fringes of the yard to lure a new wave of bargain seekers.

Sending a contradictory message were the several 'Do Not Touch' and 'Children <u>Must</u> Be Accompanied By An Adult' signs on the tables containing breakable objects. At least a dozen customers had already descended on the sale.

Liz greeted us with open arms—literally. "Jennet! Leonora! Thank goodness. Everyone except Sue and Laurence DeVille found something else to do today."

She waved her volunteer list in her face, like a fan. "Beach dates, allergies, unexpected company, poison ivy... I never heard such a litany of lies. Commitment is meaningless these days."

"We can only stay for two hours," Leonora said quickly, which was the time we'd signed up for.

We had luncheon plans at the Spirit Lamp Inn, after which Leonora had a date with Deputy Sheriff Jake Brown.

"So there'll only be five of us working the sale?" Leonora asked.

"Three, really. Sue is going to stay on the porch guarding the cash box, and DeVille drove to Ellentown to pick up a litter."

"An entire litter?"

"Six sweet innocent collie puppies from an unplanned breeding. It's a disgrace, but hopefully we'll find homes for them. They're so cute at that age."

Liz had been unloading donations from a box and arranging a set of Albert Payson Terhune books around a framed print of a tricolor collie and a pony. "Does six dollars sound right for the books?" she asked.

"It's hard to tell," I said.

They were in fair condition with no jackets and smudged covers, but there was a nice assortment that would complete somebody's Terhune collection. Or serve as an introduction to the heroic

Sunnybank collies for a small child. The small child who was banned from attending the sale unless he was accompanied by an adult.

"Start with six dollars," I said. "See how they sell and adjust the price."

"What do you want us to do?" Leonora asked.

"Circulate. Watch that nobody pockets the smaller objects. Say something nice about the collie stuff."

"We can do that," I said, longing for Liz to finish stacking the donated books on the table so I could peruse the titles.

As Leonora and I drifted away toward a line of small furniture, I said, "Be on the lookout for anyone acting suspicious."

Since the thefts appeared to be common knowledge among League members, I'd told Leonora about them. "This is our best chance to catch the thief," I said. "It may be our only chance."

"He wouldn't dare strike again."

"Or she. It's mostly women at these sales. I think there's a good chance somebody will try to steal something with so few people in charge. So we have to be extra vigilant."

That was easier said than done. The crowd increased, and the temperature soared. Customers and lookers milled around like students out of their assigned seats and soon began to look alike to me. Dressed in jeans and Capris, stretchy tops and flip flops, they complained about the heat and the prices and even the quality of the homemade lemonade.

I kept a lookout for the belligerent woman from the last sale who had threatened to sue the League for child abuse, but didn't see her, or her obnoxious little boy, or any child at all. Liz' warnings had taken effect.

In a quiet moment, I chose a set of collie coasters for myself and one of the Terhune books and took them up to Sue.

"How's business?" I asked.

"Good. Better than the last sale. I hope we can unload some of this stuff. We need the money so badly."

"The new puppies should bring in adoption fees," I said. "I hope they're healthy and…"

I broke off, my attention riveted on a woman in an aqua sundress with auburn hair piled on top of her head and long turquoise earrings.

"What's wrong?" Liz asked.

"That woman looking at the hats. I know her."

"So do I," Liz said, "and I wish I didn't. She's a total—uh—witch. That's Mrs. DeVille."

Forty

"Cruella?"

"No, Charlotte. Hey, I never made the Disney connection. That's funny."

"I know her by a different name," I said. "Linnea Haver."

"Of the haunted Haver House? But Linnea Haver is dead. She died last year in a car accident."

"So I found out later."

"I don't understand. Why would Charlotte DeVille use a false name?"

Why indeed?

"I didn't realize Laurence DeVille had a wife," I said. "He acts like a single man."

"He's a married flirt. DeVille usually goes places alone. Charlotte isn't interested in collie rescue or anything else. Just herself."

"Why did you call her a witch?" I asked.

"Because she has a mean streak. She's snooty and totally unpleasant. Any number of reasons. I advise you to steer clear of her."

Unfortunately that wouldn't be possible.

At present Mrs. DeVille was about five yards away from me trying on a pink sun hat in front of a mirror. I started to weave my way through a surge of shoppers, avoiding sandaled feet and bodies that clogged the makeshift aisles Liz had attempted to create.

Someone grabbed my arm, a woman wearing oversized sunglasses with yards of yellow material wrapped around her heavy-set body. "Excuse me, Miss, do you have any baby clothes?"

I had no idea but didn't think so. "Look over there," I said. "By the lemonade stand."

"I'm trying to find little shirts with pictures of collies on them and maybe matching caps. It's for a shower gift. Oh, and fabric flowers. Do you have them?"

"Yes, well, whatever we have is out on the tables."

I turned and saw a speck of turquoise walking down the street. In those few minutes, my quarry had escaped. Could she have seen and recognized me or simply decided that the yard sale held nothing to tempt her?

I could hardly leave my post and run after her.

The pink hat had been tossed carelessly down on top of the others. I stopped to turn it right side up and give it back its proper place on the table.

If the woman who called herself Linnea Haver was Laurence DeVille's wife, it should be fairly easy to find her again, and I intended to do so.

~ * ~

In the light of a sunny June afternoon, the Spirit Lamp Inn shed its mystique and otherworldly ambience. Sunlight streamed through every sparkling window, and the furniture gleamed. The waitresses wore new uniforms—crisp pink gingham with ruffly white aprons. Very appealing, very country. Not one of them looked familiar. I'd never known a restaurant to have such a turnover in wait staff.

"What are you going to say to Charlotte DeVille?" Leonora asked as we sat over sandwiches and iced tea.

"Ask her why she pretended to be Linnea Haver and told me that fantastic story about her sister disappearing in the wildflower meadow."

"That could be dangerous."

"It depends on what she's up to. Mrs. DeVille is definitely tied to the Haver place. She had a key."

"Maybe she has a legitimate claim to it. What if she's the heir?"

"That won't explain the lies."

Leonora took the red plastic pick out of her sandwich, and it began to fall apart, a quarter of toast leading the way for a slice of tomato. She reached for her fork. "How are you going to find her?"

"Sue Appleton will have addresses for the League members. I'll assume Charlotte DeVille lives with her husband."

"When you track her down, I'd better go with you," Leonora said. "Just in case there's trouble."

"I'll call Sue as soon as I get home."

"School's out and the mystery is heating up."

"Which gives us plenty of time to go sleuthing at leisure," I said.

~ * ~

I reckoned without other complications. Brent appeared at the door that evening in time for dinner. It was unusual for him not to bring a contribution to our meal or table.

On his way to the grill, Crane quickly added a third steak to the plate.

"Not for me," Brent said. "I don't want anything to eat."

"Nonsense. You'll join us. Crane's cooking, and I baked a fresh peach pie for dessert."

"I came to tell you the curse is alive," he said.

He could only be referring to *Ada's Litter*. I thought we'd heard the last of that infernal painting.

"What happened?" I asked.

"It's Eskimo. Another one of my animals was stricken. This has a cause, though. It's carelessness, pure and simple."

I closed the door, and the dogs danced around him as he found his way to his favorite chair. Sky and Misty settled at his feet. I waited, thinking of that magnificent white horse and his lively dark eyes.

"Since when are you careless with your animals?" I asked.

"Since never. It was Jay, a new kid I hired. Said he knew all about horses. Grew up with them. All lies. Or if he knew better, he just didn't care."

"Well, what happened?"

"It's called scratches," he said. "Jay put Eskimo in his stall when his legs were still wet. His ankles got inflamed. It looks terrible."

That didn't sound so serious to me. Apparently it was.

"Can it be cured?" I asked.

"The others are drying them now and putting medication on. He's on oral meds too. He should be better in a week. I let Jay go," he added. "Putting a horse in his stall with wet legs is a violation of Horsemanship 101."

A chill seemed to settle in the room, the kind of chill that couldn't be warmed by a ninety-degree temperature outside. It told of awaiting disaster and deep secluded graves.

"Did you bury the painting's ashes?" I asked.

"Deep in the ground, far away from the stables…miles from my house."

"Well, then… Eskimo is going to be all right?"

"It's going to happen again," he said. "Something. Sometime."

"Maybe there's a waiting period for a curse to die?"

Crane came in from the grill and sat with us. He glanced at the clock, then at me. I knew I wasn't making sense, but when had the haunted painting ever made sense?

"I suppose people make mistakes," I said, remembering the package of marshmallows tossed in a game during the bonfire. "Especially young people."

"Jay is twenty, Jennet. I know what you're saying, but you can't afford to make mistakes around animals you love. Would you forget and leave Misty locked in a hot car? Or go out for the day and leave the dogs' water dishes empty?"

I shuddered. "Not if you loved them. Obviously Jay didn't. It's too bad you have so many horses. One or two, and you could take care of them yourself."

"Yes, and I was going to expand. If I'd lost Eskimo like I lost the *Sky Dancer*..."

He trailed off.

"You said Eskimo is on his way to recovery."

"I was arrogant and stubborn," he said. "I didn't want to admit that an insentient object made of wood and canvas and oil paint had supernatural powers. It went against everything I believed in, and so I waited. Too long."

This was a new, defeatist Brent, one I didn't recognize. But the quickest way to wear a person down, the most direct route to his heart, was through the animals he loved. Napoleon. Eskimo. One on his way to recovery. The other... I wasn't sure about Napoleon.

"Let's try to counteract this so-called curse with faith, good wishes, courage, medicine... Anything in our arsenal."

I wasn't exactly sure what that meant in a practical application, but it sounded good, and when Crane served the steaks and I brought out the salad—which were the only two items on the dinner menu—Brent seemed to look a little happier.

Forty-one

After Brent left, I found myself wondering whether *Ada's Litter* had any gruesome surprises in store for me. I thought of all the time I'd kept the painting on the buffet, leaning against the wall but not hanging on it, inviting disaster until it finally came in the form of flames and destruction. A fire that could have been fatal if Candy hadn't alerted us to danger.

All that time my collies were in harm's way.

"What's the matter, honey?" Crane asked.

I told him.

"I'm not convinced what happened to Eskimo has anything to do with a curse," he said. "Although for some reason I don't understand, that painting is bad luck."

I agreed with him. Brent might be over reacting. Not about Eskimo, but about the curse.

"I work with kids a little younger than Jay," I said. "I know how unreliable they can be. In Journalism, for example, they lose ad copy, they miss deadlines. You name it. Some of my second year students still can't grasp the concept of *deadline*."

"They'd learn soon enough if they had jobs on a real newspaper," Crane said.

"So Eskimo is the victim of a young stable hand's carelessness. Napoleon may get better and Brent's bite… I didn't notice it."

"Neither did I. Maybe it's gone."

"Certainly *Ada's Litter* is gone. That reminds me, I should let Aura Lee Larkin know what happened to her painting."

She would be happy that it had been tossed onto a bonfire. I also wanted to hear her thoughts on any lingering effects. On this subject I was more than a little paranoid.

Usually when I talked over a matter that disturbed me with Crane, or Camille, or Leonora, I felt better about it. Not this time.

My runaway imagination saw *Ada's Litter* impossibly restored to wholeness and life, rising out of the ground, waiting to beguile another owner with its sentimental charm.

All foolishness. After a long hot day, after my stint at the yard sale, I was tired, impressionable. I'd have to share the idea with Lucy. She could turn it into an award-winning novel for young readers.

"Try not to worry," Crane said, exhibiting once again his ability to read my mind. "The painting isn't coming back."

"I'll try," I promised him; and I meant it. The reign of the haunted painting was over. At last. *Evil, RIP.*

~ * ~

That night I dreamed. but not about paintings rising from the ground. I was driving in the fog, lost in a part of Foxglove Corners I had never explored. Unfamiliar country roads.

Take me home…

Instead they took me to a meadow where wildflowers of all kinds grew to so gigantic a size they appeared to have sprung from alien seeds.

How can I see flowers in the fog?

This is a dream. Anything is possible.

Like the cobalt blue door, visible in the total white-out, partially, tantalizingly open. All I had to do was step over the threshold and I'd know all the secrets. For instance, why Eskimo was housed in the barn, along with Breezy.

I was out of the car, moving on, crushing down plants, pushing the taller ones out of my way. On through undulating waves of white condensation.

"Stop! Don't go any farther!"

It was a familiar voice. I hadn't heard it in a long time, but I recognized it. Terra Roman was speaking to me from her grave.

I came awake with a start, my heart pounding, ribbons of moonlight pouring through the window. The dream was wrong.

How could a dream be wrong?

Terra had been cremated, her ashes scattered over Lake Huron. She didn't reside in an actual grave.

But a dream can be whatever it chooses to be. It can mix elements and end in mid-scene, as this one had.

Terra would still have a voice.

No, she wouldn't.

I turned in the bed. Crane lay beside me, sleeping deeply. Crane who had told me not to worry. He couldn't tell me not to dream.

For the love of heaven, go back to sleep. Try to analyze a dream that's already dissipating, try even to remember it, and you'll be awake for hours. There's school tomorrow...

No, school's out. Still, I wanted to get more rest.

At times, dreams tell you something you can't figure out in your waking hours. My mother had believed that. Lucy Hazen believed it too. In the Bible, angels were always sending people warnings in their dreams.

Tomorrow I'd go back to the meadow where the alien wildflowers grew and see if I could find the blue door.

~ * ~

"I've been thinking," Leonora said the next day as we waited for Annica to bring our pancake breakfast. "You can't go to Charlotte DeVille's house and start interrogating her. She'd slam the door in your face. Maybe call the police. That's what I'd do."

"I don't plan to be belligerent. I'll have to think of a subterfuge."

"You can say you're collecting dog food for the Rescue League."

"As Laurence's wife, she'd know we don't do that. Besides, Liz says Charlotte DeVille doesn't care about collie rescue."

"Let's see, then. We could meet her on neutral territory, accidentally on purpose."

"Like the yard sale. Too bad it's over. For a second I thought I was seeing a ghost. Then I didn't have time to react."

Leonora sighed. "An accidental meeting is impossible. We don't know her habits, where she goes, anything about her except that Liz thinks she's a witch."

"I could invite the two of them somewhere as a couple, but she didn't accompany Laurence to Sue's barbeque," I said.

"That was for members."

Annica set our pancake plates in front of us and slipped into an empty seat with a cup of coffee for herself.

"I'm taking a break," she said, with a clink of her seashell earrings as she settled herself. She looked like a creature from the sea this morning, in a dress of pale blue with her hair flowing in red swirls over her shoulders.

"What are you talking about?" she asked.

I drenched my pancake stack with maple syrup and began eating while Leonora explained our brainstorming session. "We have to question Laurence DeVille's wife in a way that won't antagonize her. To make it more difficult, we don't know her."

"I know where they live," I said, "but I can't just show up without a good reason."

Suddenly I thought of one.

"Laurence went to Ellentown to pick up a litter of collie puppies yesterday. They're probably still at his house. I'll ask to look over the litter for a friend who wants to adopt one."

"Why wouldn't this friend pick out her own puppy?" Annica asked.

The idea began to take shape in my mind. "She can't. She lives in Ohio and doesn't want to drive all this way unless the League has exactly what she wants."

"That's good," Leonora said. "But don't we usually take the puppies to a vet first and put their pictures up on the League's website?"

"Usually, but being a member of the League, I'm going to claim special privileges for my friend."

"And this friend... What kind of puppy does she want?"

"I'll make it simple. A healthy sable and white female with a good temperament."

"Then you'll have to ask your real questions diplomatically," Annica said.

"I'll be surprised to see Linnea Haver again. This should work."

"If she's home," Leonora pointed out.

"And if Laurence is home alone?"

"Then I'll think of something else. I'll play it by ear."

It was going to work. I felt certain of it, and as soon as we finished breakfast, we'd drive to Lakeville and look for the address Sue had given me.

Forty-two

The house was on Kendall Boulevard, a red brick ranch with a yellow-sided second story that looked as if it had been added on as an afterthought. Probably that was what had happened as it towered over its neighbors.

The front lawn was bare in places and burned yellow; the shrubs grew in every direction obliterating their natural shape. The geraniums in the hanging basket were crying out for water, and the blinds in the front windows were drawn.

In all, the house had a discontented look.

"This is the address," I said, slipping the piece of paper back in my purse. "I hope Mrs. DeVille is home." I rang the doorbell and waited.

"I don't see a fence." Leonora peered around the side of the house. "How can Laurence keep his rescues here even for a day?"

"And I don't hear any puppies yapping."

The neighborhood was steeped in the deep silence of a hot summer afternoon, the only sound, the hum of air conditioners. One was running inside the house. I rang the bell again

The door opened halfway, and Linnea Haver—also known as Charlotte DeVille—stood before me. She wore a white sundress and the most unpleasant expression I'd seen in a long time. Her hair, twisted into a simple bun, was coming undone, but it was her shiny blue nail polish that captured my attention. It made her hands look predatory. Like claws.

"No soliciting," she said sharply.

Remembering the part I'd given myself to play, I feigned astonishment.

"Linnea Haver! I didn't think I'd ever see you again. I tried so hard to find you. There's something you have to know about your barn."

She stared at me, not the slightest hint of recognition in her eyes. She was a good actress.

Oddly, I detected a glint of contempt in that hard stare. It was almost as if she had known me at some forgotten time in my past, as if I had thwarted her in some way, which was impossible.

"I'm not Linnea Haver," she said. "You have the wrong house."

The door began to close.

"We met a few weeks ago at the old Haver House on Deer Leap Trail," I said. "You told me about your sister, Grace. About how she disappeared in the meadow."

I was good too.

"I have no idea what you're talking about," she said. "I'm Mrs. Laurence DeVille, and I don't know anyone named Linnea Haver. Now if you'll excuse me..."

The door was closing.

"There's something else," Leonora said quickly.

I reminded myself of my excuse. The puppies. By now I was truly curious about them.

"It's uncanny, but you resemble someone I know," I said. "They say that everybody has a double out there in the world."

She didn't respond. Just stared.

Undaunted, I continued. "Actually I came for another reason. I'm Jennet, and my friend is Leonora. We're from Collie Rescue. Liz mentioned that your husband brought a litter of collie puppies down from Ellentown. I have a friend who wants to adopt a sable female, and I'd like to see… "

Again she stared at me, eyes hard and contemptuous. Her hand with those blue nails tightened around the doorknob.

"There are no puppies here," she said. "I don't like dogs."

"But you're Laurence DeVille's wife?"

"So I said."

"What happened to the litter then?" I asked.

"I have nothing more to say to you. Good day."

She slammed the door in my face.

"That did not go well," Leonora said. "Let's get out of here before she calls the police."

We hurried to the car. I only hoped she wasn't inside looking through the window, jotting down my license plate number. But I had nothing to worry about. We hadn't done anything illegal.

"I don't understand any of this," I said.

I started the car and drove to the end of the boulevard where I made a right turn. Soon I would be in a familiar section of Lakeville, far away from Charlotte DeVille.

After a while, Leonora said, "Are you sure that incident at the Haver house really happened? Because it sounded pretty strange when you told me about it."

"Of course I'm sure. She drove up while I was at the barn and demanded to know what I was doing on her property. We introduced ourselves and sat in the kitchen drinking bottled water. She told me how her sister had disappeared while planting the meadow. She heard the weeping too."

It was important that I capture every detail of the memory. I desperately needed vindication because just for a second I was beginning to wonder.

Could I possibly have made a mistake? This woman, Laurence DeVille's wife, looked like the person who had identified herself as Linnea Haver. But the encounter at Haver House had been a while ago. At the yard sale, I'd seen her from a distance. A woman with auburn hair, possibly tinted. On neither occasion had I noticed the color of her eyes, which were blue and as hard as stones.

Give her the benefit of a doubt, I thought.

"It happened," I said.

"If you say so."

But did it? Or had that strange, strange place woven a spell around me, giving an imagined incident the colors of reality? Was, I, in other words, losing my grip on sanity?

No. Everything about that day was too real. The noxious taste of warm water, dust motes floating in the air, the story of a thin air disappearance, the fragrance of a thousand wild flowers drifting in through the open window...

I caught myself in time. There had been no flower fragrance, no open window. The air inside the Haver House had been close and stuffy, barely breathable, exactly what one would expect in a house closed up for a long period of time.

"You're always seeing ghosts," Leonora said.

"Not always."

"Okay. Often, then. Maybe you saw the spirit of Linnea Haver."

"Who happens to be a mirror image of Charlotte DeVille."

I glanced at her, noting the mischievous smile.

"You saw a zombie," she said.

"That's something Annica would say. We should stop at Clovers again and get her input."

There was a stop sign ahead. I knew where we were.

"I saw Charlotte DeVille at the Haver property, no matter what she says," I said. "She chooses to deny it. Why?"

"That's one more mystery to solve."

The whole affair, including today's visit, was odd, yes, but I refused to start doubting myself. Something else was going on. The encounter at Haver House aside, what I needed to do as soon as possible was to check with Sue Appleton.

Supposedly Laurence DeVille had left the yard sale to drive to Ellentown, a fair distance from Lakeville, and bring back a litter of unwanted collie puppies to place in Rescue.

Where were they?

Forty-three

Sue Appleton leaned on the redwood plank fence that enclosed her horse farm. Her fair skin was burning beneath the flowing gauzy top she wore, but she didn't seem to be aware of it. I'd told her what Leonora and I had discovered at the DeVille house. Not about my suspicion that Charlotte DeVille had masqueraded as the deceased Linnea Haver, though. That was a separate matter.

"I don't understand," Sue said.

"That makes two of us."

"Laurence DeVille should have five collies at his house, not counting the new litter," she said. "That's eleven dogs."

"Laurence's wife claims they don't have any," Leonora said.

"Not exactly." I didn't like to correct Leonora, but in this case, details were important. "She said there were no puppies. There's no fence around the yard and no noise. My guess is that there aren't any dogs in that house."

"But you're not sure," Sue said.

"Pretty sure. What dog doesn't bark when somebody comes to the door? And Mrs. DeVille came right out and said she doesn't like dogs."

"Where are Laurence's collies then?"

"Could he have found homes for them and neglected to tell you?" Leonora asked.

Sue bristled. I imagined she was mentally skewering the absent DeVille.

"That would be contrary to our procedure. The adoptive owner pays for the dog. The money goes straight into the treasury." She frowned. "Laurence hasn't turned in any money for ages, but every now and then he tells a funny anecdote about one of his dogs or mentions a problem. Naturally I assumed he still had them all."

Meanwhile the treasury was virtually empty.

"Five collies at two hundred and fifty dollars a dog amounts to over a thousand dollars," I said. "That's more money missing."

Sue stepped back from the fence and pushed a strand of hair out of her eyes. "It never occurred to me to check on the League members and their foundlings. I don't think Terra ever inquired either, and there was never any trouble."

She must have, I thought. Otherwise the operation would have spiraled out of control.

"Who decides which dogs go to which League member?" I asked.

"There are volunteer lists," Sue said. "We've always been informal in the League. Usually people keep the dogs they rescue, if they can. If not, Terra found foster homes for them."

"And they should report each rescue?"

"Yes, so I can keep a record of every collie from rescue to adoption. We keep that information to update our website."

"So the collies Laurence had would be described on the website. They'd be available for adoption?"

"That's how it works."

"What would happen if someone was interested in one of Laurence's collies and he couldn't produce the dog?"

Instead of dealing with that tricky question, Sue gazed into an azure blue sky as if to find the truth in its depths. "Not everyone is free or willing to drive miles out of town to pick up surrendered collies. Laurence has always been generous with his SUV and gas. Not to mention his time."

"Still, you have to investigate him," I said, "because something doesn't add up. How did you learn about the Ellentown litter?

"From Laurence. A friend of his alerted him to their plight."

"Which means it might not be true. But why would he lie about rescuing a litter?"

It didn't make sense. If Laurence had his own agenda, why would he tell Sue about the puppies in the first place? Did he want Sue to think he was doing his job as collie rescuer when he was doing the opposite?

"I'm going to believe there's a good explanation for all this until I know otherwise," Sue said. "I just remembered. Laurence mentioned that he had one of those invisible fences installed."

"All right. So he has a fence. There's still Mrs. DeVille. How can he bring rescues home when his wife doesn't like dogs?"

"That woman doesn't like anything except herself. But you have a point, Jennet. Then there's the question of the depleted treasury. I just hope Laurence isn't the guilty party. He's been such a strong supporter of the League. I don't know how we'd operate without him."

Leonora glanced longingly toward the car. "I should be getting home."

"Me too." I was suddenly aware of how tired I was. I was discouraged too, feeling that the Lakeville Collie Rescue League had failed me and the dogs.

With Terra's murder, the League had begun to fray at the edges. Now the tear was larger and might ruin the entire fabric. I hoped that wasn't the case, but it didn't look promising.

Missing money. Missing dogs. Possibly a broken trust. A litter of collie puppies unaccounted for. The babies were the ones I was thinking about.

"I'll find out what's going on," Sue said.

~ * ~

Leaving the current mystery in Sue's hands, I dropped Leonora off at her house and drove home to give the collies an hour of playtime before dinner. But the day was hot and the air heavy with humidity. Soon they were congregating at the kitchen door, panting and wanting to go back inside.

Candy punctuated her desire with a soulful howl.

I poured the last of the lemonade and checked my notebook. 'Call Aura Lee Larkin' topped the list. Taking my drink into the living room, I dialed her number and was surprised when she answered, being used to setbacks.

"Jennet," she said. "I was just thinking about you."

I told her about Brent's belief that the curse had been responsible for the recent problem with Eskimo and about the bonfire.

"I'm so glad the painting is gone," she said. "And I don't see how it can make a stable hand neglect a horse's care. But then I didn't understand how I created a monster either. There is something, though. Do you remember Margaret?"

"The girl in the painting. Sure."

Aura Lee considered Margaret the source of the evil that permeated *Ada's Litter*. For her own demented reason, Margaret had set fire to her family home, killing her family—most of it anyway. Since that time, she'd been living in an institution.

"What about Margaret?" I asked when Aura Lee remained silent.

"I've heard she's very ill. They don't expect her to live much longer."

"That poor unhappy woman. What does that mean for those of us who owned *Ada's Litter*?"

"I'm not sure. Maybe nothing, but I thought you'd want to know."

The painting had been destroyed. If Margaret died, surely the last seed of evil would die too. *Margaret, RIP. Evil, RIP.* Did she still think the collie Ada was alive and with her? I hoped somewhere, somehow, they'd find each other.

I might as well challenge Fate.

"I don't intend to worry," I said. "And I hope Brent doesn't either. It's high time the curse, or whatever it was, to be over."

But I half hoped Fate wasn't listening.

Forty-four

The dogs saw Sue Appleton walking on Jonquil Lane before I did. Candy and Raven dashed off the porch to give her a traditional collie greeting and escort her the rest of the way to the house.

She sank into a wicker chair and smiled at Misty who dropped a blue ball in her lap. It was the least enthusiastic smile I'd ever seen. She looked as discouraged as I'd felt yesterday when we'd discussed the DeVilles.

"I'm afraid I found our bad apple," she said.

Anticipating what she was going to say next, I waited for the details.

"I went to visit Laurence DeVille today," she said. "No one was home. There were no dogs barking and no invisible fence. You were right about that, Jennet. There's a 'For Sale' sign in the front yard. The house is offered by Three Lakes Realtors."

"So fast? I was just there yesterday."

But Leonora and I had stood on the porch the entire time. If the house was empty of furniture, we wouldn't have known it. And thank heavens Leonora had accompanied me or I'd begin to doubt that encounter had really taken place.

"He may have left town with the League's money," I said.

"It looks that way."

"But there could still be a rational explanation for his behavior."

"For his lies? For the non-existent invisible fence? I tried to go through it. Nothing stopped me." She tossed Misty's ball into the front yard, and Candy, Misty, and Raven bounded down the porch steps in pursuit.

"I wonder how long this has been going on," she said. "If only I could talk to Terra. She'd know what to do."

"Well, you can't. You're president now."

Candy, who had captured Misty's ball, dropped it at Sue's feet. How nice to be a dog and let others worry about the welfare of the canine race.

"I took the pictures and introductions of the collies Laurence was supposed to have off the website," Sue said. "What do you suppose happened to them?"

"I've dealt with dog thieves before," I said quietly.

"But Laurence… I can't believe he'd stoop that low. He said he wanted to be involved in collie rescue."

"That's a good place to be for a dog thief." Even as I spoke, I felt a trifle uneasy about indicting DeVille in his absence. "Maybe we shouldn't leap to the worst scenario. What if he placed them in forever homes himself and kept the money? That's bad enough. but not as horrible as selling dogs for nefarious purposes."

"Nefarious purpose. We both know what they are. I guess it's my nature to assume the worst. Since he just took off without a word to anyone, what else can I think?"

It was time to throw in one of my favorite sayings. "Forewarned is forearmed. I'm glad we caught on to DeVille's game when we did."

"When you and Leonora did," Sue said. "I didn't have a clue."

"I never liked the man, but I didn't have any premonitions about him. He was just so loud and obnoxious. As for his wife…"

I needed to tell Sue everything I knew about Charlotte DeVille. In my opinion, it was no longer a separate matter.

"A few weeks ago I met Mrs. DeVille out at the old Haver place on Deer Leap Trail. She gave me to understand that her name was Linnea Haver, and she had a key to the house. Yesterday she denied it ever happened. By the way, Linnea Haver died a year ago."

"Oh, no," Sue said. "This is more involved than I thought. What do you make of that?"

"Nothing yet. Give me time. What are you going to do about Laurence?" I asked.

"Go to the police. Report a swindle. Or should I call it a scam?"

"Whatever you call it, if the DeVilles are gone, the money's gone with them. The collies are gone, too, and the puppies…"

"With everything I've found out, who knows if there ever were any puppies? But DeVille's five rescues are real. If anything bad happened to them, I don't know what I'll do. It's just so unfair. They came from horrible situations and were supposed to go to good homes eventually."

"I'll do anything I can to help you," I said. "Crane is a deputy sheriff and I know Lieutenant Mac Dalby of the Foxglove Corners Police Department."

Maybe I shouldn't have mentioned Mac. Like Crane, he didn't approve of my meddling in police matters. He could be condescending and difficult, for all that he was Crane's best friend. Well, this wasn't a police matter yet, and maybe Mac would say there was nothing he could do to find the DeVilles and get back our dogs and our money.

After all, what proof did we have that Laurence had done anything wrong? It would be his word against ours.

"No one will ever trust us with a collie they can't keep again," Sue said. "I think it's time for the League to fold. I know I'm a failure as president."

"This didn't start with you," I pointed out. "Terra was oblivious, too. DeVille was clever to infiltrate the League and ingratiate himself with the members."

We were rapidly sinking into gloom, which was no way to proceed.

"I have sun tea," I said. "Let's relax and brainstorm. Our first order of business is to find out what happened to Laurence's rescues. Then we'll see if we can figure out where he went."

~ * ~

My assignment was to go back to Kendall Boulevard and interview the DeVille's neighbors. Meanwhile, Sue would contact the dog pounds and shelters in the area. It didn't seem likely that DeVille would turn around and leave a dog in a shelter. Where would be the profit in that? But it was all we could think of.

The next morning, I took Candy and Misty with me as icebreakers and drove to Kendall Boulevard.

Finding neighbors home proved to be virtually impossible, but finally I came across a friendly woman, Mrs. Clayton, watering her plants. As I'd hoped, she was a dog lover. She stopped her work to admire my collies and talk to them.

Mrs. Clayton knew Laurence DeVille slightly, having run into him with one collie on one occasion. She had been walking past his house while he was trying to coax a timorous collie into his SUV.

"He was losing patience with her," Mrs. Clayton said. "I felt so sorry for the poor dog."

That was a side of DeVille I'd never seen, but it fit with the emerging picture of the man.

"She was such a pretty little Lassie dog. Very thin and skittish. She wouldn't let me pet her. Then he picked her up and threw her inside like she was a sack of potatoes."

I winced at the image her words created. "Didn't you object?"

"It wasn't my dog. What could I do?"

I could think of several responses. But I said, "You saw only one dog? I thought he had five."

"You can't have five dogs in Lakeville," she said.

I knew many people broke that law. Usually they got away with it unless someone was determined to prove they were harboring more dogs than the city allowed.

The skittish collie sounded like a rescue. DeVille should have been coaxing her out of the car, not into it. Where was he taking her?

I was afraid of that answer.

"Did you ever see the collie again?" I asked.

"No, but I'm too busy to sit around and spy on my neighbors," she said, picking up her watering can. "Anyway, I see the house is for sale. I guess the people are gone. I heard they were just renters. So it doesn't matter, does it?"

There was no one left to ask. At this time of day people would be at work, possibly on vacation or simply not answering the door to a stranger. I counted four houses for sale on the block besides the DeVille place.

Whatever the reason, the boulevard was singularly quiet. Doors remained closed, blinds and drapes and curtains covered windows. There was nothing sinister about the dearth of activity on the boulevard; it only felt that way.

Defeated I walked back to my car and drove out of Lakeville. There didn't seem to be anything more to learn in DeVille's previous neighborhood.

~ * ~

Sue was despondent. "I've called every dog pound and shelter in this part of the state. No one has DeVille's collies."

"And all I have is an eyewitness account of Laurence coaxing a female collie into his SUV. The neighbor I questioned doesn't remember seeing any other collies on the boulevard."

"That must have been Clover. She'd been abused when she came to Rescue."

"Did you call the police?" I asked.

"Your friend, Lieutenant Dalby, was out, and the officer I talked to wasn't very helpful."

"There's not a lot they can do at this point," I said. "I think you should call another meeting of the League. An emergency meeting."

"I'll have to do that, but not just yet. I'm going to meet Liz later today. Hopefully she'll have some ideas."

"Let me know what she says," I said.

I suspected Sue still hoped we could find DeVille and recover the missing dogs and the stolen cash. I didn't share her optimism, and I didn't know what else we could do.

The money had probably already been spent, and the collies… Well, in all likelihood the collies were gone. Poor abused Clover and the others. I swallowed a giant-sized lump in my throat, felt tears run down my face.

Halley whimpered and pressed her body against mine. My dear first collie, the most sensitive and intuitive one. Misty, my puppy, brought me her ball, confident that it would cheer me.

Why hadn't I been able to see Laurence DeVille for the lowlife scum he was?

At the barbecue he had tried to shift the blame for the Rescue League's stolen funds to Terra. Being dead, she made an excellent scapegoat. Lowlife scum always did that.

A surge of anger washed over my tears. If there were still a chance for the collies, I had to be strong, and I had to make DeVille answer for his crimes.

Forty-five

The next night after dinner, I fllled Crane in on DeVille's deception. We sat in the living room with our collies around us, and my desire to help DeVille's canine victims flared to new life.

"It's your word against his," Crane said, "but if this man is stealing and selling dogs, that's illegal. We can nail him on that."

"We have to find him first."

"We?"

"The law, I mean."

"That's better."

"Sue Appleton made out a police report," I said.

"There haven't been any lost dogs in the neighborhood lately, have there? Only the five missing rescues?"

"Not since Breezy."

And the lightning flash collie in the wildflower meadow. Why should I think of that now? It might well have been an imprint of a past animal. In other words, a spirit. Or a trick of the light. Or my imagination.

I'd meant to return to the Haver property someday soon, but life had other plans. The burning of the haunted painting, Brent's horse, Eskimo, and the problems of the Collie Rescue League. Now that nothing dramatic was happening—that is nothing that I knew of— why not drive out to Deer Leap Trail again?

It was tempting. It was also looking for trouble. But to me trouble was the DeVilles, husband and wife. Surely they wouldn't hide so close to Sue's horse farm.

"I wonder why DeVille chose this particular time to run away," I said.

"Maybe his lease on the house was up. The owner wanted to list it."

"In that case, wouldn't he tell Sue and give her his new address? Instead he cut ties with the League and left us with a slew of unanswered questions."

"He couldn't continue to con you indefinitely," Crane pointed out. "In time somebody would have gotten suspicious."

"Now he'll go somewhere else," I said. "He'll offer his services to some other rescue group or shelter and charm them and end up causing more heartache for everyone. Most of all the dogs."

Unless he was stopped.

"Let the police take care of DeVille," Crane said. "You can investigate your ghosts."

I couldn't help smiling. How matter of fact he was when giving me permission to investigate the denizens of the other world.

Or was he being condescending?

I glanced at him as he picked up the *Banner*. I didn't think so. Not tonight.

"Thank you for the idea," I said. "That's what I'll do. Go on a nice old-fashioned ghost hunt and invite Annica to come along with me."

~ * ~

For the first time since she'd opened Clovers, Mary Jeanne intended to close the restaurant for a week's vacation. As this was the last day, the selections in the dessert carousel were sparse, but Annica had saved us two pieces of lemon meringue pie. Life was good.

Annica was elated at the freedom. She claimed her summer course in Restoration Drama was a snap so this was a double vacation for her.

"I don't remember Restoration Drama being a snap," I said. "That wasn't my favorite century."

"To each his own." She tossed her head, and her favorite seashell earrings clinked. "Let's take pictures at the Haver House this time. We may get lucky and catch a ghost on film."

"Okay, and we can have lunch at the Spirit Lamp Inn. That's a pretty ghostly place, but they don't allow cameras."

"Drat," she said. "They want to keep their ghost all to themselves. How incredibly selfish! When can we go?"

"How about tomorrow around noon?"

"It's a date."

I gathered my take-out dinners and wished Mary Jeanne a happy vacation. I was going to miss Clovers' desserts. Well, I'd just have to bake more of my own.

~ * ~

We approached the Haver property at eleven-thirty. From the road, it looked the same as it always had, perhaps a bit more colorful. Dozens of bright hues contrasted sharply with the white house and brown barn. I wondered if Aura Lee Larkin knew about this place, if she'd ever transferred it to canvas.

"So many flowers," Annica said. "I'm surprised someone doesn't pick them."

"This is off the beaten track."

"Not for everybody. It's like this whole meadow is protected somehow. Like we trespass at our own risk."

"Protected by what?" I asked.

"Some magical force."

"Do you still want to stop there after lunch?"

"Well, sure. I was just making an observation."

I thought about what she'd said. The flamboyant colors certainly tempted me to gather a bouquet or transplant one of each of the varieties to my own yard. All those gorgeous wildflowers would bloom and die and appear again next spring stronger and brighter and more invasive than ever.

To protect the ghost that mourned in the meadow.

"I'll take pictures from the porch," Annica said. "The colors will show up beautifully against that old barn. Maybe I can enter it in the *Banner's* Summer Garden Contest."

"It's not your garden," I said.

"Who has to know?"

We left the Haver property behind and came to the crossroads, scene of the accident that had taken the lives of Linnea Haver and her sister, Grace.

To die so close to home… How heartbreaking. Would they have had time to think of their home?

Not if they'd died instantly.

No one knew for certain when the Haver sisters had perished or if one had preceded the other in death. They might have lingered, gone into shock, possibly tried to free themselves from the wreckage.

All on a foggy day.

The air was clear today. the sun bright and the sky pure cerulean. A breeze blew in through the open windows, bringing with it the sweet smells of woods and wild plants and flowers. And just a hint of smoke and ham. Or was it bacon?

We were practically at the Inn's front door.

"Let the fun begin," Annica said.

Forty-six

The dining room of the Spirit Lamp Inn retained the fresh wholesome look I remembered from my birthday dinner. The centerpieces were banana yellow and white carnations, and the waitresses wore peach gingham to match the tablecloths. A ghost would dissolve amidst all the cheer.

To complete the picture, the cook's collie drowsed outside, framed by hydrangea bushes and clearly visible through the window alongside our table. She truly did look like the wounded dog I'd attempted to rescue, although my memory of her had begun to fade.

"I wish we could see the room where the girl disappeared," Annica said.

"We could ask, if I remembered the number."

"Let's ask anyway."

"Why don't we wait and see if our waitress is the talkative kind?"

Miraculously she was. Cheryl brought menus and water and didn't hesitate when Annica quizzed her about the Inn's resident ghost.

"The lady in the blue raincoat?" Cheryl said with a teasing smile. "She comes back to the Inn to look for her traveling companion who vanished one stormy night. But—that's just a story they tell to bring in the paranormal crowd."

"So it isn't true about the disappearance?" I asked.

"That's part of the story. It never happened.

I didn't believe her. There's at least a grain of truth in every legend. "Could we see the room the girls had?"

"Sorry, no. It doesn't exist anymore. The owner remodeled the Inn a couple of decades ago, and the room was absorbed in the process."

"That's too bad," I said. "Think how much a tour would add to the ghostly mystique."

She looked puzzled. "I guess so, but we can't undo the past. The specials today are split pea soup and a ham sandwich on rye," she added.

"Too salty," Annica murmured. "I'd be thirsty all day if I ordered that."

We perused the menu in silence for a half minute in search of a perfect entrée; then Annica said, "What do you think about the room disappearing just like the traveler?"

"It's odd. Why keep the story alive with a key element missing? They can tell us anything they want to. We need to take our own tour of the Inn."

"How do we do that?"

I'd thought about it and come up with a good idea. "Pretend we're writing a feature story about the Inn for the *Banner*. Unless they're as touchy about reporters as they are about amateur photographers, that should work."

"I like it," Annica said. "Or we could just wander up to the next floor and hope everyone stays downstairs?"

I imagined being discovered, being arrested, trying to explain. Crane would be incredulous, Mac condescending. "Do you really want to do that?" I asked.

"Umm, not today."

Outside, the collie got up, stretched, and followed the shade to another part of the yard. We ordered chicken salad sandwiches. When Cheryl brought our lunch, she said, "You were asking about ghosts."

"Yes?"

"You should check out the haunted house down the road, the one that looks like a nursery. The rumors are starting up again."

"What kind of rumors?" I asked.

"They say there are lights in the house when no one's there. They turn themselves on and off."

"What's the point of that?" Annica asked.

"It just happens. Usually you need a hand to turn lights on. These are ghost hands."

"You'd think somebody would investigate," I said. "Vagrants might be camping out there."

"People are superstitious about that place. They don't like to get involved."

"Traveling lights," Annica said. "That sounds like an interesting phenomenon. Her eyes were sparkling with the thrill of the haunt. That is, the hunt.

Mine must be sparkling, too. Any activity at the Haver House was worth investigating.

~ * ~

"Next stop, Haunted Acres," Annica said as I pulled into my usual place near the barn.

"It looks quiet today. Way too quiet."

"Don't ghosts sleep in daytime?" she asked.

"That's vampires. This is an uneasy quiet."

"What does that mean?"

"It's ominous. Something is restless."

I studied the old farmhouse. If ever a structure looked haunted, it was the Haver House. The last storm had brought down a small forest of deadwood, and wind had blown branches onto the porch. The ghostly hand that turned lights on and off hadn't bothered to pick up a broom or rake.

"We're here at the wrong time," I said. "There's no need for lights in the daytime."

"I'll need the sun for my pictures." She climbed the steps to the porch and aimed the camera at the barn.

After taking pictures from several different angles, she said, "I'd like a close-up of the woods, but the flowers in the meadow grow too thick. They're so tall and intimidating."

"Just take one of the house from the barn. A picture won't show mashed flowers."

"Stay where you are, and I'll take one of you in front of the house," she said.

"Wait. I'll hold a few of these larkspurs."

As I bent to pick my makeshift bouquet, a small gleam caught my eye. A coin lay in the shadow of a tall leafy plant. Or jewelry or… I picked it up.

A tag, the kind a dog wears on a collar. It was shaped like a bone. Squinting in the sunlight, I read the writing: *Lakeville* and *Matheson*.

"What did you find?" Leonora asked.

"A dog tag"

"I wonder how long it's been here."

"It looks shiny and new." I slipped the tag into the pocket of my denim skirt. "It's proof. I don't know what it's proof of yet."

But it felt important. In fact, it seemed almost as if I now possessed a crucial missing piece of the meadow puzzle.

Some inner voice urged me to leave this place with my find and regroup. Never one to ignore inner voices, I said, "If you have all the pictures you want, I suggest we go on home. Nothing is going to happen today."

"Some ghost hunt," Annica said. "One dog tag. No spirits, not even a whimper in the meadow, and one ghost story debunked."

"Don't forget you have your pictures. We can come back another day."

In the dusk, I thought. Not too late. When the daylight dims and reality starts to blur. When the unreal shows its face.

She brightened. "And we'll keep coming back until something happens."

Forty-seven

Between my dogs' barking and Leonora's broken sobs, I could barely understand what she was saying. The collies and I were outside where it was uncharacteristically noisy as Gilbert drove his riding mower over the grounds of the yellow Victorian.

With one hand I held the kitchen door open, and the dogs dashed inside, Candy carrying the prized Frisbee in her mouth. Here the hum was somewhat muted, and the tone on the cell phone was clearer.

"It's Wafer," Leonora was saying. "She's so sick."

"What's wrong?"

"She's been throwing up all day. I'm afraid… Do you think she was poisoned?"

Wafer, one of my previous rescues, had been lured out of the woods with Christmas cookies. She still had a claim on my heart, but Leonora had fallen in love with the winsome collie and adopted her. Wafer never strayed far from Leonora's side when they were out of the house.

"How could that happen?" I asked.

"I don't know, but I'm afraid. She hasn't thrown up since I've had her. Could she have eaten some small animal?"

"The way you watch her, I doubt it. You'd better take her to the vet."

"That's why I'm calling," she said. "Could you go with me? I'm afraid to go alone."

This was the third time Leonora had mentioned being afraid. That was unlike her. Under normal circumstances, she could weather any storm calmly and ably. But I knew that when our dogs are concerned, emotion takes over.

"You shouldn't have waited so long to call me," I said.

"I kept hoping she'd get better. I'll drive," she added.

"No, I will. You may need help getting Wafer in the car."

"That's right. She didn't want to walk, and I can't carry her alone."

I glanced at my watch. It was three o'clock. Crane wouldn't be home for four hours, but Camille was. She'd look after the dogs. And dinner? Crane could grill steaks. I'd throw a salad together. There was half a pie left from yesterday for dessert.

"I'll leave now," I said. "You get together a blanket, towels, water, a bowl—whatever you think Wafer will need."

I gave the collies fresh water and biscuits and wrote a quick note for Crane. Now to call Camille, my ever-reliable dog sitter and make sure my cell phone was in my purse. I didn't know when I'd be coming home.

Since Annica and I had visited the Haver acres and I'd found the dog tag, life had slowed down in Foxglove Corners. Brent's horse was on the mend, and I'd stopped worrying about any lingering effects of that haunted painting. In truth, the days verged on boring.

I knew it couldn't last.

~ * ~

When I reached Leonora's pink Victorian house, she and Wafer were on the porch, Leonora sitting on the top step, Wafer wrapped in a blanket lying at her side. The hapless collie looked so still and sick that it broke my heart. Leonora's eyes were red from weeping and her face was flushed. She hadn't even applied lipstick, a rare omission.

"I think she's going to die," Leonora said.

I laid my hand on Leonora's arm. "You can't know that, but she's very sick."

Together we carried Wafer to the Taurus and settled her on the blanket I'd spread in the back seat. Leonora sat beside her, stroking her head. "It's all right, baby," she said softly. "You're going to be all right." To me she said, "She doesn't hear me. Her eyes look funny. They're glazed over."

"Well, she's sick, Leonora. Fasten your seat belt. I'll drive as fast as I dare. And be quiet with her. Don't let her sense that you're upset. We're going to Doctor Foster?"

"I called ahead," Leonora said.

Mentally I mapped out the quickest route to the Foxglove Corners Animal Hospital. Wafer needed a smooth ride, but rural roads were uneven and occasionally rocky, a necessary evil for those who live in the country. As if to prove my point, a large branch materialized in my path. I swerved to avoid it.

Leonora said, "Jennet, we're pretty sure Laurence DeVille is up to no good with the collies. Do you think he hurt Wafer?"

"No," I said quickly. "What I think is that DeVille is selling dogs. Why would he want to make one sick?"

"For revenge? We ruined his business."

"You haven't interacted with him," I said. "He probably doesn't even know who you are, and I'll tell you again. Wafer is never out of your sight. DeVille wouldn't have had the opportunity to toss her a piece of bad meat—if that's what you're thinking."

What I was thinking was equally disturbing. If DeVille wanted revenge, I was his natural target, and I had more dogs than Leonora. Also, had I been too quick to assume the curse of the painting had been neutralized? To be sure, Wafer was Leonora's dog now, but I loved her, and once she'd been mine.

He couldn't know that, though.

Dogs get sick all the time. Sometimes even a top notch veterinarian can't explain a particular illness or disease. And dogs die. That doesn't mean that a curse is working against them.

"How is she doing?" I asked Leonora.

"The same," she said. "Jennet, I can't lose her."

I gave her the only answer possible. "You won't."

~ * ~

Nothing is grimmer than a waiting room when a dear one is in another part of the hospital. Animal or human institution, the fear and suspense are the same.

I could never work for a vet.

Doctor Foster was busy, but she'd taken Wafer into a room as soon as we arrived. Now we sat quietly on a hard wood bench, Leonora like a statue carved in stone. With every passing minute she seemed to grow paler. The adoption crates were empty, the other dogs aloof, and the magazines on the rack uninspiring.

How long had we been waiting without a word?

A canine cry shrieked through the room. A red and white spaniel whimpered and tried to climb up on the bench. His owner scooped him up and set him firmly in her lap. He promptly started squirming to be put down.

"I'm going to call home," I said, and moved to the small vestibule closed off from the rest of the hospital by a door.

Crane answered on the third ring. "Hi, honey. I've been getting worried. Are you still at the vet's?"

"Yes, but Wafer is in a room. They didn't tell us anything yet."

"Don't worry about us," he said. "I took the dogs for a walk, and Camille brought over a casserole. Just keep in touch."

"I will. Goodbye for now."

I slipped the phone back into my purse and glanced out the window. Where had the daylight gone? The air outside had thickened; it had a murky quality. My black Taurus was the only car in the lot. Were we the last clients? Leonora and Wafer and I?

It was only six o'clock, and I should have been getting hungry, but all I felt was a little ill. I had a trace of a headache. No wonder after a mad dash to the hospital and the attendant worry.

I'd eat when we knew that Wafer is going to be okay. When we brought her home. After we rallied our forces for one more defense against the curse that continued to plague us.

No. There was no curse. Just an ordinary canine malady that Alice would diagnose. She'd prescribe medicine, Wafer would recover at home, and I'd stop thinking that every unfortunate happening in my life and the lives of my friends could be attributed to a rogue painting.

Heartened by the knowledge that all would soon be well, I went back to the waiting room to join Leonora.

Forty-eight

Later, after what seemed like hours but couldn't have been, Alice brought a drowsy Wafer out to the now empty waiting room. Alice had already given us the good news. Wafer wasn't going to die.

I never thought she would. Obviously Leonora had.

"Then she wasn't poisoned," Leonora said. "Are you sure, Doctor?"

Alice smiled. "Reasonably sure."

Alice had run tests, prescribed medication for nausea, and told Leonora to watch her carefully and call the hospital the day after tomorrow.

As if Leonora would do anything else.

The bad news was that Alice couldn't tell us what had made Wafer sick. "It could be anything," she said, invoking images of an environment ravaged by pollutants and deadly organisms. "Wafer is a strong dog. I expect her to make a full recovery."

When Alice left us to give Wafer's file to her secretary, Leonora said, "I'll always wonder if Laurence DeVille had something to do with it. Wafer was never sick until we went to see his wife."

"DeVille may be guilty of crimes against canines, but I don't see how we can lay this at his door."

I held Wafer's leash and talked soothingly to her while Leonora wrote a check.

"Now let's get you home, baby," I said. "You and your mistress need a nice long sleep."

Lenora stifled a yawn. "Bringing a dog home from the vet has to be one of life's happiest experiences."

One by one the lights in the animal hospital began to go out. I thought of calling Crane, but I would be home soon. I wondered what kind of casserole Camille had made and whether Crane had already eaten.

I opened the door and stepped out into waves of floating fog. While we'd been inside the hospital, the world had turned white.

Leonora gasped. "Where did that come from?"

"Ground mist," I said. "It's going to be with us for a while. It's thick enough to cut with a knife."

"Did they predict this?" she asked.

"They might have. I didn't pay attention to the forecast this morning."

In the past, being unaware of approaching storms and tornado warnings had gotten me into trouble. But this was just fog. Dense fog to be sure, but I could drive slowly and turn on my lights. I'd have to do that if I hoped to see the road. I couldn't see it now. In fact, I couldn't see the Taurus.

But everything was going to be all right. The worst part of the day was over.

We found the car. I started the engine, turned on the lights, and we stood in a small yellow pool with a wobbly collie between us. Once again we settled Wafer in the back seat. Leonora smoothed the blanket over her and yawned. "I can never thank you enough for coming with me tonight, Jennet. I'd have been lost without you."

She was probably right. I'd never seen Leonora in such a state. "That's what friends are for," I said.

~ * ~

I helped Leonora get Wafer into the house. The collie had reached the end of her endurance. She flopped down in the vestibule and closed her eyes.

"Do you want me to help you carry her to her bed?" I asked.

"I'll leave her here till she's ready to wake up. I'm going to sleep on the sofa tonight."

"If you're sure you're okay, I'll be on my way."

She thanked me again, and I went back out into the fog.

The drive from the animal hospital had been harrowing, slow and strange as we moved through the still, white world. I expected the way home would be the same, but I was anxious to get back to Crane, my own dogs, and the casserole Camille had prepared for us. Now that the crisis had passed, I realized I was hungry.

The route from Leonora's pink Victorian to my house was fairly straightforward. A network of country roads and three turns to Jonquil Lane. In good weather, I would be home in fifteen minutes. Double that tonight.

But I was no stranger to fog. Once I'd found a body on a lonely country road which had brought my life to a shuddering stop. More recently, I'd heard a shot, followed a wounded collie, and seen a blue door beyond swirls of white mist.

Pray God tonight would be a simple journey home with no trauma or drama because I had exhausted my stores of energy with Leonora and Wafer.

For a while the ride was uneventful. I inched forward, listening for the sound of another vehicle, hoping the deer would stay out of the road. Eventually a light flickered ahead of me in the distance and disappeared. Moments later, a sign loamed out of the fog: 'Road Closed Ahead'. Another few yards and I'd have run into it.

Dealing with a detour in Foxglove Corners could be tricky on a clear day. Cautiously, I turned the car around, all the while doing some quick calculations. I could approach Jonquil Lane from one of three different directions, all of which would take me out of my way.

I tried to picture the roads that ran parallel to the one I was on at present. My mind seemed to freeze, and they all ran together. I couldn't even remember their names. Even if I could visualize the lay of the land, every landmark, every road sign, every light had been lapped up by the hungry tongues of fog. But as long as I was going in the right general direction, I should be all right.

Don't panic. Think!

At last I came to a crossroad, turned, and drove on, my eyes fixed on the small slice of roadway visible ahead of me, hoping to see another light or a crossroad. I saw nothing but fog, and it dawned on me that I'd been driving far too long.

Pull over, I told myself. *Way over. Turn on the emergency lights in case someone else is on the road and call Crane.*

There was no way I was going to be home at a reasonable hour. Suddenly I wanted desperately to be in my own home safe. Crane ought to know where I was.

I didn't know where I was.

Crane would know about the fog, though. All he had to do was look out the window. At some point he'd call the animal hospital. Maybe he'd already done that. He would reach their answering machine and worry. I should have called him from Leonora's house.

Better late than never. I pulled over onto what I hoped was the shoulder, switched on the inside light, fumbled in my purse for my cell phone, and dialed. It rang five times and went to voicemail.

I left a message: 'I'm on my way home. Not sure where I am. The fog is terrible. Well, you know that. See you soon.'

Okay, I told myself. *You're somewhere between Leonora's house and Jonquil Lane. You've covered this territory countless times. You know the way. It's just that fog changes everything and you can't see.*

I steered back to the road, kept driving, and my thoughts turned in a grim direction. I might have crashed on an alien world where the air was thick and white and impossible to breathe. Perversely, I remembered Brandemere, that storied road where unwary travelers reach the end of the earth and drop off of the planet.

That was one of Foxglove Corners' more chilling little legends. I didn't need to remember it now. Anyway, pedestrians were the ones who suffered this gruesome fate, not drivers.

Fog not only changes the landscape; it creates its own dark magic, distorting reality and stretching distances to the breaking point. The road went on and on. I shouldn't have been driving so long without reaching a familiar road. Unless I'd somehow made another turn without being aware of it.

Impossible. It only seemed that I'd been driving forever because I was nervous. In any event, I had only one option: to go on. The possibility that I was lost was unacceptable.

~ * ~

I saw lights behind me before I heard the sound of a motor. First, pinpricks of brightness, then a dazzling burst that bore down on me like a monster. A horn blared, and a dark bulky shape sped past me. Not a car. A truck with a maniac behind the wheel. Who on God's earth would pass another car in white-out conditions?

Shaken, still hearing the horn's echo, I steered to the right, to what I hoped was the shoulder, and saw woods, wreathed in folds of white, their trunks dark and ominous. I reached in the backseat for the bottle of water that Leonora had brought for Wafer and left behind.

I needed a few minutes to quench my thirst and regroup. Driving blind had taken a toll. My mouth felt as if it'd been stuffed with sand, and my hands ached from gripping the wheel so tightly. I unclenched them and let water trickle down my throat.

There. That was better. Infinitely better, and the fog seemed to be thinning, floating all around me in long white shreds that wrapped themselves around trees. I hadn't been able to see woods before this.

A glance at the dashboard clock told me that I'd been driving for forty minutes, which meant I'd veered far off my course. I could only hope that the worst of the fog was behind me, that any minute I'd see a landmark that would point me toward Jonquil Lane and home.

A shot fractured the unnatural stillness. A shot. Then a yelp. Of pain?

Just like the last time, everything the same except for the time of day.

Everything?

Glowing through shredded curtains of white I saw a bright blue door.

Forty-nine

This, I thought, was too weird. It was as if the fog had picked me up and deposited me on the very edge of the Haver property while duplicating the events of that first visit.

For what purpose?

I couldn't think of one, unless this was a genuine case of déjà vu.

In reality, though, that wasn't what happened. I had become disoriented in the fog. Anyone would, especially when confronted with a road closure. I'd driven miles out of my way with near zero visibility and ended up here. Coincidentally. Because no matter what strange happenings unfolded in the fog, this was over the top.

To decide to stop the car so close to the wildflower meadow that had captured so much of my time and attention was undeniably uncanny.

I drank the rest of the water and set the bottle on the floor.

All weirdness aside, at least I now had a clear idea of my location. If the fog proved to be thinner in this part of Foxglove Corners, the rest of the drive home should be a breeze.

Are you serious? Nothing in your life is ever a breeze.

What should I do about the blue door?

Turn it over to the police, along with my theory. Before I drove on, I'd call Crane again and Lieutenant Dalby. Mac had to investigate the painted door while it was still there. That was my only possible next step because there was no way I was getting out of my car.

A howl interrupted my impromptu planning. Mournful and bone-freezing, it was the eeriest sound in creation, conjuring visions of wolves and moons—and Candy. Suddenly the night filled with barking, all of it centered in the barn.

Realization hit me with the force of a plummeting boulder. The stolen goods inside the barn were alive. A cache of abducted dogs. I should have guessed. The dognappers who had targeted Foxglove Corners soon after my arrival there had stashed their canine captives in an isolated barn where they awaited pick-up. I hoped by some miracle DeVille's rescues were inside.

This knowledge didn't change anything. Even if I hadn't heard the barking, I didn't have to investigate to know what I'd find around the barn: more crushed wildflowers, spatters of cobalt blue paint on the leaves, and maybe another tag fallen from a dog's collar. Evidence.

Let Mac handle it. As he'd often reminded me, he was more than capable of keeping law and order in Foxglove Corners. I was a lowly female civilian who'd chanced to discover a covert and illegal operation.

I checked to see that the car door was locked—it was—and made my calls. Crane still didn't answer. Mac was out. Were they together? Unlikely but possible. No matter. Any officer on duty could handle the matter. But he had to hurry. It would be a disaster if he arrived to find the barn empty.

Now to drive home as fast as safely possible. I stepped on the accelerator and steered back to the road. Yes, the fog was thinner here. Not quite pea soup. A gauzy broth. Still hazardous, but…

Something stirred in my peripheral vision.

On the other side of the road a dark animal form moved. It was a dog, a collie as black as night haloed in my headlights. It rose and waited for me to make the first move. Was this the dog who had yelped? If so, it had been shot. But it didn't seem injured, only skittish. Shot *at* then.

All of my safe, sane planning collapsed in a heap. I cast off my role as amateur detective and became what I was at heart, a rescuer of lost and desperate collies, in any condition. In any circumstance.

Leaving the car running, I opened the door and approached the dog warily.

A hurt or frightened dog can be dangerous. Proceed, but with caution.

That was what Terra always said, telling us over and over what we all knew.

The black collie gave a tentative bark. Its tail moved about a quarter of an inch. I didn't think it was hurt. Frightened, yes, but willing to trust the human who came out of the fog.

Most dogs are trusting, even when man has betrayed and brutalized them.

I came closer. There was no blood, no sign of a wound. This time the shooter had missed his mark. The dog, a male, was wearing a green collar which meant he was someone's pet, strayed or stolen. With the presence of multiple dogs barking in the barn, my guess was stolen.

Somehow this one had escaped his captors.

"Good boy," I said. "Look at you. Lost in the woods. Would you like to come home with me?

He stepped back, whined, then bared his teeth and growled.

"No? Okay. No pressure."

Leonora had brought a package of cookies for us to eat while we waited at the animal hospital but had been too nervous to open it.

Some time ago, Wafer had followed the lure of Christmas cookies right out of the wild and into civilization. The same magic might work on the black collie. I'd just go back to the car and get it.

"Here's hoping you're hungry," I said.

The collie growled again. A twig snapped. Magnified in the silent fog-enshrouded world, it sounded like a gunshot.

Understanding its significance, I whirled around. A great pain exploded on top of my head. I fell back onto the damp ground.

Then there was nothing.

~ * ~

Flowers filled my dream. All colors, all sizes, all scents. They grew wild in the meadow, careening into one another, crowding out the weaker varieties. The giant ones frightened me. They were taller than I was, some of them as tall as young trees.

I couldn't see over their tops. I might have been in a cornfield or a forest, and my head hurt.

"I'm not going to school today," I said to no one in particular. "I can't work with such a violent headache."

All around me blossoms continued to open: bright orange, deep pink, golden yellow, purple, a blinding array of color like computer-generated flowers in a futuristic movie. Impossibly vivid colors burned my eyes and sent new waves of pain zigzagging through my head.

I waited for them to subside and prayed to wake up.

~ * ~

It's good to return to consciousness. Not so good when someone is pounding on the top of your head with an iron mallet. I felt ill, nauseated from the fragrances of a thousand flowers mixed with the strong easily identifiable smell of wet dog. Gradually the sweet floral scents evaporated, leaving behind the doggy odor.

I was lying on a hard floor, and I was alone. In the barn?

Too late. They'd moved the dogs out. I'd been too late to save DeVille's rescues, the black collie at the side of the road, and all the dogs who had sensed my presence and barked their desperation from the barn.

My assailant had approached me quietly in the dense silence of the fog and struck me with something hard while I was talking to the collie.

The dog had known. Where was he now?

I tried to move, to rise. The pounding in my head increased.

Not yet. It's too soon. Lie still.

A weak sliver of light crept under the door. I must have been in the barn all night, dreaming of strange flowers. How in the name of everything that's holy was I going to get out of here? What would Crane think had happened to me.

Wait! What about the police? I'd called them. Help might be on the way this minute.

That hope died a quick death. They had come, found an empty barn, and gone, apparently not seeing me. Maybe the blue door had already been painted over.

This night had gone from weird to hopeless.

I lay back down on the hard dirt floor and tried to will the pain away, tried to figure out how I was going to break out of this prison. Because there had to be a way. There usually is. I just had to find it.

Fifty

The barn had been built without windows. Even if they had existed, there was no way to reach them, for the structure was empty. No handy stool or chair or ladder stood by to offer me an easy access—to nowhere. Only a few stray strands of straw and fluffs of dog hair remained, and what could I do with them?

The door was probably locked. Summoning what was left of my strength, I pushed and pounded on it.

Yes, locked.

Fortunately the door was an imperfect fit. It allowed faint light and a whiff of air to seep through from the world outside. I wouldn't suffocate, but I couldn't get out either.

Panic closed bony hands around my throat. I couldn't fill my lungs with air. Couldn't breathe. I *would* suffocate. Trapped in a box. Entombed.

Slow down, I ordered myself. *It's not happening yet.*

Eventually somebody would find me. Judging from the sliver of daylight, the fog would have lifted. A passerby would see my car, empty and abandoned, with the keys inside and my purse. And a cell phone. If that passerby investigated. He might just drive past.

Dear God, I don't have anything in my pocket. Not even a candy bar or a tissue or a tin of aspirin. There's aspirin in my purse.

I sank down on the floor and wondered if I had a concussion. I was finding it difficult to keep track of my thoughts. Most unsettling, it seemed that I wasn't really alone in the barn.

Was that a jingle of tags clinking together? It was gone now, but I'd heard it. A whimper now in a far corner, a cold nose pressed against my forehead? Something of the dogs who had been trapped in the barn before me lingered in the unmoving air.

If only I had a real dog for company. The collie I'd thought to rescue. My resourceful Candy.

The lightning flash collie? If my situation hadn't been so deadly, I would have smiled at that notion. An invisible dog wouldn't help me now.

Positive thoughts might.

I remembered… How could I have forgotten my call to the Foxglove Corners Police Department? Mac would hear of it. Crane would realize I must have been in the vicinity of Deer Leap Trail to have seen the blue door. They'd know where to find me.

So all was not lost.

It gave me comfort to think of Crane listening to my message, calling Leonora, getting in touch with Mac. They'd find my car parked at the roadside, search the house and the barn, every step bringing him closer to me.

But a whole night had passed.

Why wasn't he here?

~ * ~

I heard voices. At first, they were so far away and indistinct that I thought I was imagining them. Then they came closer.

A man and a woman, I thought. I couldn't understand what they were saying but sensed it wouldn't be good for me.

I forced myself to stand. To meet the enemy head-on. On my feet. If they expected me to be cowed into submission and pliable, maybe unconscious, they'd be in for a surprise.

Be ready for anything. When—if—they open the door, dash past them to freedom.

It wasn't much of a chance, but it was better than nothing.

I waited. No one was talking at the moment, but I heard a faint click at the door. A key turning in the rusty lock?

And another sound, a distant siren, sliding down the scale only to rise in a high keening. The most beautiful sound in the world.

Thank God, thank God.

A muffled curse. The door creaked open. Rude light flooded the barn. Squinting at the onslaught, I saw a tall woman with a lavender scarf tied around the lower part of her face. Her black hair, twisted into a bun on top of her head, had a newly-dyed blue shine in the light.

She held a gun in her hand.

"Come on," she said. "Get a move on. Out of here."

I took an unsteady step toward her, toward the gun. "Who are you?"

"Move! Hurry up!" She shoved the gun in my ribs. With her free hand, she grabbed my arm. "To the house."

The siren screamed.

My eyes fastened on the oversized tee shirt she wore with tight fitting blue jeans. I knew that shirt and the slogan emblazoned on it: *I (heart) My Rottweiler.* I had seen it once in a nightmare.

"Where's the man?" I asked.

She ignored me.

The siren screeched closer, louder, blasting my eardrums. Any minute, it would come into view. I glanced at the road.

Stop! Please! Don't pass by!

My car! It wasn't there. I'd left it at the side of the road.

With her own desperate glance at the road, my captor pushed me into the field of flowers toward the house. Through the open front door, into the living room, into dimness and musty air. Just as she slammed the door, the siren died. At the house. It had stopped.

Through the dusty windows I saw lights flashing on Deer Leap Trail. A police cruiser. At last!

But was it too late?

~ * ~

Emboldened, I said, 'You're Charlotte DeVille."

Charlotte with dyed black hair and unfashionable casual clothes. A shirt with a remembered slogan. Where had I seen it before?

"Or Linnea Haver, whichever name you're using today. And where's the man? Where's Laurence?"

"Shut up!" She pulled back a curtain. Dust drifted down. Through the window I saw an officer tramping through the wildflowers to the porch. Not Mac. Another man went in the other direction and opened the barn door.

"Up the stairs," Charlotte said, brandishing the gun. "Quick!"

I stood on the first stair, grabbed for the railing, thick with the dust of ages.

"I can't," I said. "Can't climb... My legs..."

An imperious pounding cut off my words. Charlotte backed up to a door at the foot of the stairs and yanked it open. "In here then. Make a sound, and you're dead." She raised her voice to a witch's shrilling. "Coming! Hold your horses!"

The closet was marginally smaller than the barn. It seemed to be empty. I felt the jab of wire hangers and heard a light scratching. I couldn't take a proper breath.

Hold your breath, then. Inhale dust. Save your strength.

I figured Charlotte's threat was a bluff. She would have to open the door. If I cried out for help... Well, the officer had a gun too.

His voice boomed out clearly. "Sorry to bother you, ma'am, but we're looking for a young lady who went missing sometime last night..."

Now!

"Help! Help me! I'm in the..."

The gunshot drowned out the rest of my sentence.

280

Fifty-one

A gunshot isn't that loud, and I didn't think it should have an echo, but I seemed to hear it reverberating in the country stillness. With each reverberation it grew louder.

I had to know who had fired the shot, even if it meant becoming the next victim. If the shooter was Charlotte DeVille, my chances of escaping a bullet had just plummeted to zero.

But there were two police officers. Two men. One shot.

I opened the closet door. The policeman who had knocked on the door lay on the porch, bleeding from a chest wound. The other was running across the wildflower field to the house. The gun lay on the floor. Charlotte was gone.

I leaned against the wall. A sudden dizziness washed over me in waves. The scene on the porch winked out of focus, turned dark, burst back into vivid color.

What was wrong with me? I had to stay conscious and lucid, had to answer the officer's questions. He'd reached his partner and bent over him, saying something I couldn't make out. His voice seemed to come from a great distance. It sounded hollow.

Dear God. Did he think I'd pulled the trigger? I had to make him understand. I was the wife of a deputy sheriff. I'd never shoot a policeman.

"The woman who fired the shot assaulted me," I said. "She locked me in the barn. I've been there all night. I—I'm sick."

My voice sounded hollow, too. It took a tremendous effort to add: "Her name is Charlotte DeVille. She and her husband have been stealing dogs. They kept them in the barn."

The policeman wasn't listening to me. He was calling for help, and I was babbling. Another minute and I'd be talking about a door in the fog.

"I have to sit down." I looked for a likely place. A wood rocking chair, a sofa draped in a dingy sheet, the window seat—like everything else in the Haver House covered with dust.

I chose the rocker.

Where could Charlotte DeVille have gone? I didn't remember seeing another vehicle in the short time it had taken us to walk from the barn to the farmhouse.

Was she still in the house? With a shudder, I glanced up the staircase. These old farmhouses had plenty of hiding places: small rooms, shadowy nooks, doors in unexpected places. There was the whole outside. She might have dropped the gun and run into the woods. But why would she discard the gun?

Still, there had to be a car. She couldn't have flown in and out on a broomstick.

Why not? She was a witch. Someone had called her one not too long ago. Someone? Who?

The officer stood over me. "You're Jennet Ferguson, right? Deputy Sheriff Ferguson's wife? We've been looking for you. Are you hurt?"

"The DeVille woman hit me on the head with something," I said.
"Why?"

"I was trying to save a dog. I'm in Collie Rescue, and I saw this tri. That's tricolor, black, tan and white."

No, that couldn't be the reason for the attack.

"I found out what she and her husband were doing," I said. "I know what the blue door means."

He fixed me with that condescending look all policemen have in their repertoire. He was blond, like Crane, younger, not so handsome.

"Will your partner die?" I asked.

"Not if I have anything to say about it."

"I can't imagine why she shot him. All she had to do was say she hadn't seen me."

"Hang on," he said. "The ambulance is on its way. You can tell your story later, when you're less confused."

"I'm not confused. It all makes perfect sense. It's just that my head hurts so much I can't think straight. Do you have any pain killers I could borrow?"

"Wait till you've been checked out," he said.

"Oh," I said, "before I forget. My car. It's a black Taurus. It was right over there." I pointed to the verge. "And the dog was across the road. I guess they got him."

For the second time that morning, I heard a siren's wail.

They could come inside to tend to me, but I wanted to see if I could walk. I could, albeit my steps were unsteady. I went outside, took a deep breath of fresh country air, and stood next to the fallen man. His partner had administered first aid. When did he do that?

Maybe I was confused. Certainly I was frustrated. This encounter hadn't worked out the way I'd hoped. Charlotte DeVille had disappeared, robbing me of my chance to confront her. She hadn't even answered my question about Laurence.

As for the dogs who'd been in the barn, where had they taken them? And that T-shirt. *I (heart) My Rottweiler.* Why was it so familiar?

Things had gotten hopelessly muddled since Charlotte had forced me out of the barn at gunpoint. I hoped the doctor would give me something to make them clearer.

~ * ~

In a tiny hospital cubicle, I lay, quiet and safe and relatively pain free. I was waiting for Crane. In that state, I finally remembered the story of the T-shirt with the emblem: *I (heart) My Rottweiler.* The memory took me back to my first winter in Foxglove Corners. Leonora and I had taken refuge from a snowstorm in the Cauldron, a dive with an unsavory reputation.

There we met the dognapper, Al Grimes. We didn't know he was a dognapper at the time. We *did* know he was trying to strike up an acquaintance with me, an enterprise I promptly squelched. He used to wear a T-shirt with that distinctive message on it. It turned out that he really owned a Rottweiler.

Grimes was in prison now for the murder of the town's veterinarian and attempted murder (of me), and there he remained. So far as I knew.

Charlotte DeVille's shirt couldn't possibly be the one he had worn. There must be hundreds of them out there.

Charlotte. I recoiled at the unfairness of it. I'd had an opportunity to stop her in her tracks. Well, not much of an opportunity. She'd slipped off the canvas, wounding a policeman in the process. I might never see her again.

I had failed the dogs. If only I could have alerted the police while they were still in the barn, before that DeVille woman grasped the upper hand.

On the verge of tears, I closed my eyes and let the fiasco at the Haver place dissolve around me.

~ * ~

"Jennet! I thought…"

I knew that voice, and I knew what he'd thought. I opened my eyes.

"I've been waiting forever, Crane," I said.

"It's only been a half hour. We found your car at Sally's Country Oven. We were looking in the wrong places. How do you feel?"

"Okay, I guess. I don't have a concussion. You said 'we'?"

"Mac and me and Brent. Everyone's been looking for you. Even Leonora. She blames herself for you being on the road last night."

"It just happened," I said. "She and Wafer needed me. No one's to blame except Charlotte DeVille."

"Hey, Jennet." Brent emerged from the shadows by the doorway. "You gave us quite a scare. I for one didn't think you'd stop at a restaurant on a foggy night."

"You thought the curse of the painting had caught up with me," I said.

"At least."

"Maybe it did." I turned to Crane. "I want to go home. How are the dogs?"

"Restless. Pacing and whining. You'd swear they knew you were in trouble. I had to hogtie Candy to keep her from following me."

"They were with me in spirit," I said. "Candy and all the dogs I tried to help. That black collie in the road. The dogs the DeVilles stole." It was worth saying again. "I want to go home."

"Just as soon as the nurse says it's okay," Crane said.

"Did they find Charlotte DeVille?" I asked.

"Not yet."

"How about Laurence DeVille?"

"Those two disappeared."

"I think she came to the barn to kill me," I said. "Then she heard the siren. Those young officers saved my life, turning up when they did. But I won't feel safe until she's behind bars."

In the company of the bravest men I knew, I could sense danger's stealthy approach. It would be the haunted painting's last hurrah.

Fifty-two

I came home to the jubilant greetings of my collies and my familiar surroundings. The green Victorian farmhouse on Jonquil Lane was paradise, a safe haven. It had everything I needed for a happy life: a place to brew tea, a refrigerator filled with food, my own comfortable bed, and a caring friend across the lane. I never wanted to leave it.

My husband was there and his locked cabinet of guns, and my own gun that I'd bought for protection but never used.

I was home, but in my dreams that night I struggled to breathe in a locked barn or airless closet. In a nightmare, a gunshot broke apart the threatening silence and a man lay bleeding on the porch of the Haver farmhouse.

Sometimes, in other dreams, I was the one who bled.

I'd been terrified when I was in Charlotte DeVille's trap and was still afraid. Maybe more so now that the danger was over, because I didn't know where she was. Which meant she could be anywhere.

"Out of the state, if she's smart," Sue Appleton said. "I can't believe Laurence pulled the wool over our eyes for so long. Terra would turn over in her grave."

Terra didn't have an actual grave, but that was beside the point.

Sue had come to visit me the morning after my rescue, having heard the story from Leonora. She'd brought a colorful bouquet picked from her garden. We sat on the porch eating blueberry coffeecake that Camille had baked that morning.

The collies lay in their favorite spots on the porch. They looked drowsy but I knew they were on guard, especially Candy, who kept her eyes trained on the lane and barked at every minor disturbance in the environment.

Anyone would think the dogs knew of my secret fear that Charlotte DeVille and her husband hadn't left the state at all, but were lurking in the woods waiting to set Act Two in motion. All six of them, even Misty the puppy, stayed close to me and followed me in the house, wherever I went. I should have felt safe. To a point, I did.

They didn't want me to leave the house for fear I wouldn't return, and I was happy to oblige them.

I reached down to give Halley an impromptu pat on the head. Immediately Misty was at my side, looking for her share of attention. Candy shifted her gaze to the lovefest that didn't include her.

"What if Terra knew?" I asked.

"What do you mean?"

"I've had a lot of time to think lately. Suppose Terra suspected Laurence of stealing dogs and surprised him at the Haver barn? She might have threatened to turn him in. What if he killed her, then spread the rumor that she had stolen Rescue League money?"

"That could be. But you can't prove it."

"Not at the moment."

The more I thought about it, though, the more sense it made. We had a viper in the League, and the viper had a wife coiled in the background. I had no doubt that Charlotte had intended to kill me.

Perhaps Terra had been the first victim. The search for her killer had stalled.

We owed it to Terra to clear her name.

I had another thought that I kept to myself. Perhaps Terra was the mourner in the meadow, the spirit who had met her death among the wildflowers and wept for her lost life. After all, they'd found her body close to the Haver property, in the woods of Deer Leap Trail.

I was happy to lay the murder at the DeVilles' door. Charlotte or Laurence. Either one could have done it.

"I'm afraid this trouble is going to tear the Rescue League apart," Sue said.

"It shouldn't. There's still a need for rescue. We may lose a few members, but we'll attract others."

"Liz says we've become a halfway house to horror. Rather melodramatic but apt. I'll never forgive myself for letting Laurence keep those collies."

"We had one bad apple. No, two. The apple and his wife."

"Don't count Charlotte. She was never in the League. But if that cop she shot doesn't pull through, she'll be guilty of murder."

"He's going to make it," I said.

After Sue went home to teach a riding lesson, I kept thinking about Charlotte, kept seeing her dyed black hair and the scarf she assumed would hide her face and especially her Tee-shirt proudly proclaiming '*I (Heart) My Rottweiler.*' Again, that shirt led me to a memory of Grimes and the long-ago showdown that could have ended in my death.

"Can you find out if Al Grimes is still in prison?" I asked Crane that evening.

"The dognapper? He's serving a life sentence for murder."

"Without parole?"

"That's right. I'll check it out, but if he died or escaped, they'd let me know about it."

I told him about the Tee-shirt Charlotte DeVille had been wearing, a detail I'd forgotten to include when narrating my misadventures of the previous night.

"When Leonora and I visited her at her house, I had the feeling, just for a moment, that she knew me from some time in the past and bore me a grudge. I'm pretty sure we never met before that day. I wonder if her wearing that shirt is a coincidence."

"There must be thousands of those shirts floating around, one for each breed," Crane said. "You can probably find one that says *'I (Heart) My Collie'.*"

"It's just a thought," I said.

But it wouldn't leave me.

~ * ~

Crane wanted to take me out to dinner. So did Brent, who suggested a grand celebration at the Hunt Club Inn. Leonora invited me to lunch at Clovers.

"You know Annica will feel left out if you don't tell her everything that happened," Leonora said.

Wafer had recovered, and Leonora still felt guilty for asking me to drive her to the animal hospital on a foggy night.

"There wasn't any fog when we left," I reminded her. "And Wafer was sick. What else could I do? I might as well blame the collie I stopped to help."

I didn't want to think of his possible fate. I didn't even know his name. A barnful of stolen collies. A litter of puppies torn from their mother. Rescue dogs who thought they had a home. That I hadn't been able to save them grieved me. That I was loath to leave the safety of my home was worrisome.

That was why Crane insisted on going out when I planned to bake a ham for dinner. Why Brent wanted to celebrate. Why

Camille had suddenly remembered a gift she had to buy at the Green House of Antiques and didn't want to go shopping alone. It was probably the reason for Leonora's desire to connect with Annica at Clovers.

Coffeecake and flowers. Invitations and assurances that I wasn't alone. My friends were worried about me, too.

"All right," I said. "There's no law against going out to eat twice in one day."

Leonora and I would be together. Nothing could possibly happen to us. That is, to me.

Fifty-three

Clovers was another familiar place where I felt safe The dessert carousel crammed with pies and cakes, the menu with its offerings of comfort food, the green theme that gave the restaurant its cool woodsy atmosphere—all combined to reassure me. There was safety outside my house, safety in numbers.

Leonora and I sat in my favorite booth with a view of the woods. Soon Annica joined us for an impromptu break, which she arranged to coincide with our visit. The third cup of coffee and the last dessert on the tray were for her.

There was safety in the company of friends.

Annica gave a mighty put-upon sigh. "You have all the adventures while I'm working or in class. My life is so dull. Serving the public and studying for tests. Bah!"

"I wouldn't describe what happened as an adventure," I said. "Certainly it wasn't fun. I came close to getting killed, for heaven's sake."

"Whoever thought collie rescue would be dangerous?"

"Not I."

At least I never anticipated the kind of danger I'd encountered.

Annica took a sip of her coffee. "Mmm, that's good, if I say so myself. I made it." She turned to her pie. It was chocolate meringue, my all-time favorite. Leonora and I had generous pieces of our own. "And this will be good, too. It's Mary Jeanne's special recipe."

"Chocolate pie is what I need to restore my spirits," I said.

"Mine too. Now here's a coincidence. We had a woman with jet black hair in for dinner yesterday. She complained about everything and left Marcy a nickel tip. Can you believe that?"

Leonora and I exchanged glances. "That sounds like Charlotte DeVille," I said.

"Her hair had to be dyed, or she had a wig on. No one has hair that black at her age. She was wearing a scarf around her neck, too. Just like the one you described."

"Was she with someone?" I asked.

Annica shook her head. "She was alone and taking up a whole booth during rush hour. Mary Jeanne said we couldn't ask her to move to a small table. That would be antagonizing a customer. But there was a line a mile long. The lady seated herself," she added.

Leonora said, "If it was Charlotte, why wasn't Laurence with her?"

"Any number of reasons. I'm surprised Charlotte would come here. You'd think she'd keep out of sight after what she did."

Clovers was popular with the police. For all Charlotte knew, she was wanted for murder. After all, she had shot an officer of the law. Any savvy killer would be in another county by now with her hair dyed red.

Maybe Marcy's customer wasn't Charlotte. Still, a bit of my complacency drifted away. Clovers might not be so safe after all. As for Laurence, he was an enigma. Just before she'd come for me at the barn, Charlotte had been talking to somebody. If her companion was Laurence, where had he gone?

He's somewhere out there. Biding his time. The two vipers waiting to strike again.

Well, that was good. Didn't I want that confrontation with the murderous pair, alone or together? How else would I have even the slightest hope of finding the missing dogs? How else would I explore a possible connection between Al Grimes and Charlotte DeVille? Not to mention solving Terra's murder.

Doing all that seemed overwhelming to me. I felt my energy draining out of me, along with my complacency.

If only this fear would go away. I couldn't afford to be afraid. Not if I wanted to continue to live happily with myself.

"You're quiet today, Jennet," Annica said. "Didn't you like your sandwich?"

Before I could answer, Leonora said, "I'll bet her head is aching again. You'd better call the doctor, Jennet."

Annica set her fork down, with half of her pie still to be eaten. "Do you think Mrs. DeVille did permanent damage to your brain? I knew a woman who got hit on the head like you did. She was never the same after that. She kept saying these little yellow monsters with dinosaur faces were out to get her. She ended up... Well, her story didn't end happily."

"Really, Annica," Leonora said. "That's not very encouraging, and those monsters are just silly."

I had to nip Annica's enthusiasm in the bud. "I'm all right. Just a little tired. I haven't been sleeping well."

"Let me get you more coffee," she said. "No, wait. That has caffeine in it. How about switching to herbal tea? Mary Jeanne just brought in a tin of Georgia peach."

Not surprisingly, I was getting a headache. Next I'd be seeing little yellow monsters lurking in the shadows.

"Just a water refill," I said. "And thank you."

~ * ~

Leonora pulled up behind the Taurus and left her car running. "I'm sorry you didn't enjoy lunch, but it was good for you to get out of the house. You can take a nap so you'll be rested for your dinner with Crane tonight."

Dinner tonight. Oh, yes. I didn't feel like going out again, but how could I disappoint Crane? He'd already made reservations at the Adriatica. Besides, I wasn't in the mood to cook dinner either.

"I'll call you tomorrow," I said and fumbled in my purse for my key. This was a purse I hadn't used all season and I was unused to the various compartments. My old one had been recovered, along with my cell phone, with the car, but imagining someone plowing through my possessions, I'd retired it.

I walked around the Taurus to the kitchen door, relieved to be home. That nap was a good idea.

Something was wrong.

I felt it before I realized there were no collie faces in the window, no excited dogs with their noses pressed to the glass.

There was no welcome home barking

This was a first. This was—ominous. It was like coming to the wrong green Victorian farmhouse on Jonquil Lane.

Panic moved with me, across the walkway. I turned the key in the lock and opened the door to silence.

"Halley!" I cried. "Candy, Sky... Where are you?"

I looked into the dining room, then the living room, calling their names. "Raven, Gemmy, Misty!"

I stepped on Misty's blue ball, losing my balance. I grabbed for the banister, righted myself, glanced around.

This was the right house. There was no doubt of it, for there was my favorite chair, the cabinet that housed Crane's gun collection, my collie pictures on the walls, the heirloom candlesticks that had belonged to Crane's Civil War era ancestress on the dining room table.

But no collies.

All right, this could't be. When I'd left with Leonora for lunch, they'd been napping in the kitchen. Six large dogs couldn't just disappear.

In Foxglove Corners, anything is possible, a wicked voice whispered. *Your collies wouldn't be the first to vanish.*

Fear had me in a choke hold.

Okay. Don't panic yet. They have to be somewhere in the house. Clown collies playing a canine trick on me? All of them?

I called their names again, backtracked to the kitchen where I found their water bowls still full. One of the biscuits I'd dispensed before leaving lay under the table half chewed. Another first. My dogs loved biscuits.

A glance out of the kitchen window told me that both Camille's and Gilbert's cars were gone. Surely they hadn't taken them anywhere.

I pulled my cell phone out of my purse, imagined myself telling the police, "I came home and found my six dogs gone. The doors were locked…"

I'd better check the front door.

Locked.

In that instant I remembered my stolen car, the keys in the ignition. Anyone could have made a copy of the house key. Charlotte? Laurence?

Anyone could have entered the house and taken my dogs, locking the door behind them.

Okay. Now it's time to panic.

Fifty-four

Panic wasn't going to help me. I had to think clearly, to figure out what had happened and take action. Maybe there was a way to reverse this horror.

First, how likely was it that anyone could remove six large dogs from a house? Halley, Sky, and Misty, possibly. Candy and Raven? Never. Gemmy? I didn't know.

If both Camille and Gilbert were gone, a thief could work quickly and undetected. Still, my car was parked in front of the house. Who would know I'd left with Leonora? Unless someone had been spying on me.

Laurence and Charlotte.

None of this helped, but strangely it didn't feel as if the dogs were gone. They were here, somewhere. Unseen, unable to respond to my call, but here.

Try to explain that to the police.

Above my head, a floorboard creaked. There! I knew it! They'd gone upstairs for something. All of them? Yes, as a pack. For some unfathomable reason. Even though they preferred the first floor? Even though they always barked when I came home, never failed to welcome me?

Yes. I wanted desperately to believe that.

Calling them again, each one by name, I started to climb the stairs, moving slowly because I didn't know what waited for me on the second floor. What if it wasn't a dog who had walked across the board?

Go back for the gun!

As I turned, I saw a crumb spill on the stairs. Crumbs on the floor didn't last long with dogs in the house... I blinked and looked again. They couldn't be there. I'd vacuumed this morning and hadn't seen anything but dog hair.

Wait a minute! Crumbs? From what? There was nothing in the dogs' reach that could leave crumbs.

But the evidence was in front of my eyes. The landing was a mess with chunks broken off from a yellow cake or cupcake pieces. Lemon-colored frosting was smeared into the fibers of the runner and even on the wall.

I raced up to the second floor. Misty lay across the doorway to the guest room, her face covered with yellow frosting. Her eyes were closed. She didn't move when I touched her head. My little puppy.

No, no, no...I steeled myself to look down the hall. It was strewn with bits of cake and dogs, all of them lying as still as death. I fell to my knees beside Candy.

As still as death.

I touched them, spoke to them, let my tears fall on them. They were still warm.

My dogs had been slaughtered in their own home by an intruder dangling irresistible chunks of poisoned cake before their noses.

By Charlotte DeVille. Or Laurence.

Dogs love bones and biscuits. Cake is infinitely better and never offered. Except as a lure offered by a stranger. They would never resist the treat.

Red-hot rage burned in me. It blurred my eyes and turned my blood to ice.

I'll find them. I'll make them pay. If it takes the rest of my life, everything I have...

Another board creaked. The study door swung open, and Charlotte DeVille stepped into the hall gun in hand, too-red lips arranged in a smug smile.

"You did this," I said.

"I admit it, but they're not dead. Just sound asleep. I have better use for dogs. But for you, Jennet Greenway, I have no use at all."

Not dead. Sound asleep. Those were the words I heard.

There was hope for them, then. But for me? The next few seconds should tell the story. And if they were to be my last few seconds, what would happen to my precious collies?

They'd be carted away to an unspeakable fate.

I should have called Crane and the police as soon as I realized the dogs were missing.

Jennet Ferguson, long time member of Collie Rescue. She saved many abandoned dogs from certain death and gave them forever homes. Ironically, she couldn't save her own.

Now that pestiferous inner voice was creating my obituary.

I stood up, faced Charlotte DeVille. She still wore her barn outfit, those tight-fitting jeans and the infamous '*I (Heart) My Rottweiller*' Tee-shirt. A blue scarf twisted its way through her jet black hair like a snake. I felt as if I were looking into the face of evil.

Evil, RIP.

No such luck. The curse of the painting had caught up with me.

I eyed the gun. Charlotte's hand was steady, her eyes cold.

"What did I ever do to you, Mrs. DeVille?" I demanded. "We never even met until a few weeks ago."

"No, but you've been a thorn in my side for years."

Keep her talking. She wants me to know something, or she'd have pulled the trigger by now.

"Snooping, interfering, ruining our business," she said.

"And your business would be…?"

Ignoring that, she said, "We have a mutual friend."

"Laurence?"

"That jerk! No, not Laurence. He was just a convenience."

"Who?"

"Do you remember Al Grimes?"

Dognapper, killer. The *'I (Heart) My Rottweiler'* man. I would never forget him. There were times when he still invaded my dreams. Always leering, towering, threatening. Times when I could still feel his hands closing around my throat.

"It was a long time ago," I said.

"He mattered to me, and you took him away. That was only the beginning of your campaign to destroy me."

Better not to remind her that Grimes had brought his confinement on himself when he'd committed murder.

"My husband will be home soon," I said. "You'd better go while you still can."

"And leave without doing what I came to do? Not a chance. Let that fine husband of yours come home and find his wife dead and his dogs gone. Maybe that'll make up for what you put me through." She turned her head. "What was that?"

A missile launched at the kitchen door. A multi-ton weapon attacking the wood door. I knew that sound. It was Raven.

She who had once refused to set foot in the house now reacted violently to being shut out. I couldn't remember how many times I'd said, "She's going to break that door down."

But Raven was in the hall with the others, locked in a deep drug-induced sleep. I looked at Misty again, counted collies.

No, she wasn't!

I remembered now. Raven had been out on one of her jaunts when I'd left for lunch. I never worried about her because she had access to the Victorian dog house that Crane had built for her.

She never threw herself at the door a single time. She kept doing it until it opened for her. Suddenly I had hope, even though Charlotte still had the gun. She was shaken and uncertain. I could build on that.

Charlotte had gone pale, those lips blood-red in a marble-white face. "What's that noise?"

"That's probably my husband at the door. You'd really better go, Mrs. DeVille. Out the front door. You know Crane is a deputy sheriff, don't you? And don't forget to leave my key."

She turned and raced down the stairs, slipping in a frosting mess on the landing, making a frantic grab for the railing. I followed.

As we reached the first floor I heard a crash that sounded as if someone had broken a wall down. A black collie tore through the house, snarling, giving the impression of a starving wolf who had spied a walking steak.

Charlotte raised the gun, but Raven was quicker. Grabbing the hall runner on which Charlotte stood in her mouth, she yanked it out from beneath Charlotte's feet. With that distinctive witch's screech I'd heard before, Charlotte fell on the hardwood floor. She was as quiet as the dogs lying asleep upstairs.

The gun flew across the room. Gingerly I picked it up.

"What a good dog, Raven," I said. "You're an amazing dog!"

She wagged her tail proudly.

I glanced at Charlotte. I didn't think she'd give me any further trouble, but I was going to be sure. I pressed nine-one-one on the cell phone. Then telling Raven to watch the witch, I went down to the basement for a length of strong rope.

Fifty-five

Someone was knocking on the door.

It couldn't be the paramedics. They didn't arrive in silence and rap politely. I tightened the last knot around Charlotte DeVille's wrists and decided it would hold her. She hadn't regained consciousness.

I wasn't sure how I felt about that. I didn't want her to die but needed her to be immobilized. Well, she didn't look dead. She was still dangerous, though. Still evil.

I glanced out the window, half afraid to find Laurence DeVille on the porch. Instead there was Brent holding a gorgeous bouquet. He saw me and waved. Salvation! Brent would help me. We'd have to transport all five dogs in the Taurus. He'd driven his sports car.

I flung open the door. "Brent, thank God you came. You're the answer to a prayer."

"I just brought you a little cheer-up bouquet…" He looked beyond me to the fallen woman and Raven taking her guard duty seriously. "What happened here?"

I took the flowers and set them in the nearest empty vase. "That's Charlotte DeVille, the woman who shot the policeman yesterday. She came to kill me."

"But you killed her instead?"

"Not quite. Raven pulled the runner out from under her, and she fell. She hit her head on something, probably the floor. Anyway she's unconscious, and I confiscated the gun."

I hadn't straightened the rug. It lay in an untidy heap, separated from the pad.

"Just another harrowing day in Foxglove Corners," I said

I must be in shock to speak so flippantly of a near-death experience.

"Why did she want to kill you?" he asked.

"Because collie rescue interferes with dognapping. She was going to do it at the barn yesterday when the police showed up."

Quickly I told him about the plight of my collies. "She said they were just sleeping, but I don't trust her. She put something in cake and fed it to them."

He swore. "I'll start carrying them downstairs. I'll drive your Taurus, Jennet. You hold Misty on your lap."

"I guess we have to wait for the ambulance," I said.

As if on cue, I heard a siren. Judging from the sound, it had just entered Jonquil Lane. Good. My dogs needed care, and I didn't want to waste another precious moment on this vile woman who had endangered their lives.

~ * ~

When I knew my dogs were going to be okay, I allowed myself to fall apart. By then I was alone in the house that had seen a parade of strangers trooping in and out.

The last hour—could it only be an hour?—had flown by. The young officer who had been searching for me arrived with another partner in the wake of the ambulance. Then Crane appeared out of nowhere. I hadn't seen his patrol car turn in the driveway, hadn't even had a chance to call him yet.

He held me close. I felt his heart beating through his uniform and heard the fear in his voice although he tried to conceal it.

"You're sure she didn't hurt you, honey?" he asked.

"It was touch and go there for a few minutes before Raven took over," I said. "Remind me not to scold her for throwing herself at the door again."

"I'm going to bring home a thick juicy steak from the Adriatica for her."

"You'll have to bring six of them because the dogs will be back home by then."

"They will be," he said softly.

While Crane and Brent exchanged hurried words, I went back inside to give Raven fresh water and get my purse. The door lay on the kitchen floor, hinges torn away, glass shattered.

Anything could get in. Even though the monstrous woman was on her way to the hospital or in jail. I didn't care which. I still had to take precautions.

I felt fears flowing again. For a broken door. For wood and glass, part of my house. A person had a right to be safe in her own home.

Crane had followed me into the kitchen. "I'll patch it up. We'll have it fixed tomorrow and buy a new strong door. You take care of the dogs. Fowler will stay with you."

He and Crane lifted the five collies tenderly into the Taurus, and Brent took us to the animal hospital while Crane drove off to finish his shift. Brent waited with me while Alice examined them, ran blood tests, and gave them I.V.s.

By late afternoon they began to emerge from their stupor. Later still, they were walking, which meant I could take them home.

Alice and her assistant led them out on leashes. Mostly they were still drowsy, but Candy and Misty wagged their tails vigorously.

"Here are your beautiful collies," Alice said. "As good as new."

"How about if we stop at Clovers for take-out on the way home?" Brent said.

"Thanks, but you've done enough. Besides I just want a sandwich."

"Even now that you know the pooches are going to be all right?"

"Even now," I said. "All I want is to go home. I think they do, too."

"We'll have a real celebration dinner tomorrow now that we have more to celebrate. You choose the place."

He laid his hand on mine, and I noticed that the bite was gone. His hand was as clear as if it had never been marred by a strange, inexplicable wound.

~ * ~

I ate my sandwich in the living room with the dogs sleeping peacefully where they'd first lay down on coming home. Every now and then I glanced at them, hoping to find at least one pair of eyes looking at me. I had to believe Alice's assurance that they'd be fine tomorrow.

Tomorrow the whole house would have to be cleaned from top to bottom to rid it of Charlotte's malign presence. Not today, though. I was too drained. Still, how would I sleep knowing she might have been in our bedroom pawing through my intimate possessions, defiling them?

As soon as I finished my late lunch, I climbed the stairs again and conducted a thorough room-by-room search.

Charlotte had left nothing behind, not even a whiff of the spicy perfume she wore.

Nothing except her purse.

I found it in the study, a plain denim shoulder bag open as if the owner had just pulled an object out of it.

Unabashed I spilled the contents out on the desk and examined them. Compact, lipstick, coin purse, wallet, hairbrush, keys...I recognized the copy she'd made of my house key and extracted it from the ring.

She had five hundred dollar bills in her wallet and a pink post-it note: Redbrook Farm, Route 2, Redbrook Road, Hemlock Junction, MI.

Oddly the paper seemed warm as if it had just been handled. Which was impossible.

The rural address was obviously important, a clue. Could it be another place where the unscrupulous DeVilles kept stolen dogs?

Probably not, but it was worth investigating. I slipped it into my pocket, intending to give it to Crane when he came home.

This was a mystery that refused to end.

Fifty-six

"Charlotte and Laurence weren't married, and DeVille was an alias," Crane said.

"Next you'll tell me Charlotte borrowed her name from Cruella DeVille."

Crane smiled. "She may have. The two of them were partners in the dog theft business. They may have worked with Al Grimes in the past."

"She clearly knew Grimes."

Crane and I sat together in the living room with our dogs. I'd vacuumed the drug-laced crumbs from the stairs and hallway and banished all traces of Charlotte from the house with furniture polish and lavender-scented spray. Little by little, the five afflicted collies had begun to perk up with the help of prime rib roast sliced into their dinners. Our home belonged to us again.

I reached down to ruffle Raven's fur. "DeVille is such an obvious name for a dognapper. Charlotte wasn't too bright to advertise her secret trade."

"No one suspected her until you came along."

Crane gave me too much credit. I didn't suspect her until the end.

"She blamed me for Al Grimes being in prison," I said.

"Where he still is."

"And she blamed both Terra and me for trying to break up her dog stealing ring. I'm convinced that's why Terra was killed. She found out about it. Charlotte will probably blame Laurence, but I'll bet Charlotte pulled the trigger."

Once I'd turned the investigation over to the police, the secrets started falling like dominoes.

Charlotte's real name was Charlene Davis, which was close enough to her alias. I supposed she was telling the truth when she'd told me that Grimes had mattered to her, although what attraction he could hold for a woman escaped me.

Laurence was dead. His body had been found on the Haver property behind the barn. Of course, Charlotte denied any involvement in the murder. I liked to think she'd killed him over a disagreement on what to do with me. Perhaps we'd never know unless she confessed.

"Don't they say that the female of the species is deadlier than the male?" Crane asked.

"Charlotte/Charlene was definitely deadlier than Laurence."

Best of all, thirty-seven dogs had been liberated from the Redbrook Farm just in time, as no one had come to feed them for several days. Among the captives were five collies—Laurence's missing rescues—and six collie puppies. Various shelters were scrambling to care for them. The adult collies went to Sue who was busy finding foster homes. Liz had taken in the puppies. Fortunately all of the dogs survived.

"I still don't understand Charlotte's connection to the Haver House," I said.

Crane had an explanation for that. "Charlotte befriended her neighbor who inherited the property after the Haver sisters died. When he moved into a nursing home, he gave Charlotte a key and asked her to check on the house from time to time. She saw the possibility of using the barn to store stolen dogs until they could be moved."

Which brought me to a final question. I'd assumed Charlotte or Laurence had painted the door blue as a signal to a confederate who picked up the dogs. Who was this shadowy third person?

"That'll have to stay a mystery for now," Crane said.

I'd sent Charlene's purse back to her and hoped never to see or hear from her again. If she was convicted of Laurence's murder, that hope would become a reality.

The story occupied the front page of the day's *Banner*.

"Once again, all's well that ends well," I said. "Foxglove Corners is going to be known as an unhealthy place for dognappers."

Which was better than being famous for unsolved disappearances and ghosts.

~ * ~

In the evening the Spirit Lamp Inn had a mysterious shivery ambience. Gone were the blue gingham uniforms, the yellow and white centerpieces whisked away. Candlelight flickered, shadows swayed when the black-clad waitresses moved, and it was easy to believe the Inn's resident ghost would make her entrance at any moment and mingle with the guests.

I said, "I don't believe 'the woman in the blue raincoat' is just a story kept alive to draw customers to the Inn."

"Neither do I." Lucy glanced around the dining room. "I heard their waitresses keep quitting. They claim they see things that shouldn't be there. I love this place," she added.

Brent refilled our wine glasses. "It gives me the creeps," he said a little too loudly. "But Jennet wanted to come here. She deserves to have her own way for capturing Cruella DeVille."

Crane squeezed my hand. "That she does."

Once again I was being offered unearned credit. "That was Raven, Brent. I had a special reason for wanting to have dinner at the Inn. I wrote a note to be delivered to the cook."

They all looked at me, waiting for an explanation. I wasn't sure my missive would do any good, but I had nothing to lose. My dogs were healthy again and happy in their own homes. All the stolen collies had been freed from Redbrook Farm. One more victory could make the outcome perfect.

I'd already given the note to our waitress, but I knew its contents by heart: 'Several times I've seen a collie at the Inn who looks a lot like the picture of a dog named Breezy on a "Lost Dog' poster. If this collie was a stray, you might want to check with the owners. They offered a reward for her return.'

"What do you think?"

"Who's going to give back a dog they want to keep?" Brent asked. "Assuming the cook's collie is this Breezy."

"It's a kind gesture, Jennet," Lucy said.

"Ever the collie rescuer," Crane added.

"It may come to nothing, but I think it's worth taking a chance," I said.

Then our waitress was serving our dinner, fried chicken all around with a fabulous lemony dessert to come. The good feeling that surrounded us was practically tangible.

"I think the curse of the painting is finally gone," Brent said. "Napoleon is over his spell, Eskimo is back to normal and our Jennet has emerged from the outskirts of hell. Yes, it's over!"

Lucy took a deep breath. "I feel that, too."

"I knew it was over when Raven broke down the door and took out Charlotte or Charlene," I said. "She'd been out wandering. How did she know I was being threatened inside the house? How could she possibly know that?"

"Magic," Lucy said.

"Naah." Bremt shook his head. "A dog has a sixth sense. Collies think. They'd have to think to take care of their sheep."

"Jennet and her collies are on the same wave length," Crane added, sounding for a moment like Lucy.

I raised my glass. "Let's drink to Raven. Without her I wouldn't be here."

As I took a sip of wine, a strange picture formed in my mind. Miles away on Brent's property, the ashes of *Ada's Litter* settled unhappily into the earth.

Meet

Dorothy Bodoin

Dorothy Bodoin lives in Royal Oak, Michigan. After graduating from high school, she worked as a secretary for Chrysler Corporation Missile Division in southern Italy for two years. A graduate of Oakland University in Rochester, Michigan, with Bachelor's and Master's degrees in English, she taught secondary English until leaving education to become a full-timewriter. Dorothy is the author of the Foxglove Corners Cozy Mystery series, six novels of romantic suspense, and one Gothic novel. She is a member of Sisters in Crime.

VISIT OUR WEBSITE
FOR THE FULL INVENTORY
OF QUALITY BOOKS:

http://www.books-by-wings-epress.com/

*Quality trade paperbacks and downloads
in multiple formats,
in genres ranging from light romantic comedy
to general fiction and horror.
Wings has something for every reader's taste.
Visit the website, then bookmark it.
We add new titles each month!*